A Staged Murder

Jo A. Hiestand

Cousins House

St. Louis, Missouri

Cover and Interior Design by Cousins House

This is a work of fiction, and is produced from the author's imagination. People, places and things mentioned in this novel are used in a fictional manner.

First printing: Hilliard & Harris 2005 as *Death of an Ordinary Guy*
Second printing: Copper Ink 2013 as *Death of an Ordinary Guy*
Third printing: Cousins House 2017 – completely edited, revised, revamped as *A Staged Murder*

ISBN: 978-1544695150

Visit us on the web at: www.johiestand.com

Published by Cousins House
Printed in the United States of America

Dedication

For my parents, Carol and Douglas Hiestand.

Acknowledgments

This novel is the work of many people other than the author: professionals and supports. Among the professionals, I thank Inspector Tony Eyre and Detective-Sergeant Robert Church of the Derbyshire Constabulary, who guided me through the intricacies of British police procedure; Dr. Robert Paine, for medical information; Margaret Elliott, who helped me to my first break; Shirley Kennett, who showed me the importance of subplots and a side-kick; Nicole St. John, the Sister who's been there/done that and offered advice on what not to do; Alan Bamford, Brian Coombs and Jed Flatters, for Guy Fawkes celebration information; and to Brian Coombs and David Doxey for keeping the English language pure. Thank you, also, to Cindy Davis, who took on the task of editing this edition—which she did quite well!

Supporters are equally important, supply emotional support and encouragement throughout the novel's birth. I thank friends Chris Eisenmayer, Paula Harris, and Esther Luttrell, who were never too tired to lend an ear or shoulder.

I am grateful for everyone's help. Any mistakes in facts, however, are entirely mine.

Jo A. Hiestand
St. Louis, March 2017

Author's Note: The Peak District consumes a vast portion of Derbyshire, which is where this series is set. Its hills, valleys, rivers, moors, and woods seem to ask me to plant a mystery or two within its beauty. As do the peculiar customs clinging to the villages and towns. I obliged, and my Derbyshire Constabulary CID team was born.

A word of explanation about this 2017 version, however... *A Staged Murder* was originally published in the early 2000's as *Death of an Ordinary Guy*. I discovered more than a decade later that it had never been edited, simply put out as my manuscript came to the publisher at that time. I was mortified and angry when I learned about that this past year. I apologize to those who read the book; it was my first mystery and should have been corrected, which applies to the others they duly put out. To compensate as best I can, every book featuring Taylor and Graham is now being professionally edited and revamped. I hope the new versions (published under the series title A Peak District Mystery) are much better and worthy of your time.

Cast of Characters

The Villagers
Arthur Catchpool: owner of Catchpool Manor
Gilbert Catchpool: Arthur's uncle
Ramona VanDyke: Arthur's fiancée
Liam VanDyke: Ramona's son
Byron MacKinnon: Arthur's secretary
Talbot Tanner: the village odd jobs man
Evan Greene: publican of The Broken Loaf
Mason Conway: owner of the gift shop
Kris Halford: friend of Steve Pedersen
Derek Halford: Kris' husband
Lyle Jacoby: vicar of St. Michael's church

The Tourists
Steve Pedersen: American tourist, Kris
Halford's former fiancé
Tom Oldendorf: American tourist

The Police of the Derbyshire Constabulary
Brenna Taylor: Detective-Sergeant
Geoffrey Graham: Detective-Chief Inspector
Mark Salt: Detective-Sergeant
Margo Lynch: Detective-Constable
PC Byrd: Detective-Constable

1

"The last four to die included Guy Fawkes, the great devil of it all. Having asked the King for forgiveness, he crossed himself and was hanged. A pathetic ending to a daring plot."

Quiet, born of distress and shock, stifled the listeners, who clustered on the village green, mesmerized at the waiting woodpile. Morning slipped into afternoon, and the November sun shone through the leafless woods to the west.

"The plot was discovered when one of their group, a Catholic peer, was warned," the speaker continued. Byron MacKinnon, a ginger-haired Scotsman in his late fifties, was secretary to the local lord-of-the-manor. He was good at his job, I had heard, and from what I could judge, good as a guide, showing the manor's bed-and-breakfast guests the delights of the English countryside. He glanced at the two men and went on. "His absence from Parliament saved James I's life and led to Fawkes' exposure and death."

The two Americans stared at the fire circle, then at the wooden platform to their right. The planking, raised several feet off the ground, served as a stage. A rock band was slated to perform there this evening, and it seemed they'd hold nothing back from their performance. Besides the piles of fireworks, a straw-filled effigy of Fawkes hung from a neighboring tree limb.

What purpose it would have in the show, I could only guess.

Even if it served as a traditional part of Bonfire Night, it seemed out of place near the stage, a suggestion of the chaos that could result during the performance. And just as out of place in this peaceful village, Upper Kingsleigh, nestled in the heart of England's Dark Peak District. I felt out of place, too. And underused, for I was itching to prove myself by investigating a burglary or missing person case. Something for which I, Detective-Sergeant Brenna Taylor, could get noticed. Something more dynamic than nursemaid to a stack of wood and a straw-filled effigy. But we were few on the ground this November weekend, and a policewoman's lot is not always a happy one.

Several junior school-aged children ran across the green, their chant echoing off the buildings opposite us.

"Remember, remember   the   5th   of November.

The poor old Guy.

A hole in his pocket, a hole in his shoe.

Please, can you spare us a penny or two?

If not a penny, a ha'penny will do.

If not a ha'penny, may God bless you."

The end of the rhyme faded under laughter as the children ran into the edge of the forest, leaving the area quiet but for bird song.

A dangerous combination for me, as bird watching was one of my hobbies. And while it didn't rank with playing guitar, it took my attention away from my job at times. Which was evident if you looked at the reprimands in my personnel file or talked to my colleagues. But I closed my ears to the redwing's 'chiree, chiree' and turned again to the three men. A moment later the silence shattered when one of the Americans laughed.

I stared at the group, wondering what I had missed.

Byron, straight-faced, gestured to the huge oak. "That's why every 5ᵗʰ of November we make a straw-filled effigy of Guy Fawkes, which we call the Guy. It's usually hoisted at the beginning of the celebration. The note listing his offenses to the Crown, and warning other potential traitors is then read aloud—"

"I won't be able to understand a word if it's in Old English." Tom, one of the Americans, screwed up his mouth. Middle-aged and destined towards fat in later life, he was already developing the jowls of an English bulldog. He pulled his baseball cap farther down on his head before shoving his hands into his sweatshirt pockets. "All those thee's and thou's and hear ye's..."

"We've put it into modern English." Byron exhaled loudly.

"Nothin' turns me off faster than thee's and thou's," Tom muttered, gazing at me in an attempt to find sympathy from a kindred spirit.

I wasn't the partner for him. History has been a favorite of mine since my early school days. And while I struggled reading Geoffrey Chaucer's *Canterbury Tales* in their original Middle English text, I reveled in such books as the King James Bible. The old language evoked vivid images our contemporary speech didn't. Thee's and thou's and hear ye's held out a hand to guide me back to my ancestors, which wasn't a bad thing. Too bad Tom couldn't feel that.

"The Guy is then lit with a torch—"

"Hope there's no dead grass around. Straw

and clothing falling down might start a fire. You got pails of water handy?"

Byron exhaled heavily and continued. "And then the bonfire is lit with the torch."

"Looks like those guys are gonna do the lighting." Tom nodded toward a trio of twenty-year-olds placing microphone stands on the stage and pacing off distances. Another member of the group extracted coiled cords from a battered metal case. He dropped a cord at each stand before lighting a cigarette and sitting on the edge of the platform. All of them wore maroon-colored tee-shirts featuring a graphic of a white comet on the front. When they began the mics' sound check, Steve turned back to Byron.

"All this over this religious thing? Religion or politics. Folks still get riled up over that stuff." Steve looked to be the same age as Tom—aging baby boomers relinquishing their fight to retain their teenage physique, and succumbing to the pleasures of couch and cuisine. Yet the battle was not quite over. While his stomach shook slightly when he walked, his shoulder muscles screamed of weekly workouts. His hair, too, had refused to shift tones, still a dark brown. All in all, he hadn't gone to seed as quickly as Tom. And he seemed less bothered by the cold—his nylon jacket unzipped, his head bare. "In those days they were pretty much the same thing, weren't they?"

Byron's knuckles whitened, and his jaw muscle tensed.

"Damned injustice, I call it," Tom said. "You've got a Catholic king so all Catholics get favor at the court. A few years later, when the Protestants are in vogue again, they get the royal handouts and titles."

"Sounds nutty," Steve said. "Burning straw dummies for four hundred years."

"It's not so much the burning," Byron said, his voice hardening, "as it is the tradition."

Steve asked if anyone had been visited by Guy Fawkes' ghost.

Tom made the mistake of asking why he wanted to know.

"'Cause if so, they'd really be in the spirit of the thing." He laughed while Byron and I exchanged glances.

"When's this start again?"

"The program normally begins with the lighting of the Guy, the straw effigy," Byron said, his tone strained. "Lighting the bonfire, and eating roasted potatoes follow that. However, there's been a change of plans. Instead of beginning at seven o'clock, the event starts earlier this year. At four o'clock." He took a deep breath, his neck muscle throbbing.

"Something special going on this year?" Steve consulted his watch.

"Don't know about special, but it's unusual. A musical program."

"You don't normally have music? No patriotic songs, like 'Rule Britannia' or 'God Save the Queen' or 'London Bridge is Falling Down'?"

Byron exhaled slowly and glanced toward the stage. "It's not anything traditional. Just the opposite. It's a rock group." He winced as he said it.

"Yeah?" Tom smiled and stepped closer to Byron. "What group is it? Anyone we've heard of?"

"I don't recall the name. I was just informed of this."

"That's probably them there." He took a step toward the stage, but stopped as the group got out their guitars and started tuning up. The twang of amplified tones sailed over our heads.

Steve nodded toward the Guy hanging from a large bough of the nearby oak tree. It cast a dark gray shadow on the wooden floor of the stage. "Is that why the Guy is hung already? Something to do with the musical group?"

"I believe so. I've not been told any particulars."

"They going to light it? It's so close to the stage, I just wondered."

"I very much doubt that will happen." Byron walked over to the effigy and grabbed one of its feet. The slight swaying motion stopped. "The tradition is for the villagers to burn it just before the bonfire."

"Sounds screwy," Steve said. "All this way for a glorified weenie roast."

2

A pale moon shimmered in the fading sky, painting the giant oak and everything within the perimeter of the fire circle, in silvery tones. One or two early stars winked in the blackness, confirming their existence. Lanterns, already lit and dotting the bonfire area, seemed to mirror heaven's arrangement. The magical atmosphere broke when Arthur Catchpool, owner of Catchpool Manor, walked up to Byron, who was standing near the unlit fire. Both men were dressed in tweeds and corduroy, lending a decidedly "country squire" air to the coming drama, and I momentarily wondered if a horse and carriage would appear.

I'd been on duty all afternoon. No one had gone near the woodpile, so I felt confident the bonfire would be free of firecrackers. Which would please Arthur, the village council, and other concerned residents. The rumor that rockets, pinwheels and bangers were crammed into the wood stack and would explode when torched seemed to be unfounded. Or at least nipped in the bud by my presence. A police officer hanging around an area tends to deter would-be miscreants. So I mentally patted myself on the back, thought what a blameless job I'd done, and waited for seven o'clock and the lighting of the Guy and the bonfire. I was in a hurry for my assignment to end, and all I wanted was a hot cup of tea and a chair.

"I see the *omnium gatherum* has already begun." Arthur looked at the people milling around the stack of wood. His voice rose as he fought to be heard over the music blaring from the makeshift stage. "Night looks clear, too. Nice for once, no rain."

Arthur Catchpool, a slight man in his early forties, could have easily been mistaken for the straw Guy in the lantern-lit darkness, had it not been for his obvious vitality. Though not a lord of the blood, he had bought Catchpool Manor some years ago, saving it from the wrecking ball and the village from a slow death. Now manor, lord and village survived, if not prospered, and enjoyed the influx of tourists who came for the three-day celebration of the Catchpool Dole, Mischief Night, and Guy Fawkes festivity. Hardly surprising, for there were few villages or towns left that celebrated Guy Fawkes as thoroughly as Upper Kingsleigh.

"Might've been better if it'd rained us out."

"What?" Arthur blinked, then nodded. "Oh, yes. I see. We'd be spared…*that*."

As if on cue, the band finished with a flourish of drums, cymbals, and screeching guitars. The lead guitarist shouted his thanks into the microphone, and the group walked off the makeshift stage amid enthusiastic applause from the under thirty year-olds.

"Yes. *That*." Byron sniffed loudly, as though detecting a bad odor, and watched the band members head toward the pub. "We would've escaped with our hearing intact if it had rained." He glanced at the dark clouds moving toward the moon. "Nothing seems to ever go right, does it."

"Not so as you'd notice." Arthur rubbed his arms and watched a group of teenagers running after the band members.

"If you don't mind me asking, sir, what brought all this on? Rock bands aren't part of Bonfire Night. It leaves a kind of..." Byron seemed to fish for an appropriate word that would convey his displeasure and still keep him employed. "...disharmonious atmosphere to the tradition."

"I couldn't agree with you more. But I felt I had no choice. Ramona begged me to let Liam and his group perform tonight. I was trapped. I said yes—very reluctantly—and prayed for a short performance and rain." He glanced heavenward. "Unfortunately, my prayer wasn't answered."

The look Byron gave his employer made me wonder if Ramona held more sway with Arthur than the man would admit. Maybe it was another example of blind love.

"I know there's a proper time and place for such performances." Arthur moved two mic stands to the side of the wooden platform and disconnected the microphones. "But personally, I didn't think it mixed well with this custom. Tradition has its place, too, and I see nothing wrong with keeping it the same each year. Those who like Bonfire Night as it is will show up. Those who want a rock concert will leave us alone. Poor old Guy Fawkes must be turning over in his grave."

If there's anything left of him, I thought, but I silently agreed. I was a stickler for customs.

"A lot of the villagers didn't like it, sir." Byron nodded to a few of the older residents who were obviously talking about the concert, their heads bent together and their gazes shifting from Arthur to the backs of the retreating rockers. "You can't just do anything in the name of progress and have it accepted."

"Or successful. Well, at least we know not to do it again next year."

Byron opened his mouth but said nothing. I wondered if he was going to make a comment on either Arthur's or Ramona's marital status.

Arthur was about to move to the torch area when Byron grabbed his arm.

"What do you—" Arthur began, only to follow Byron's nod. He groaned as Talbot Tanner, the village odd jobs man, walking up to him. "A hell of a time for this. We're about to start." He glanced at his watch.

"You want me to corral him?" Byron asked.

"No. I'll shake him off as quickly as possible. Another minute more or less..."

"Trouble is, he rabbits on more than a minute. He's here about the Dole, I assume." Byron stepped back as the older man stopped inches away from Arthur and tapped his forefinger against Arthur's chest.

"I don't know how you sleep at night." Talbot's eyes narrowed, drawing up his cheeks and giving him a look older than his sixty-four years. "You're giving away the money that should be mine."

"How do you suggest we change it, Talbot? It's written out, nice and legal. I can't go against my grandfather's will and hand over the money to you."

"You could do. No one need know."

"That wouldn't be exactly ethical." Byron

stepped closer to the man. "According to Henry Catchpool's will—"

"Will be damned!" Talbot exploded, grabbing Arthur's jacket.

I took a step forward, wondering if the man wanted me to intercede now that Talbot had become physical. Byron saw me and shook his head.

"I'll prove it." Talbot released Arthur's jacket. "I'll prove to you and the whole village that I'm entitled to that yearly dole money. I'm goin' to search tonight, and when I find the proof, I'll see who my real friends are. Aw, hell!" He turned quickly, spat on the ground, and strode toward the oak where the straw effigy hung.

Byron eyed me, silently mouthed 'thank you,' and guided Arthur to the torch area. Minutes later the traditional Bonfire Night program began. It was typical of most village entertainment: this year's songs cutely interpreted by the pre-teen group, jokes and riddles by the younger set, and a painful violin solo by an older man who—the vicar explained—had just begun lessons last month.

I glanced at the faces nearest the violinist. They shone golden in the lantern's glow, an array of the listeners' emotions and physically expressed opinions. As one teenager yawned open-mouthed, I thought of my first piano recital and the family members who sat watching me. In my childhood innocence I'd never questioned if they'd wanted to be elsewhere, that my parents might've cajoled them into supporting little Brenna's performance. Trapped into listening via kinship. These disinterested villagers endured the violin music through good manners and neighborly respect, and I admired them.

The song ended in a drawn-out single note,

quivering between sharp and correct pitch. The man tucked his instrument beneath his arm, bowed, and merged into the crowd.

As the applause died, the vicar bent over and tugged at the wooden torch pushed into the ground near the woodpile. Cotton batting covered in layers of paraffin-soaked gauze topped the stick giving it the grotesque appearance of a giant cotton swab. He held the wooden torch as high as he could, letting everyone see and snap a few photos if desired. Then, from somewhere in the darkness behind him, a match scraped against something rough. The smell of sulfur filtered downwind, and a small blue and ochre flame bored a hole into the blackness. The flame moved forward as if floating through the gloom. There was a stronger scent of kerosene as the cotton batting ignited, and the vicar's thin face leapt out of the dark, bathed in crimson, gold and yellow. He slowly walked forward, his ink-black robes one with the night, his shadow bobbing behind him while the torch flames danced. The instant he struck the torch into the base of the gigantic woodpile, the crowd cheered.

Without a word, the vicar walked over to the huge oak. He handed the burning torch to Byron, who held it over his head and angled toward the top of the ladder. The bright ochre flame threw a woman's slender form into silhouette against the blackness of the night sky. Quiet descended on the crowd as they watched the woman steady herself on the ladder and the effigy rotate from the massive oak limb that held it in mid air.

The woman bent forward slightly to get closer to read the declaration scribbled on a slightly wrinkled square of paper stretched across The Guy's chest and held upright by an old knife.

Its wooden hilt and naked blade gleamed in the firelight and threw hideous shadows across the whiteness of the paper. The crowd cheered, urging her on as she peered at the effigy's face. Ebony and saffron-yellow alternately washed the face as shadow and firelight flitted across the form. At another vocal urge, the woman took the torch from Byron, ready to light the straw-filled figure. Now that she held the torch, she raised it to peer at the face before her. A moment later her scream rose against the clamor as she fell in a faint.

3

"You're certain it's a person." There was a hint of a question to Graham's voice, as though he didn't believe the Murder Team, me, or his eyes.

"It gave me a start, too, sir, when I first saw it. It was confusing in the light from the bonfire and torch."

I hesitated, wanting to add something more, something that sounded very official and showed I'd done my preliminary investigation before phoning him up. But other than protecting the corpse and scene, and determining it was murder rather than death by natural causes, I could do nothing else. Protocol dictated my commanding officer be brought in to take charge. And now I wavered between letting him command and my need to astonish him with facts. But I had none yet. I felt my chance to shine before Detective-Chief Inspector Geoffrey Graham quickly fizzling.

We stood just outside the police cordon, which enclosed the bonfire area of the village green. Within its confines, crime scene investigators prowled, their bodies half illuminated by the ebbing bonfire, half submerged in night as they stepped into or out of the light, their white paper jumpsuits and facemasks brilliant against the darkness.

"It's too bad Upper Kingsleigh has need of the Derbyshire C.I.D." Graham's tone held a note of regret, as though he didn't want murder to intrude on their peaceful lives. "It's a nice spot, from the glimpse I had of it coming in. What is it...five hundred residents or so?" He glanced over his shoulder as though he could perceive the entire village population.

"Yes, sir. On the fringe of Wormhill Moor."

"Snuggling up to the Pennines. Right."

I nodded, picturing the great snaking mountain chain of the Pennines, the three hundred-mile link of towering tors, dales, desolate moors, caverns and streams stretching from midland England northward to the Scottish Lowlands. Giant vertebrae. Derbyshire's Peak District was part of the Pennine progression, comprised of Dark and White regions. The White Peak, characterized by its white limestone, gave way in the northern section to the Dark Peak, named for the dark Millstone Grit running through the moors, cliffs and peat hags. Upper Kingsleigh indeed hung onto life, as Graham noted, precariously balanced between the moorland at its front door and the forests and mountain faces at its back. A village nestled into its environment, secluded and tranquil, where not long past in its history the most difficult aspect of life was getting 'over the tops.'

As if reading my mind, Graham said, "This is usually a calm place, Taylor. It's had very few call outs, but it seems to have had quite a jolt tonight."

Ivy-wrapped stone buildings, their gray slate roofs glistening from dew, stretched the length of the road. Beyond the cluster of shops, homes alive with light pinpricked the black evening. A great stand of sycamore at the base of the church hill swayed in the gentle breeze, their bare branches grasping at the moon like a net thrown at a fish. Moonlight danced on the rooftops and in the depth of the pond, gurgled over stones in the stream, painted the foliage with silver.

Someone let a door slam and the magic evaporated. Graham wondered aloud if the baker's shop across the street would have anything left from the day's sales.

"I don't think they're open, sir." I pointed out the darkened windows.

"Then we'll have to ferret out something elsewhere."

Graham slipped on his facemask and stepped into the brightness spotlighting the corpse. The white of the footed, plastic squares used to protect the ground and give us access to the body and scene seemed to hover above the dark soil. Graham walked carefully along this path, his head down as though he was focused on every detail the land could give. Which may not be much, considering the barren hardness of the rock-and-soil composition. No such thing as a muddy footprint, in other words.

The deceased wore a brown tweed jacket, socks, tan trousers of no particular name recognition, and a blue shirt. His callused hands and weatherworn face held the physical hardships of his sixty years. Sixty years that led to this spot and this finish.

He lay on his back. Clumps of straw

haphazardly protruded from the cuffs of the jacket, obliterating his hands. Straw, pale and casting thick, black shadows under the intense police lights, fringed the lower edge of the jacket. Straw escaped from beneath the dusty fishing cap, angled at a rakish angle, and mingled with his blond hair. A small knife plunged into the corpse's chest secured a square of paper. It looked like a try-out for a Ray Bolger role gone horribly wrong

Graham squatted at the corpse, lifted a corner of the impaled paper with his pen, and peered beneath it. He seemed to speak to the body. "Rather a large knife. And an equally great rope. I wouldn't have thought a straw dummy would require such a thing."

I explained that the police surgeon and the superintendent had already looked at the body, and no one liked the look of it. "Deceased is a Steve Pedersen," I said while Graham went on with his cursory look. "American. Sixty years old. Tourist who had just entered the Kingdom a few days ago."

"Traveling with anyone, or free and unencumbered?"

"He was with his brother-in-law. He arrived in the village about the same time as a number of other tourists."

"For their three days of revelry, I expect. Dole, Mischief Night, and the Fawkes Celebration."

I wished I could have come up with a list of attractions or statistics about the village that would impress him. Instead, I stood there looking at the corpse. "They do very well in the tourist trade, yes, sir. At the moment Upper Kingsleigh hosts several Britons and several Americans. But besides playing the tourist, Steve was here to see friends."

"So that's why he didn't melt into the vastness of London or Blackpool, say. I suspected there must be something other than Guy Fawkes to lure him off the tourist track."

"Derbyshire has a lot to offer holiday-makers, too, sir."

Graham nodded and spent several minutes examining the corpse. Without looking up, he said, "Have a look, Taylor. Let's see if you spot the same thing I did."

I joined Graham and look a closer look at Steve Pedersen. The deceased's left palm had recently sustained an injury, the skin on the heel was cut, and there was a large gouge approximately one-quarter inch square that was red and fringed with broken skin. Several cuts ran parallel to this gouge and appeared dark red, nearly brown. A large, purple bruise covered the heel. I leaned over the chest in order to view the right hand. The palm showed no such injury.

In general, the facial skin was as pale and cold as that of other corpses we had attended. Bruises at the side of the throat were overwrapped in places by abrasions and a ring of redness that followed the jaw line. There were bruises, nearly black, on the left jaw and side of the neck. A thick patch of hair near the left temple was matted with dried blood. The eyes stared vacantly at nothing, though the left pupil had dilated larger than the right one had.

An image of me in a constable's uniform flitted before my eyes, and I took a deep breath, praying I wasn't about to blunder. I said, "You referring to the head injury, sir?"

4

"Not bad for a refugee from university, Taylor. What were you reading?" He turned away before I could say I had considered majoring in archaeology. He would have laughed. Here I was twenty years later, involved with a different type of dead body. He started at the Guy, a look of disbelief on his face. "Attacked, hanged and knifed. What do we have—a lunatic, or an annoyed trio?"

"He, or they, wanted to be sure Steve was dead, from the looks of it," I said.

"I assume Steve was knocked out first—that's what the head wound suggests to me, at any rate—then the rope slipped around his neck for the hilarity of the rock concert or bonfire. Note the bruises at the side of the neck, near the ear." Graham glided over my editorial comment. "And the flap of skin and scalp where the blood has clotted. Classic signs of head trauma. I hate to assume it's a skull fracture, but..."

"From the wounds on his left palm, I suspect he may have fallen when he was hit."

"His palm taking the brunt of his fall, yes. Good point, Taylor. The Home Office pathologist will tell us if his knees or hip are bruised."

Graham handed me his pen as he stood up. "I'd almost bet my pay packet he was hit first, TJ.

Almost. But I need the money this month."

Even though it's been many years since my police schooling days, my mates still called me TJ. The initials stood for The Job, which was how police referred to their employment. And the goal I wanted so fervently that I had made no secret about it. Now I reveled in the nickname that doubled as a Right of Passage in a male-dominated occupation, and as a trophy of a once-vicious taunt. The only woman in my police class, I had endured the course and my colleagues' snide remarks, finally proving myself worthy of being a cop and working with them in the job. I'd been nervous when I first heard Graham use the initials, wondering if he were mocking me. But he used it in quiet moments between us, and I cherished the sign of his friendship.

I took the pen out of habit, clipping it onto the neckline of my jumpsuit, and watched him follow the white plastic stepping-stones to the oak.

The lads had dispensed with the tent we would normally erect around a corpse outdoors. A waste of time, that, the Super had said on viewing the scene—a jumble of grass, gravel, wood chips, fire ashes, straw, dry leaves and twigs. A hundred people coming and going all day, milling about at the bonfire, contaminating the area beyond any defense that the tent could tender.

Graham stopped beneath the great, overhanging bough and looked around the tree's base, ready to give the area the same observation he had given the corpse. He glanced at the rope that swayed slightly. "No one thought anything of the knife? Part of their Guy Fawkes tradition?" His voice sounded tired and he rubbed his eyes, looking remarkably like a small boy who had stayed up past his bedtime. "I agree with your childhood recollections, Taylor. The effigies of my youth had some sort of note pinned or stuck to the dummy, the knife borrowed from one of the villagers' households. We'd always thrown our effigy onto the fire, though. This hanging is a bit unusual, though in keeping with the historical end of Guy Fawkes."

I stared again at the wrinkled white paper, lifted from the jacket's dark background by the intense flood lighting. The note seemed to float above the corpse, except for its center where it was cruelly affixed by the knife.

"Well, sir, it's the sort of thing the villagers do each year. No one took any notice. When Ramona VanDyke—that's the woman who discovered the body—started to light the dummy, she noticed it was a person."

"It must've given her quite a fright." He stared at the rope that ran over the oak limb.

The slowly swaying form, washed by shadow and firelight, with the knife blade winking at the villagers, shimmered before my mind's eye. "Anyway, no one noticed a thing. The dummy's been out in plain view since Thursday."

"Three days ago?" When Graham turned toward me, his eyes were bright with interest.

"Yes, sir. There was nothing extraordinary about the dummy. The villagers passed it every day, whether to bring more wood for the fire, or just to see how the fire building was progressing. They were used to seeing it, so they really didn't see it."

"You see what you expect to see. Especially if you've no reason to expect otherwise."

I agreed. It was difficult to imagine someone substituting the corpse for the effigy, but it was clever.

Graham scowled, looking annoyed with the hour, the murder, and the obvious tampering with the scene. He glanced again at the bough that stretched overhead like the arm of an ancient crossroads gibbet. "Who would have thought that the mundane practice of lighting bonfires, begun on the evening in 1605, would evolve into a tradition still observed more than four hundred years later?"

"Or that Guy Fawkes would evolve into the arch villain of the gunpowder plot, when it really ought to be Robert Catesby."

He looked at me, either surprised I knew my history so well or unsure of his own.

"Yes, sir. Catesby was the leader of the gunpowder conspiracy. Not poor Guy Fawkes, whom we love to revile."

Graham regained his composure. "No wonder you turned to detection, Taylor. Your memory of the smallest detail does either your ancestral genes or your police schooling proud."

I avoided his gaze, afraid I would color. "Seems a pity to hang the blame on the wrong lad. It's like sending the wrong man to the dock."

He refrained from commenting, keeping to the investigation details. "Do we have any measurements, yet, on height of the tree limb and all the rest? I see they used a stepladder." He indicated the impressions of the ladder's feet in the earth, then gestured to the rope that ran from the limb to the deceased. The rope was about an inch in diameter, creamy white and very new. "Effigy must have been dangling damned high if they resorted to a ladder."

"Yes, sir. The rock band hoisted the dummy early for their performance tonight. They used the same bough and hanged the Guy at the same height as previous Upper Kingsleigh effigies."

"How'd Steve get down?"

"Well, sir, you know how it is…"

"I probably do," Graham replied slowly as he steeled himself for some horrendous account of crime scene destruction.

I was glad of the mask covering my nose and mouth. He couldn't see my smile. "Well, just like anybody, their first thought was to get him down in case he might still be alive."

"With that ruddy knife in him?" Graham's eyes mirrored his astonishment. He shook his head and muttered, "*Ora pro nobis*" to the universe.

I agreed that we needed all the help we could get, but inwardly doubted God would send a flaming chariot of avenging angels, no matter how diligently Graham had served his collar. And, from the office gossip, he had, even if he had been Chapel and not C of E.

In the silence following his vocal plea, two constables complained about the evening's cold. Their voices must have jarred Graham. "Sorry, Taylor. Go on."

"Well, they lowered him to the ground, hoping he was still breathing. He wasn't."

Graham snorted, his eyes back on the disarray of the corpse.

"You can't really fault them, sir. It's a natural reaction."

"I suppose."

"We can't get a measurement of the height of the body from the ground, but we can estimate it fairly accurately. We know his height, and the rope should show signs of—"

"Bloody helpful," he repeated. "Who actually lowered the body? Do we know that?"

"Talbot Tanner. Village odd-jobs man, sixty-four years old—"

"Fine." Graham waved aside the rest of my rendition.

Thinking he would find it interesting as well as pertinent, I mentioned Talbot had been in charge of constructing the bonfire, but that Ramona VanDyke had overseen the straw dummy.

"Were either Talbot or Ramona responsible for the knife?"

"Haven't gotten that far, sir." I hesitated, wanting to recite some fact about them or the bonfire or the lack of firecrackers, but they would be taken for what they obviously were: a feeble display of non-essential knowledge.

"Of course not. Early days yet." Graham bent over the body, the knife fascinating him. It seemed to whisper to him, taunt him. "It looks familiar, but I can't place it. Do you know, Taylor?" He stepped aside so I could get closer.

I squatted, peered at the knife from several angles, then stood up and said that it seemed like a scout knife. "Awfully common. I don't think it gets us anywhere."

"We probably won't find any dabs on it, either." Graham stared at the knife's short blade, the metallic rivets pimpling the wooden handle. "Well, one of the CSIs will have to deal with it. And I hope whoever does it won't make a bloody mess of it this time." Shielding his eyes from the brilliance of the working lights, Graham looked around, as if to see whom he could trust.

Unfortunately, I knew what he meant. An eager constable attached to a previous case had packaged a bloodstained knife in a paper bag, remembering the bit about allowing it to dry first, but forgetting the bit about tying the knife to the interior of a cardboard box, which prevented movement—and removal of blood—during transport. I swallowed, pitying the officer if he mucked up this one.

"Well, if we're not told otherwise, I don't think Steve Pedersen was stabbed to death." He held out his hand to me, and I, as though a sister in an operating theater, placed the pen in his palm. With a nearly inaudible "thanks," he carefully lifted the left edge of the deceased's plaid jacket. As though addressing Steve's chest, Graham muttered, "I'll give you three guesses, Taylor. Three's the magic number, but if you don't get it in one, I'll be quite disappointed with you, and strongly suggest a refresher course in Elementary Detection."

Even though I assumed he was joking, I wanted to shine, to win back my top-of-the-class status. Of course I wasn't expected to solve this case single-handedly. I mean, that's why I was partnered with him. To learn as well as to complement his skills. But I wanted him to think I had promise.

I nervously pulled all police schooling from somewhere deep within me as he gestured toward the jacket front that was bunched up slightly where the knife blade had pulled bits of it into the wounded flesh. Aside from a strand of straw and a bit of blood on the knife, there was nothing unusual about the shirt or jacket.

"Well, Taylor? What about it? Does this lack of blood speak to you?" I must have made some sort of face, for he said, "Should I be worried about your dinner?"

Praying that I wasn't about to demote myself, or look like an idiot, I said, "Bit of a giveaway, yes. Blunt force trauma of the head."

I must have answered satisfactorily, for he let the jacket edge fall back into place, got to his feet, and gave me the pen. "Can Ramona

VanDyke talk now?" He turned toward the area where she, her fiancée and the vicar had been moments before. The grassy spot was empty.

Graham swore under his breath after I explained that Ramona was given a sedative just before he had arrived. "She needed it."

He stood, clenching his fingers, staring at them as though they had held the knife. Hands were important to him, I knew from office chatter. He was a serious amateur musician. Some sort of keyboard instrument, I vaguely recalled. What was there besides piano or organ? Neither sounded quite right, and I stood there, trying to recall what the chatter had said. I had just decided to ask him when Graham sighed. "We can let the lads work I'll just have a word..."

I exited the crime scene and took off my work clothing. From the darkness of the eastern woods, I could hear Rams Dyke Creek rushing downstream to join the River Dove. I silently thanked the saint or Olympian god who ruled such things that we weren't dealing with a drowning. I had seen enough water-eaten corpses to fill the rest of my career. Which I hoped would be long, if I didn't do something stupid in front of Graham. He could be your best friend or as cold, hard-hearted, and unyielding as the police manual if he was crossed.

I shook off the water-bloated image that claimed my mind and wondered what had pulled Graham into the Force. I had progressed to fantasizing about revenge for a murdered sister when I saw him approach. His step was light and quick, full of self-assurance; his tall, lean body silhouetted against the work lights.

All this time I had been patiently waiting beyond the police tape, and lifted it as Graham joined me. His footprints were dark smears on the frosted grass, a straight trail that spoke of his completion with the scene and his determination to begin the next phase. I collected my shoulder bag from where I had stashed it near a straw bundle. "You suppose the knife will be all that difficult to trace?"

Graham disrobed quickly and handed the paper apparel over to a constable, who promptly stuffed it into a paper bag. The evening's chill had gripped him, and although he did his best to ignore it, he looked as though he was cold. And hungry. He tugged up the zipper of his suede jacket and pulled on his gloves, which were of the same color leather. I hugged my arms to my chest, glad of my down-filled jacket. We watched the frozen breaths of the constabulary team shrouding the scene, white against the glare of the police lamps. He turned back to me. "No one will own it, Taylor. You've been a copper long enough to know that. I suppose you better phone up the video team from Chesterfield. Or—" Graham stopped in his directive to study my face. My expression must have told Graham what he had suspected. "Should know better than to tell you something so obvious. They're enroute, are they?"

In spite of my wish to bottle my feelings, I smiled. It passed unnoticed, for he was concentrating on the job.

"Now, whom should we talk to first? Or is it too late? What time is it?" He consulted his watch. "Nine's not particularly late, but it will be before we unpack our pajamas."

"Well, since you asked for my vote, I suggest Arthur Catchpool. He's something of the local lord, though there's no claim to a peerage. More of a lord-of-the-manor thing."

"Great benefactor of the village, then?" Graham stared absentmindedly ahead of him into the dark village. A few lighted-up windows spoke of the houses' occupants still awake. "Probably chattering on about the murder over hot cups of tea," Graham said, then murmured something about slices of jam-covered bread, fat rascals, and blazing fires. He spoke of it as one would of a loving memory.

"He couldn't be more of a benefactor than if he guided each villager through life, to hear some of them talk. Pays for half the drinks at the bonfire, for starters."

"And who provides the potatoes?" Graham kicked one of the tubers that had rolled out from the fire area.

I felt suddenly sad, knowing these villagers had been cheated out of their evening revelry. Maybe not such a disappointment to an adult, but to a child it was probably an earth-shaking tragedy. A chestnut pop as I stepped on it. "You will ask embarrassing questions, sir."

He smiled slightly, the skin over his jaw tightening so that the scar was more visible. It was the only flaw in his otherwise lead-actor looks. "Nasty habit. Sorry. Continue."

"Well, Arthur's a likely place to start our investigation. He's converted a section of the venerable pile into a bed-and-breakfast, so we might find some of the tourists who were here at the bonfire getting ready to nest for the night."

"It'd save on returning tomorrow to question them, is what you're implying."

"Even if the tourists are soothing their frayed nerves at the Broken Loaf—that's the local pub—Arthur's still the key player, sir. He emceed the pre-fire program, handed out laurels to workers, oversaw the straw bundle delivery, paid for the chestnuts..."

"Busy man. And apart from observing

village hierarchy..." His voice trailed off. Was he envisioning the bonfire, the light-streaked faces of the villagers eagerly anticipating the food and fueling of the Guy? "Very well, Taylor. Let's see if Mr. Arthur Catchpool is still awake and, if so, if his benefaction will extend to two cups of tea."

5

Arthur Catchpool was indeed awake, and so were the others beneath his roof—family, house staff and tourists. And true to Graham's hope, Arthur did offer us tea after he settled us in his study. I curled my cold-stiffened fingers around the cup, glad of the warmth. The tea smelt of hot lemon, and the aroma of fried pork and apples hung in the air. I inhaled deeply, as though the fragrance would appease my growing hunger. It didn't, and I drank greedy as a desert-parched survivor. It nearly scalded my throat, but the temperature shocked me awake.

The room was what I had expected of a country great house—wood paneling, walls of books, accessories and portraits that went back generations. But Arthur was entirely unexpected. Instead of a robust, rotund squire, we found a slight man in his early forties, soft-spoken and dogless.

I reluctantly traded my cup for pen and paper when Arthur began his narrative.

"I'm afraid that's all I can tell you, Mr. Graham." Arthur sat opposite us, his legs crossed, his elbow on the edge of a small table. He was dressed in a patch-elbow tweed jacket and wool slacks, the knees of which were still wet from where he had knelt on the damp earth, aiding

Ramona VanDyke during her faint. A wisp of straw, just discernible, had lodged under the tassel of his loafer. Arthur's voice, high from apprehension, filled the room.

"The vicar lit the fire, then handed the torch over to Byron. He held it while Ramona climbed the ladder. Of course, we had no inkling that the dummy wasn't—" He paused to swallow, looking quite uncomfortable. "For all that went on here tonight, Mr. Graham, Upper Kingsleigh's still quieter than Lewes." He offered the village comparison with pride, as though he had to find something good in the night's horror. I envisioned the Sussex town, the lighted dummy dangling from a noose, the noise swelling until every corner of the town seemed filled with the bedlam. Arthur abruptly abandoned his speech, grabbed his shirt collar, and pulled at his tie, looking definitely paler than a few minutes ago. I was about to find him some water or brandy when he spoke again. His statement now was embellished with the bulwark of village safety statistics.

Arthur swallowed loudly, his fingers intertwined and squeezed together as though he was in earnest prayer. Somewhere within the bowels of the mansion a grandfather clock erupted in a deep voice to announce the hour. The chime echoed faintly from the opposite end of the hall.

"It was dark. Seven o'clock. We didn't look at the effigy before or during the music concert. It'd been hanging for days, so why should we look at it that evening? The whole thing's a shock. How that man ended up as the dummy—"

"You didn't know the deceased, then," Graham asked.

Arthur seemed to relax, now that the focus

had shifted from him. The flesh of his fingers returned to its normal hue, the top leg ceased its agitated bounce.

"No, I didn't." He confessed rather too quickly, I thought. I glanced at Graham, but his face revealed no hint of emotion or opinion. Arthur continued. "That is, I knew he had been a bed-and-breakfast guest here. But other than that..." He shrugged and glanced at one of the portraits, as though the ancestor would understand.

"So while you lodged Steve Pedersen..."

"Other than greeting him as I do everyone when they arrive, and inviting them to tea the first night... Well, why should I know he was going to— Well, anyway, Byron knew who Steve was, of course, and told me just before you arrived. That's Byron MacKinnon, my bookkeeper and secretary. My private life's not that demanding, so Byron fills a portion of his forty hours by keeping the books for Evan Greene, the publican, and Mason Conway, owner of the gift shop. Met him yet? Grand fellow. Anyway, Byron had a business ten, fifteen years ago before he came to work for me."

I asked why a man enjoying the freedom of his own business would trade that to be someone's employee.

Arthur shrugged. "I hate to gloat over another's misfortunes, but it wasn't until his own business failed that he came here."

"Hard cheese."

"What? Oh, yes. Rough go. He's a hard worker. Invaluable man. Also emulates the Buxton visitors' center. He keeps the pamphlets plentiful, plans day trips to local sites, lets my guests know what's happening throughout the area, and takes a group photo, which people are free to buy or not. Nice holiday reminder, and they seem to appreciate the kindness."

"Invaluable man, indeed," Graham agreed, then caught my eye. "We'll need to speak to Mr. MacKinnon."

"Of course. I'm all for helping the police."

"It's a pity there aren't more people like you, Mr. Catchpool."

"Yes, I suppose it would make your jobs easier. It's been a dreadful shock. Simply awful. I've just seen to my guests, actually, and they're taking it quite well, if you can call dealing with murder 'well.' There's a comfort in wanting it to be suicide or an accident, isn't there. I mean, it shifts the horror of an unknown lunatic lurking among us to a self-inflicted event."

"But the burden of suicide is that the survivors carry the guilt of the death." Graham, the minister, emerged briefly. "They eternally accuse and punish themselves with non-answerable questions. 'Why didn't I help more? Why didn't I spend a bit more time with him?'" He tilted his head, looking wise and paternal and otherworldly. I wondered if his words were mere ministerial dogma or pain from personal loss.

"Of course. Well, I hope you catch this berk." He settled back in his wing chair, as though waiting for the jail doors to clang shut on the criminal.

In the silence, I sank my fingernails into the chair's velvet upholstery, scraping them against the nap to create little roads in the smooth blueness. Like the villagers' lives, I thought, staring at the uneven fabric. An event hits and ruffles everything. I smoothed out the fabric with the flat of my hand as Graham said, "I would've thought that Steve would've stayed with his friends, the Halfords." He looked at me for confirmation of the name. "Or don't they have the space for a guest?"

"Actually, he did stay with them. After his second night here he left us. I don't know why he didn't go straight to Kris and Derek, but that's where he ended up."

"Nothing like mother-in-law come to visit?" I suggested.

"The only mother-in-law is in America, and she hasn't been over for ages."

"Fear of flying, then?"

"I have no idea, miss. If you want to know anything in that vein, ask Kris. I don't know her mother very well."

"So." Graham set the teacup on the table and leaned forward slightly, his brown eyes bright with interest. "Steve checked into your B and B Thursday. He stays that night, as one would expect, but checks out on…"

"Saturday, after breakfast," Arthur said. "He stayed here the two nights, I believe. Fortunately, Derek and Kris remodeled a bit a few years back. It would've been a sticky wicket trying to squeeze a guest into that cottage of theirs. But it turned out to be worth every pound I lent them. The house is quite nice. Anyway, we had the graveside dole on Friday. Steve presented himself to the Halfords afterwards." Arthur seemed a bit flustered sorting through the progression of days and events.

"I've heard about the dole, but I don't know particulars."

"Nothing much to it. My great-grandfather set it up. We assemble every third of November in the churchyard. Derek and I are the principal performers, if you will. *A maximis ad minima.* We're also the last performers in the succession of this fantastic tableau. Have been since— Well, I suppose I should start at the beginning if you're to make any sense of the whole thing."

Graham assured Arthur we would appreciate it.

"It began more than a century ago. 1915, actually, when great-grandfather ran over Derek Halford's grandfather. Well, not himself," Arthur corrected as Graham registered bewilderment. "My great-grandfather's carriage ran over Derek's grandfather. Broke his leg. Damaged the carriage somewhat, too. Unfortunate."

I offered my opinion that it was very unfortunate for Derek's grandfather also.

"What? Oh, yes. Rough go for Halford. Great-grandfather had him seen to, of course. Best medical attention and all that. But for some reason, the leg refused to set properly, and Halford limped the rest of his life. Great-grandfather, of course, felt just awful about it." Arthur shifted slightly in his chair to study a portrait of a white-haired older man. The painting hung, gilt-framed, next to an equally white-haired man who bore unmistakable family resemblance. Arthur's likeness was two frames down the line, presumably next to his father. I wondered what would happen if Arthur had no children or the wall became filled. "He had this consuming sense of duty. The whole thing haunted him terribly, so on his deathbed he provided in his will for Halford. The family was to get £300 annually, payable on the date of great-grandfather's death. It was to run for three generations." Arthur bent forward and lowered his voice, the parentheses almost visible. "I suppose great-grandfather figured the remembrance of Halford's accident would be passed down through successive generations. Vivid enough, certainly, for a father to relate to his son, never mind village gossip helping it along."

"And the son," Graham ventured, "is the present dole recipient, Derek Halford?"

Arthur nodded. "That's why this dole is so unique. Most run on to perpetuity. Ours will die out with Derek."

"Interesting. So what happens? You hand Derek Halford his money and you all go celebrate in the pub?"

"Nothing quite so normal. No. We gather in the churchyard, Derek recites a verse great-grandfather wrote. It's a foolish bit of scrap, but according to the will it has to be said."

"And it is..." Graham prompted.

Arthur looked at the carpet, as though pleading it should open up and receive him. "First the crutch to heal the bone, then the purse will me atone. As the bone and mind set, so must do the man. Sire to son this passes on. Son to son will see it gone till the last of three my charity will span." He looked at Graham, as though waiting for judgment. "Derek holds a pair of crutches over great-grandfather's grave. A symbolic gesture, you understand, merely a stage prop. Though it's oddly prophetic because Derek did need crutches for a while, years ago. He still limps. The vicar then hands me a small brown leather pouch with the dole in it. I hand it to Derek. Then we all troop down to the bonfire area and Derek throws the crutches onto the woodpile, ready for the bonfire lighting on Guy Fawkes Night. Silly, isn't it? There's all the bother about getting the money from the bank, driving Buxton or Chesterfield or somewhere to buy a pair of crutches, digging out the leather pouch... Silly. Whole thing only takes five minutes, but we have to perform."

I said I thought it quite a nice, civilized

ceremony. "It's refreshing to hear someone has enough moral fiber to stand accountable for his actions."

Arthur silently consulted great-grandfather's portrait again. "Anyway, Friday we had come down to the bonfire for the last bit, and when it was all over, Steve pops up in front of Kris and announces he just happens to be alive and over here." Arthur recrossed his legs and looked rather upset. "I must say he chose a bloody awful way of doing it, but there you are. Kris fainted from the shock of seeing him. Well, she would, wouldn't she, after believing he had died years ago? Steve went home with them, though he returned here to sleep. Then he checked out Saturday and spent the rest of his time with them. What an unpleasant way for a holiday to end."

"Bad way all around," I agreed. "Mrs. Halford enjoys their friend's stay, then winds up being present at his death. Very unpleasant."

"Have you any thoughts why Steve Pedersen should be murdered?" Graham said.

"Who's murdered?"

Though decidedly slurred, the statement was understandable, and drew our attention to the newcomer in the doorway. Propped up like a limp sack of potatoes from the bonfire, a man slumped against the doorjamb. One hand was wrapped around the edge of the door, the other hand wrapped around a glass. He uttered his question again, this time to the door.

Obviously embarrassed and annoyed, Arthur rose quickly. Glancing at us, he mumbled an introduction. "This is my uncle, Gilbert Catchpool. He's visiting for a few days."

As if editorializing, the wood-cased clock on the mantle belched the half-hour, then settled into silence.

Uncle Gilbert lifted the glass to his lips and, as though using the glass as odd binoculars or telescope, staggered into the room, barely consuming more whiskey than he spilled. He paused at the couch as Arthur rushed up to him.

Remarkable. No family resemblance at all, I thought, scanning the paintings on the wall. The Catchpools were, without exception, angular, bony people. Brunets and redheads. There were several noses that seemed to pass themselves from father to son, and an occasional cleft chin, but the verification of Catchpool splendor and lineage rested in the eyes. Dress altered with the generations, but those large, close-set eyes linked them. And Gilbert Catchpool either echoed the maternal line or was a throwback to an earlier branch, I thought, for everything about him was round. But his round hazel eyes had taken on a definite red hue, as had the circular spot of pale skin at the back of his head. An emphatic stomach rolled down his substantial frame, threatening to overflow the confines of his belt.

Gilbert's free hand dug into the back of the sofa for support, giving him the appearance of someone leaning into a cyclone. He swayed slightly, alternately blinking and pulling back his eyelids, trying to focus his eyes and mind. Like a bully clamoring for a fight, he demanded our names, and to know who had been murdered.

"Steve Pedersen's been murdered," Graham replied from his chair.

Gilbert squinted at his nephew, as though the name and circumstances nagged at him from somewhere within his mental morass. "Do we know him? Did I murder him?"

6

Blushing, Arthur laughed, glanced at Graham—who wasn't laughing—and said, "No."

To which question, I wondered.

Arthur turned to Graham. "He gets like this, I'm afraid. You mustn't pay him any mind."

I stood up and made a move toward them. "Anything I can do, Mr. Catchpool? Help you get him situated?"

"What?" Arthur blinked as wildly as his uncle, then pulled a smile from some inner resource. "Thanks all the same. I'm accustomed to this. He's used to me. It might confuse him if you came along."

Nothing would confuse that old sot, I thought. What you want to say is that it'd be embarrassing for me, being a woman, to help tuck Uncle into bed.

"Thanks anyway, miss."

I nodded, reclaimed my chair, and scratched Gilbert's name into my notebook.

"Was your uncle at the bonfire tonight?" Graham's question halted the Catchpools' progress across the room.

Arthur turned toward Graham, his hands on his uncle's shoulders, his mouth open. Gilbert stood facing the door, continuing his mumbled questions while Arthur related Gilbert's activities.

"I don't know when he was there. I know he came before the fire was lit. I saw him. So did most of the people, I suppose."

"His question about killing Steve—"

Arthur laughed again, and said it was just his uncle's drunken talk. "It's piffle. He's talking nonsense. He's had too much to drink. He didn't even know Steve. Uncle's staying with me in this section of the house. I doubt if he even knows who my B and B guests are."

"Will he remember anything about his evening when he wakes tomorrow?"

"Should do." Arthur glanced at Gilbert. "Depends. Some nights he drinks more heavily and remembers nothing. Or he might recall everything. You know how it is."

Graham thanked Arthur, then watched the two leave the room. He turned to me, eager to play 'what if.' "Could just be the idle talk of a drunk."

"Could be just an act, too. Wanted to know what we've deduced so far, so he thinks he'll barge in here, maybe crash in a chair and eavesdrop. Only his upstanding nephew—"

"He could've eavesdropped outside the door," Graham reminded me.

"He couldn't hear as well. We weren't exactly shouting."

"No doubt about his having a pull or two. He didn't get that complexion by standing under the moonlight."

"Arthur was in an awful hurry to get Uncle G away from us. Embarrassment, fear, or change of plans?"

"There you've got me, Taylor."

Quarter of an hour later, Arthur was back in his chair, decidedly less flushed and breathing normally, and replying to Graham's original question about motive for Steve Pedersen's death.

"I haven't a clue. As I said, he didn't know anyone except the Halfords. Byron can get you a list of the guests' names, if that would be helpful. Perhaps he had made an enemy among them. I don't know. People do get a bit uptight and on others' nerves when they travel."

"We can suppose almost anything at this stage," I mumbled as Graham stood up.

Arthur quickly got to his feet. He seemed relieved the grilling was over. "Would you like a work area? I've got any number of rooms that might be suitable. I suppose you'll be needing something like that."

As I moved toward the door, Graham thanked Arthur for the offer. "I'll see if we can get a room at the pub. That usually suits our purpose. We really prefer to work away from anyone's home. We come and go at such unorthodox hours."

"Yes. Less disturbance all the way around. Well, if there's anything more I can do..." He saw us to the door and waved enthusiastically as we got into our car.

"What'd I say about eavesdropping?" I asked. "He probably offered the room so Uncle G could keep an eye and ear on us. Then he'll know how to change his story when we question him."

"Has anyone ever told you you've got a detective's mind?"

"First I've heard it mentioned, sir."

Graham's fingers lay loosely across the steering wheel, drumming out a steady beat. I wondered if he was mentally playing a favorite piece of music. I glanced out the window, not wanting him to know I was curious about him. A faint fragment of a tune escaped his lips. So, he likes Handel. And the keyboards in Handel's day were the organ and harpsichord. Was that the instrument office gossip had joked about? I recalled catching the tail end of one joke as I entered the canteen one day—Graham in a white wig and asking about key information and if anyone could handle it—but at the time I had assumed it was linked to his ministerial career. Graham at the harpsichord was a different image than I would have conjured up. I glanced at my own left hand, surreptitiously pressing the fingertips against my thumb. The calluses from years of guitar playing were hard, unlike the softer touch needed for stroking harpsichord keys. I knew that much from my brother.

I looked at Graham's hands again. Did harpsichord and guitar sound good in duet? I was about to ask Graham when he said, "It's not too awfully late, Taylor. Just gone ten o'clock. What say you sharpen your interviewing skills and tackle the Halfords. The female link is vital at times. Women convey sympathy, understanding, patience. I'll see about that incident room. I hope I didn't just turn down the only available space in the village."

"We can always plead stupidity. It wouldn't surprise a lot of people."

Derek Halford showed no surprise when I identified myself at his door. He's probably expecting the entire village to be interrogated, I thought as he hurriedly straightened the afghan covering an upholstered chair.

The room carried the house's exterior harmony inside. A wall of bookshelves, flowered draperies, and pastel colors blended to soothe the senses. A large picture window looked out into the Halfords' back garden. I began with my usual apology at having to bother Derek at his hour and under these circumstances, and then inquired about their emotional state.

He crossed the room quickly and turned off the telly, cutting off the actor in mid-sentence. He blushed, as though normal human activity was a sin under the circumstances, picked up the evening's newspaper and his jacket from a chair, and motioned me to it. He dumped the items on the floor near the couch, seemingly oblivious to the small table near my chair, and sat down.

"I suppose we're all right. Though it was a hell of a shock." He glanced at the staircase leading to the upper floor.

I nodded, wondering how many more times in this investigation I'd hear that phrase.

"I was dumfounded when Steve came up to us at the dole. We'd just about gotten over the shock and joy of his resurrection, I guess you could call it, only to find him like this at the bonfire. It was terrible for Kris." He shook his head.

I could only guess at his wife's emotions. I had been there, and it had jolted me. Kris had known him. What she and Ramona were suffering was more than grief on hearing of a death. I stared at the used mugs on the table and wondered how Derek had forced Kris to drink anything. She had been hysterical at the bonfire.

"Those tablets from your police surgeon were just what she needed. Thank her again for me, won't you? It's been a hell of an evening, and tomorrow's not going to be much better. Kris will be awake, and have to deal with the memory."

I nodded, knowing the grief that would settle on Kris.

"We'd only known Friday evening that Steve was in the village. We invited him over after the dole." He paused, probably to see if I knew about the dole. When I asked no question, he continued. "We got on so well together, and there were forty-some years to catch up on. Well, it was natural that we asked him to bed down here."

"And that was…" I nudged, waiting to see if I would get the same answer as Arthur's.

"Saturday. We had two days with him." Derek's voice broke, and he reached for his handkerchief.

"I understand Steve was both your and Mrs. Halford's friend. You had no idea he was coming, then?"

Derek shook his head. He muttered that they had known Steve when they had all attended university in America, but they had no idea he had scheduled a visit to the U.K. "We thought he had been killed in Viet Nam during America's war. That's what makes this so devilishly hard. We just got him back, and lost him again."

"And you hadn't seen him or heard from him for all that time. I can well imagine your shock at his reappearance."

"He just walked up to Kris after the crutch bit of the dole. Just said hello, as if we'd just parted yesterday. Hell of a hello. What if Kris had keeled over from a stroke?"

"Why had he kept quiet all these years? Had he lost your address?"

"He explained that." Derek stuffed the handkerchief into his jeans pocket before grabbing a photograph from the end table and handing it to me. "Steve." He stopped suddenly, as though he was aware I'd seen Steve Sunday afternoon. "Anyway, he said he'd landed in Nha Trang in 1975 and was captured nearly immediately. Years later we discovered he'd been listed MIA, but at the time he thought of himself a

POW. He got back to America in 1983."

"That's an eight-year hole in his life."

"When he returned he was hospitalized."

"Wounded?"

"Mentally.   Spiritually.   Emotionally. However you want to put it. Aphasia."

"It'd be hard to cope with losing your memory."

"Harder getting it back. Though it's easier in some ways than having your leg hacked off, so you won't be confined to crutches or stared at the rest of your life as a handicapped—" He worked his palm over his left thigh. "I'm sorry. Sometimes this damned leg hurts like hell."

"Recent injury?"

"Car accident. Not as life shattering as many." He tapped the top of the photo's frame. "Steve explained his aphasia. It was brought on by the trauma he'd gone through being POW. Though he appeared to be perfectly normal, he said he couldn't remember much about that segment of his life. While he'd been in hospital he'd been a mental vegetable, unable to speak or write. It was like living inside a bottle, not making sense of anything."

"So that's why he couldn't contact you. What took him so long to locate you? Had he just been released when he arrived here?"

Derek shook his head. "He was released in '86 with a clean bill of health, a hearty handshake and a sincere 'good luck' from the physician."

"Even a criminal gets a new suit when he's released."

Our conversation lapsed, and in the silence I heard the wood flooring in the hall pop as the house cooled. Derek didn't stir, perhaps accustomed to the sound, perhaps concentrating on the evening's event. His gaze returned to

Steve's photo and I felt the tension building the room. "So when he returned home…" I suggested.

"He learned from his mom that Kris and I had married the previous year. He smiled bravely, counted his blessings, took a deep breath, got married and started a business."

"Takes guts. What did he go into?"

"Local, commercial deliveries. He eventually owned a couple small jets and a fleet of vans. The smaller shipments from small companies who wanted stuff flown overnight. In Missouri, Illinois, Kansas. Oh, I don't know where all."

"And Steve came over here without his wife?"

"He told us she had died a few years ago."

I slowly relinquished my study of the photo and looked at Derek. "He brought this with him, I take it?" When Derek nodded, I handed it back. "It's a nice remembrance."

"We don't need to remember right now. I'm near to shoving it into a drawer. I don't think Kris—" His face reddened as he sought an explanation. I wanted to tell him I understood, that it's sometimes more painful seeing the loved one daily and not being able to be with him. But I let my elementary counseling slip by the wayside. "In a month, perhaps, when all this is less painful, I'll dig it out, but not now." He practically slammed the photograph onto the cushion beside him. "At university we were inseparable—a Three Musketeers thing. It was hard to say for a while who Kris loved more." He took a deep breath. "There was a fourth to our party. Kris' roommate. I was rather keen on her at the time. I considered marriage."

"And did you marry her?"

"No. My infatuation wore off, though I thought I was headed that way. We were a constant couple. Anyway, Kris naturally teamed up with Steve, didn't she? They were planning to wed, but then he leaves for Viet Nam and is captured."

"Rough."

"She waited ten years for him, but never received a hopeful word. This is so hard on her, so unfair. After all this time..." His voice hardened as though all the injustice of the past and this terrible evening had conspired to wreck his wife's life. "This dreadful affair coming on the shock and delight of recovering Steve. And of course, there was the perpetual row earlier tonight over the dole money. That's expected, but it's none the less stressful on the both of us."

"Perpetual row?" I asked, my mind racing back to Arthur's scant information. "I was led to believe it was a short little ceremony. It shouldn't warrant stress or a row, I wouldn't think."

"Well, you don't know much about Talbot Tanner. He makes a Sunday school picnic an ordeal."

I mentioned that I had heard a bit from Talbot earlier that evening.

Derek shook his head. "What you haven't heard is how hot and bothered he gets each year."

"From the dole?"

"That and his renewed surge of patriotism, I guess you could call it. He walks around the village, cornering people, reminding them that we owe our present way of life to Guy Fawkes and the ensuing events. That we should put more emphasis on thanking our forebears than on the festivities. Says we've turned it into a carnival. But he's totally daft about the dole. He claims *he*, not *me*, is the rightful recipient of the Catchpool dole. He'll yammer to anyone who gives him the least concerned look. Bit of a pain, but there you are. Unfortunately, if I want the dole, I have to keep a stiff upper and ignore Talbot's ranting, which gets downright ugly at times."

"The dole must be worth a fair amount, for you to put up with an annual whine like that. I think I'd be rather tempted to chuck it. I can't stand conflict."

"Well, I think it's worth the few days of grief. £300 may not be a king's ransom, but it's very nice."

"So Talbot thinks—"

"The man's a lunatic!" Derek snapped. "He side-stepped normality years ago. Claims some type of relation to me, but of course he's never bothered to bring forth any evidence of this fantastic yarn. Instead, he continues to gripe and complain that it should be him up there every third of November. Honestly, the man wants mental care, the way he talks on about it. I don't mind so much for myself, but I'm concerned about my wife. She hates any kind of emotional outburst in public, and that's Talbot's forte. The man's totally round the twist."

"He's not violent, is he?"

Villages aren't as peaceful and cozy as they appeared. They held all the human emotions harbored in cities.

Derek snorted and leaned forward, his hands on his knees. "Who's to say, if Talbot gets angry enough? We've seen the occasional temper tantrum, heard the string of vulgarities, but usually Talbot's an easy-going chap."

"Except around the third of November," I reiterated, wondering if a full moon made it worse.

"He seems to have it in for me personally.

And for Arthur, though Arthur's as innocent of the dole's regulations as I am. We just show up, do our bit, and I collect the money. Yet Talbot looks at the both of us like it's some huge conspiracy against him. I tell, you, miss, I wouldn't be surprised if some Mischief Night or Guy Fawkes Night I fall into a trap that Talbot's laid for me. He's a queer one."

"Maybe Steve wandered into some trap Talbot laid for you. Since he was a close friend of yours, would Steve have felt some kind of honor or duty to protect you from Talbot? I assume he was in the village long enough to hear Talbot's usual ravings."

Derek considered the question for a few moments. "I suppose so, though I don't recall Steve overhearing the row. The most recent one was after dinner tonight. Outside the pub."

No wonder I hadn't heard it. "Do you know where Steve was?"

"I can't recall off-hand. You see, Steve's war experience scarred him. He had a real fear of sudden noises. They evidently pushed him back into that war mode. We never saw that, but I don't doubt his word. Why lie about it?"

"Why, indeed. Plenty of men have that affliction, unfortunately. It's a common occurrence of war. I believe it used to be known as 'shell shock' in the First World War."

"It must be awful, knowing anytime you could lose your equilibrium."

"I've heard it takes some of them like that. A fragrance, a scene, a sudden noise just waiting to trigger a memory and reaction that's become ingrained."

"Steve and Talbot were going to check the torch and lanterns for firecrackers." Derek's voice had been rising during his explanation. He paused, looking at me, not saying that the obvious place, the bonfire, was under my jurisdiction and shouldn't have needed checking. He continued in a lower voice. "If Talbot started that stupidity about the dole, and Steve heard some firecrackers exploding from kid's play or even that rock band..." Derek glanced at me, as though we were thinking the same thing.

"I know." I stood up. "If Steve snapped, perhaps Talbot had to kill him in self-defense."

7

"Is that how you made sergeant grade?"

The question, though a joke, came from the sober lips of my friend, Margo Lynch. She was a constable, ten years my junior, and was learning from me as I was from Graham, though I was certain Margo was getting shortchanged.

We sat on a bench outside the pub, half-filled glasses in our hands, expounding on the world in general and the murder case in particular. I shivered as I took a swallow.

"Never mind the smart remarks," I said. "What happened to your rose-colored glasses? You're supposed to wear them when you look at me."

"I take them off at sunset."

"Great. I thought you wanted the benefit of my experience."

"I do, Bren! I marvel at you."

"You'll make sergeant quicker than I did, Margo, if you avoid my bruises and mimic my laurels."

"Will I know which is which?"

I glared at her, in no mood for humor. The

hours were slipping away and I still had to talk with Graham before I got to bed. I finished my shandy. "Why am I laying my theories before you, then?"

"So you'll hear them, find holes in them, and fix them before you recite them to Graham, who will, we both know, fillet you like a piece of cod and roast you for good measure if they aren't reasonable."

She stared at me, her dark eyes serious in the light from the pub's windows. She had a good figure and a good mind, and really had no need of my tutelage, but it was great to have a friend. Confiding in Margo was like writing in my diary.

"He unnerves me at times," I confessed, keeping my voice low. My fingers went to the lapus lazuli necklace I wore. The three rectangular stones were warm from my skin.

"I think he unnerves all of us, Bren."

"I'm a competent detective, Margo. I graduated second in my class, and I've earned several accommodations. I'm usually calm and able to think on my feet, but I find myself stuttering and second-guessing my decisions when he looks at me a certain way or says something in a certain tone. When I'm around him I start to fall to pieces. And then I'm mad at myself, because I'm not like that working on my own."

Margo screwed up her mouth, as though considering the information. "I think there's a bit of hero worship in there, isn't there, Bren? Or even infatuation? Besides being smart, Graham's awfully good looking. Is that part of your problem with him?"

I shrugged, not able to sort through my confusion. Maybe it was a case of exhilaration from working with one of the best detective-chief inspectors in the Force, or an exuberance of love. I just didn't want to make a fool of myself or, worse yet, show I had burgeoning feelings for him. I hoped that my normal wisdom would return before I made a hash of my career. I said as much to Margo.

"I don't envy you, Bren. Isn't there a saying about never meeting your idol?"

"He's not really my idol, Margo. He's just someone I admire."

"And wish he'd return your love. No, don't look at me like that. Maybe that's not the right word, but you feel something bordering on that. And that makes you seem slow-witted and a bit childish at times. He knows you're smart. He knows class rankings and history of all his team members, and he chose you for his team, if that makes you feel more confidence. But I think you're treading on thin ice. Don't let him know there's something more than a work relationship between you two." She stretched and drew in a deep breath of the cool air. "You could always ask to be transferred."

"Isn't that like cutting off my nose to spite my face?"

"I don't want you to go elsewhere. I like working with you. Just be careful if you continue to be paired with him. Emotions like that have no business in the job. Especially not during a murder investigation."

I nodded. She was right; she usually was. I'd stick with the team, steel my heart, and learn as much as I could from him.

"And if you want my last thought on this, Bren, he probably realizes you're slightly nervous. It's been only a month or so. It takes time to fit in and understand your coworkers. I'm sure he'll overlook a few mistakes. Just don't take too long getting up to speed."

I sagged against the wall of the pub, a medieval relic that seemed to lean eastward. Probably to catch the first warmth of the rising sun, I thought, wondering how much colder the courtyard would be in January with the flagstones buried in snow and the roof gutters fringed in ice. The quadrant smelled of mold and dead leaves but I envisioned it in Christmas, perhaps enlivened with pine boughs and twittering birds. Now it was merely dark and dead, as though waiting for the winter solstice to resurrect it. I scuffed the toe of my shoe along the bench's base, barely aware of the cold stone at my back, deaf to the sounds around me as I mentally prepared for our upcoming meeting.

Margo drained her glass and set it down with a thud. "A couple of the tourists want to leave. I can't say as I blame them. They're nervous. They think it's some kind of strange village ritual, picking out a foreigner to sacrifice. The Vic put a fast stop to that little idea. Probably scared them into staying."

I turned my head toward her, suddenly back in the present at the sound of Graham's nickname. 'The Vicar' or 'The Vic' had been born out of ridicule, as mine had been, but had now faded into our jargon, its reason and origin nearly forgotten. In spite of my unease at my upcoming chat with Graham, I smiled.

"I can believe that. He *is* forceful."

"I wonder what he was like in the pulpit?" Margo asked it like most women ask 'Wonder what he's like in bed.'

"He probably hasn't changed much. He's still Graham. Personalities don't change, even with a new set of clothes."

"He wasn't defrocked or anything, was he?"

I listened to a dog bark and watched a light go off in a house down the lane before I shrugged.

"Well, it's a mess-up, this whole thing. Have you talked to the proprietor of the gift shop?"

I set down my glass and leaned forward, more out of habit than in trying to see across the car park. When I shook my head, Margo said, "He's nervous business will fall off."

"Because there's been a murder?"

"Sure. What do you want, Brenna—a dozen? Even one's bad for sales when the tourists get cold feet and leave. And I can't see a gift shop having that large of a profit margin. They have to sell a hell of a lot of post cards to pay the electric." She shook her head and stretched again. "Bad all around. So, what do you have for Graham?"

I told her about my conversation with Mason, practicing the confident tone I didn't feel.

"And then, Talbot tried to cover up the killing by stringing up the body? Seems like a lot of trouble. Why not just plead self-defense?"

Margo's skeptical look didn't perturb me. I was glad to have something on which to work, a challenge on which to focus my brain. "So you think it's Talbot? When did he do it? And if not him, the killer?"

"The time schedule's pretty tight." That was like saying Steve had stopped breathing. "We've got the Guy sitting out in plain sight from Thursday till time of the bonfire on Sunday. It sits there through the dole Friday, when villagers and tourists walked by it; it sits there through Mischief Night Saturday. Granted, the effigy isn't under lock and key or constant surveillance, but there are enough people strolling around the area during those three days to make a substitution difficult, in my opinion."

"But one was made."

"So, what do you think?"

"I think Graham will be happier with your success rate of zero firecrackers at the bonfire."

"Great."

"You can bring that up if things get a trifle warm, Bren. Remind him that the moronic element might have thought up something stupendous in the humor line, only your presence and vigilance—"

"Your words are a comfort in this time of trial, Margo."

"—prevented a greater mishap. After all, the moronic element never let an opportunity pass for a good joke. Especially if it causes alarm or disgust. You were saying?"

I stood up and smiled at her. "To quote our Fearless Leader, '*Ora pro nobis.*' We who are about to die—"

"Don't give me that, Bren. You're too worried about what he'll think. Just go in and talk to him. He's not God, for Christ's sake!"

"Of course I'm worried! He's my superior officer!"

"You've been placed with him to support him and learn. So make a few mistakes and learn!"

She stood up, slung my purse over my shoulder, and pushed me toward the pub door before wandering off.

Graham—tie loosened and shirtsleeves rolled up—and I sat in my room at The Broken Loaf mulling over the possibilities already forming in this case. A combination art show/Christmas bazaar had eliminated the village hall's eligibility as a rural branch of the Derbyshire Constabulary. Exuberant displays from the area's talent smothered every interior inch of that hall. So, a space in the pub served as incident room. With any luck, we'd be out of here by the end of the week, and the publican could reclaim his territory. Murder inconveniences everyone.

I relaxed considerably once we had started talking, but still struggled with unease at having Graham in my room. We observed the proprieties—he sitting in the chair and I on the bed. And even though we kept to the neutral subject of the murder, I couldn't help but wonder if I'd welcome or resist his advance if he chose to do so. I glanced at the bed, recalling times when I had wished for a romantic interlude with him, but now that he was so close, in such an intimate surrounding, I found my chest and throat tightening. I sought solace and protection in the murder. I angled the notebook toward the light. "We've got the Guy Fawkes pre-bonfire festivities starting a bit before seven o'clock." I squinted at my handwriting. "Vamsyhe, Vanoyke…"

"VanDyke?" Graham suggested. He couldn't bear any type of suffering. "Ramona VanDyke?"

"That's the lady. Thank you, sir. Usually I don't make such a mess of my notes."

Graham replied that normally my notes were the pride of B Division, and asked me to continue.

"The event starts with that rock group playing for thirty minutes or so, but the program proper starts a bit before seven, with Ramona VanDyke doing the singing honors. Most of the village had gathered by that time. I think it's probably the same each year."

"And Ramona's contribution to the evening's joy was over by…"

"Ten after seven, or close enough to it. There

was a rather embarrassing dance routine by a local girl."

"Embarrassing? She fall into the bonfire?"

"No, sir. Suggestive attire." I remembered the scanty bikini. "More in keeping with August temps and the beach, I would have thought."

Graham smiled, then asked me to go on.

"The dance was executed to music played on a portable cassette player. Following that, we have a poem read and written for the occasion, and a violin solo. That amounted to another five minutes or so. Then the vicar says his bit to the assembled mass, lights the torch, and hands it to Bryon, who hands it to Ramona."

"Who promptly reveals the effigy is in actuality a corpse, and faints. Easy and succinct."

"The rock group that played before all this began was a new addition this year."

"Oh yes?" Graham looked interested.

"Arthur's fiancée has a son by a previous marriage. He was rather keen on having his group play, and Arthur begrudgingly gave his permission."

"That sounds as if that went against tradition."

"It riled many people, and not all of them are old-age pensioners."

"Too bad it spoiled their evening. What's this got to do with the murder?"

I said that Ramona's son was adamant that the effigy be hung early. "To use as a visual for one of their songs," I explained.

"So it was hung early, against tradition," Graham guessed.

"Yes, sir. Sometime in the morning instead of hoisted immediately after the bonfire lighting."

"So we have that bit of change, and people have access to the effigy and the whole bonfire event. I wonder if everyone was where he or she should've been?"

"Meaning?"

"Meaning, if this village drama is as old as everyone says, and it varies hardly a millimeter from year to year, and all of a sudden Talbot, say, wasn't next to the vicar to hand him the wooden torch—"

"That's kind of obvious, though. Wouldn't the murderer have more brains than that, realizing it'd be a dead giveaway if he weren't where he should be?"

"Speaking of being in places, why don't you question Talbot, if he hasn't sought the refuge of eiderdown? I'll see what our landlord has to offer."

"If it's supper," I said on my way out the door, "save me something."

Talbot's cottage lay in a thick pocket of the woods, at the end of an earthen track driven clean of grass through hundreds of trips. Tree branches and leaves littered the edges of the lane, barely allowing room for my passage. Once I had to stop mid-point, the engine of my Mini idling in the quiet as I got out to drag a large tree limb from the road.

There was a rustling in the undergrowth to my left, as though I had disturbed some animal's evening foraging. But no eyes glared at me, no angry retort came. I heaved the limb into the woods, the leaves—crisp from frost—crunching under my feet. I wiped my hands on my trousers and glanced at the sky. Stars seemed to balance high overhead on bare branches, as tips of fairy wands. I got back into the car and turned up the heat, the scene seeming suddenly desolate. Minutes later, Talbot's house emerged from the gloom.

It was of gray stone, half submerged in Virginia creeper, and half hidden by elderly oaks. A kind of witch's house from Hansel and Gretel, with a large wood pile leaning against the southern side to protect it from winter's blast. A curl of smoke seeped from the stone chimney that sat in the middle of the slate roof. Two windows, like giant eyes, stared into the woods from either side of the front door. Below the windows was the remnant of a small flower garden, its wizened stalks and leaves barely visible above the forest's castoffs. The door glistened bright yellow in the glare from the car's headlights.

I found Talbot there. He looked to be in his sixties, and was as thin and gray as the weathered wood he handled for the annual bonfire. Nearly indiscernible dark eyes wedged between a craggy forehead and hollow, sunken cheeks in a long, gaunt face, producing a living likeness to a Grimm fairy tale goblin. He stood in the open doorway, a patch of moonlight catching his facial hollows. He cautiously eyed me before begrudgingly letting me inside. I took the indicated chair, aware that he still leaned against the closed door. He remained there for a minute or more, as though deciding something. When he finally crossed the warped wooden floor, his shoes clattered into the stillness.

Talbot came to a halt in front of a well-used chair, the back of his legs touching the knobby-textured fabric. His eyes fixed on me while his hand sought one of the chair's upholstered arms. Lowering himself into the lifeless cushion, he asked what I wanted. "Kind of late to be rousin' folks, isn't it?"

"Sorry if I roused you, but the light was on, and you opened the door readily enough." I surveyed the room, not so much as to prove Talbot had indeed been awake, but as to set the man in his environment and help me understand him.

It was a small room, as all rooms probably were in the small house, serving as a catchall lounge and dining room. A plate complete with dinner remnants sat on the end table, a heap of newspapers served as a place mat. Well-worn, solid furniture ringed the room's perimeter like American football linebackers. A low wattage light bulb from a floor lamp did its best to illuminate a corner. I could just discern a few books in the over-all gloom. The electric fire was on the lowest setting, barely glowing or disseminating warmth. I rubbed my arms.

Talbot noted his dinner plate, my observation, and the work clothes he still wore. Useless to pretend, I thought.

"Just talkin' general, Sergeant. Now, what's it you want? I suppose it's about the killin', 'cause I can't think of why else you'd be here."

I felt more than saw Talbot's eyes drilling into mine. Like an eagle tracking a wounded mouse. I watched a brief flash of light skate across the dark hollow that hid Talbot's eyes. Unnerving. I pushed the discomforting comparison from my mind, and settled in for the routine of gathering information. "I understand you built the bonfire."

Talbot fidgeted and shifted his emaciated body, his veined hands gripping the arms of the chair. Moments passed before he nodded, his thin gray hair slipping into and out of the lamplight like gossamer strands of a spider web undulating in a faint breeze.

"Near twelve, fifteen feet high, it was. I take my time with the buildin' of it." He settled back into his chair, his eyes buried even deeper in the shadow cast by the chair's high back. "Unlike most villages where they just let anyone throw on whatever. I take my time to see it's all set up proper. That means a solid base of the bigger stuff, then taperin' up to the smaller. Mind you, Sergeant, I can't always hold strictly to that 'cause sometimes people bring me old furniture or wood or whatever after I've got beyond the base. But I do with what I have, and do the best with what I have. And so far, there's been no complaints or mishaps from crumblin' wood."

"And probably won't ever be. You seem to have an excellent grasp of engineering. How many years have you been constructing the fires?"

"Since 1974." He screwed his eyes shut as though it was an effort to remember. It hadn't taken him long. I suspected Talbot knew readily enough; he just wanted to emphasize his importance in village life. "What's that make it? Forty-odd years? I was twelve years old when I took it over from Mr. Brains when he left for study in America. The Polytech weren't good enough for him, it seems."

"Would that be Derek Halford?"

"He takes himself off, spends four years in university and comes home with his degree. He built the fires before he left. Threw them together would be the word. Didn't build them careful like I do."

"So he left in 1974 for his university courses, and you've been in charge of the bonfires ever since."

"Aye."

"Did he ever give you a hand with it? I just thought he'd miss the fun of it. They don't do this sort of thing in America, I understand."

"They don't. It's purely British, and I can't see it ever crossin' the Atlantic like so many other things of ours has done. And no, Derek's never had a hand with the fires since he come back. Don't know if he's too high and mighty for manual labor now that he has that university degree, or what. Seems it was fine for me to do as a kid, but too common for a university-bound one."

"Maybe he has other commitments. Marriage takes a lot of some men's time."

"Don't get started with that line of thinkin'." Talbot pounded his forefinger against his thigh. "Derek didn't bring back a wife when he returned from his studies abroad. Wasn't even courtin' Kris. Don't know why he wasn't interested in the Guy Fawkes celebration. Never asked him. Anyway, I'm happy with things as they are. I enjoy buildin' the fire. And I don't want to give it up!"

I hoped the blast hadn't damaged my hearing. "You all seem to have your talents in this village, Mr. Tanner. You have the fire to see to, plus Ramona—"

"Ramona gets the dummy together." Talbot's grin slowly consumed his weathered face. "I'd say it suits her fine, seein' as how she's courtin' the village's biggest dummy!" He rolled back his head and laughed in one loud bark. "Her official part in all this is to ask at the homes hereabouts for any castoffs. But as she and Mr. Lord-of-it-All Catchpool are keepin' steady company, and will probably be married in not too many months, that could change. Arthur's a bit jealous when it comes to Ramona. Can't see him lettin' her run about, beggin' for clothes from the men. But she's a willful lady, and if I know Ramona, she'll keep on with it even when she's enthroned as Lady of the Manor."

"So it's more than keeping up an image, then."

"Can't see her givin' up that little bit of work when she gets that ring on her finger. There's nothin' to most of this work, is there? What's so damned hard about findin' old clothes?" Talbot's eyes stared out from the darkness beneath his eyebrows, daring me to contradict him.

"Nice that you have so devoted and caring a group in your village. Many places aren't so lucky."

Talbot sniffed, wiping the back of his hand across his nose. "Like I said, it's not all that bad. There's nothin' to most of it. It's a one-shot thing."

"Not like being church choir director, for instance?"

Talbot nodded and said no one would ever corner him into doing something on-going. "I've got my own things to worry about. But it's not too much to build that fire. Only takes a few hours from my year. The Big Three can bask in the limelight all they want. I like my dark corner."

"The Big Three..." I looked up from my notebook and searched Talbot's face for meaning. "Would that be Arthur Catchpool, Derek Halford, and Ramona VanDyke?"

"Missed the brass ring, Sergeant. Though Ramona will be movin' into that slot soon enough after she's married. Can't be too soon for her, either, from what I hear. She'll certainly welcome Arthur's bank account. About run through her own, she has. Wants the Lord of the Manor to increase his B and B portion to take in more payin' guests and shore up Arthur's bank account, but I can't see him destroyin' any more of his precious rooms to give over to tourists."

I said it would be a shame, from what I had seen of the Manor, for Arthur to destroy more rooms to insert en suite facilities.

"Got too many antiques, anyway. What would he do with 'em if he does over a dozen more rooms, say? Sure wouldn't pile them on the fire come next November! But as to the Big Three, now, the third is Byron MacKinnon, Arthur's indispensable secretary and convenient shoulder to Mrs. Halford, should she ever need it. And many's the time she does. That's the high and mighty trinity that rule this village, our lives, and allow us to do what they like. They've all cheated me out of my legal money, sought to cheat me out of everything due me ever since I told 'em who I really am. Ever since—" Talbot stood up and glared down at me. "But maybe you need to go now. Getting' late. I need to get to bed. Should think you'd want to, too. You've been here all day. I saw you, down at the green. Nosin' about the fire. What for?"

I explained my original assignment, stressing that I had merely been there to prevent firecracker trouble.

Talbot grunted. "Pure waste of time. We have a bit of trouble with firecrackers in this village, but not to extreme."

I wasn't certain if he meant the firecrackers were a waste of money, or if my assignment was. The ill-lit room did nothing to help me penetrate the darkness thrown over the man's face and read the emotions in his eyes.

Talbot bent forward, his hand supporting his thin frame as it dug deeper into the chair. I heard the metal spring contracting beneath the compressed chair fabric. "Government's into everybody's lives. Don't let a man breathe, go about his own business. What we need is a democratic government, individual rights, where a man ain't beholdin' to no lord—"

Somewhere in the darkness outside, a dog howled. A long, slow, frustrated howl. Give me another minute, Dog, and I'll join you. "That's probably true." I glanced at Talbot's meager dinner remains. "But I need to establish a timetable for the day's events. It'd be very useful to our investigation if you could tell me when you recall—"

"If you want to do something useful, you look into this business of the dole. You look into the dealings of Arthur and Derek, and you find the money they've cheated me out of. You do that, Miss Detective-Sergeant." Talbot's knee pushed the heavy chair forward a bit. "You nose about a bit into that Terrible Trio's goings-on and you come back here and tell me I'm wrong!"

I mumbled something memorized and noncommittal, and left Talbot in the middle of his lounge. The lone, howling dog had induced others to join him and, to me, the yelping chorus sounded peaceful compared to Talbot's raving.

8

I left Talbot's bewitched woods and the cacophonous canine chorus, wondering if the man had assimilated to the setting, or vice versa. The night had settled in with a calmness that probably belied the agitation and grief gripping Ramona and the Halfords. Beyond the blackness of the churchyard, the village green seemed to pulsate in white light as constabulary duties were still being done. A moment later I parked at The Broken Loaf, last in a long line of police cars. Graham's red Insight hugged the curb opposite the front door. Coincidence or right of rank?

Rectangles of light spilled from the pub's windows, washing the courtyard flagstones in liquid gold. An apt hue, I thought, recalling the region had been the haunt of highwaymen and criminals. The pub had catered both to them and honest clientele, storing chests of gold, silver plate and jewelry in its dim cellar. The medieval building still suggested its past through creaking floors and blackened timber, yet the publican had been careful to hide its modern appointments from the tourist eye. I paused in the courtyard, imagining a midnight call to the shutters, a clatter of horse hooves on stone. Now the air held only the familiar chatter of police business.

I turned to a noise behind me. Nothing

moved in the darkness. At the farthest end of the yard, where the light did not reach, wrought iron tables and chairs huddled in great piles, waiting for winter storage. A fountain, waterless and looming like a nightmarish creature, squatted in the near corner. I caught an odor of wet stone as I passed.

The pub's main door had been braced open to allow for the myriad trips needed to bring in equipment. I hesitated in the entrance, listening to a snatch of laughter from the public bar, unsure of where the lads were establishing the incident room. A CSI officer nearly collided with me as he pushed open the door to the private bar. Blinking at me, he jerked his head and said, "In there. He's in a lovely mood," and hurried outside. Thanking him, I followed the sound of Graham's voice and walked inside.

Computers, boxes of paper, and general office equipment sat on chairs, folding tables, stools and any available floor space. It looked more like a schoolroom at the end of term than it did a pub. I nearly tripped over a desk lamp as I walked up to Graham.

Evan Greene, publican of The Broken Loaf, threw a damp towel onto a convenient table and joined us. The sweat on Evan's dark hair and beard told of his help in converting the room from bar to temporary police workspace. He pushed up the sleeves of his black pullover and stood, hands on his hips, surveying the room.

The bar smelled of fried food and coal fires. In not too many more hours, it would also stink of smoked cigarettes and perspiration—an unfortunate occupational hazard, for it was a nice room. A painting executed in somber oils by a heavy-handed artist consumed the wall above the fire's hearth, while at its feet an accent of yellow and gold mums complimented a brass cauldron. A telly, its screen nearly the size of a car, sat diagonally in a far corner, the room's one concession to Progress, while the traditional dart board hung below a large photo of a current political leader. I was sure I could ascertain small holes in the picture, editorial comments on the state of the world. Even in the current clamor of carting in equipment, I could imagine the 'thwack' of the dart as its metal tip bit into the corkboard. The corner opposite the television sported a large sign proclaiming the meeting time of a local folksinging group. They would have to meet elsewhere tomorrow night. Not a bad room, but I felt like a fox in a hole. The dark curtains that smothered the pub's windows would have to be opened, for I already yearned for sunlight in this somber environment.

"Hard workers, your lads are." Evan watched a constable place a paper shredder on the settle near the fireplace. I wondered how much more weight it could hold, for it seemed already to be groaning under the accumulating equipment. "Never seen a group work so quick in all my life. Or so much equipment, for that fact. Guess I'm still back in Sherlock Holmes days. A person tends to think of detective work as looking about on the ground with a magnifying lens, doesn't he? Must be a hard go keeping up with all this computer technology."

"It's not all that hard," Graham said, catching my eye. "We're given a choice each year of enrolling in Open University classes for three months or sitting alongside some five-year-old for a week."

"That so? Well, the things kids know these days..." He shook his head in amazement as Graham smiled at me.

"I'd like to thank you for the use of the room, Mr. Greene. It's more help than you can imagine, having a large, secluded place in which to work. Would you mind a few questions as long as you're here?" Graham gestured toward a table. "I know it's a hell of an hour, and you're probably dead-tired, but I'd like to get as much information as I can before we all collapse into our beds. Memories are so much fresher right after the event." He smiled broadly, evoking a genuine vivacity for life and his job, and a personal charm that very few people could resist. I had heard the talk; he had developed this quality while a minister. Just because he had switched careers was no reason to abandon the talent. Graham motioned again to the table, let Evan precede him, and waited until I had joined them before asking about the evening's schedule.

"I didn't have anything much to do with it." Evan wiped his palms on his jeans. "It's Arthur's show."

"Oh? You supply the potatoes and the beer. Big enough contribution, I'd say, both in expense and time."

"I like doing it. And I can afford it, so it's no hardship."

"There are a lot of people who can afford to do things, yet choose not to. It's nice you help out. The villagers must be very grateful to you."

Evan mumbled that he supposed they were, but that wasn't why he did it. "I'm not out to prove anything, or to put myself above anyone. Wouldn't be a proper bonfire night if we didn't have our potatoes and parkin, would it?"

I smiled. The oatmeal and treacle gingerbread had been part of my childhood bonfire nights.

"Do you know when you delivered the

potatoes to the fire area?" Graham asked.

"I must've unloaded the potatoes around quarter past six."

"You didn't notice anything unusual about the fire area or the effigy, I take it."

"Other than the Guy already hung, which, I'll tell you straight out so you know, I was dead set against. It's not our tradition to have it already hanging when the festivity starts. But that son of Ramona's wanted it up, so Arthur caved in and allowed it."

"Has Liam or his group ever played at the event before tonight?"

"No. And I can't say I'm sorry." Evan scowled and shook his head. "I don't pretend to know anything about music. I can't say whether they are good or mediocre or bad. But it's the going against the Bonfire Night tradition that irks me, and I'm not alone in feeling this way. Ask most anybody there. They didn't like it."

"Did Liam or any of his band members tamper with the Guy?"

"Not likely to know that, am I? I wasn't there when they began playing or when they set up. They could've, I suppose. But why would they dress a dead man as the effigy?"

"Did they know Steve Pedersen?" I asked, anxious to follow the thread.

"I wouldn't know."

"They didn't talk together in the pub?"

Evan frowned, as though picturing the gatherings of people. "They might have, but I can't say definitely. I suppose they could've met around the stage area or bonfire earlier in the day. I wasn't there." He eyed me, implying I should've seen the meeting since I'd been on duty.

"What about when you delivered the potatoes?" Graham asked. "Did you see that the effigy had been disarranged or altered?"

Evan snorted. "I don't know. I'm not a bloody mind reader. We weren't expecting anything unusual, and I didn't see anything like that. It'd just gone sunset an hour before I got the potatoes unloaded, so it was good and black out there."

"I'm surprised you didn't have a torch with you."

"Couldn't very well handle that plus the potatoes, could I?"

I explained to Graham that Evan had left the truck headlights on.

"Parked near the circle since I came from the pub. So I was pointing away from it, toward the woods. I always park like that, parallel to the fire circle. I've been livin' here all my life, so I know the layout. I just need a hint of light so I don't step on some little feller crawlin' around!" He laughed, then said he hadn't seen anything he oughtn't to have seen.

Graham's low voice, smooth as silk, asked if anyone else had been at the green then.

"Kris Halford." Evan watched my pen skate across the notebook page. "She came over to watch the till here in the pub, and I trotted off with the potatoes."

"Came over from…"

"Her house. She lives just a minute or so away. It'd just gone six, I think, when Kris got to the pub."

"Anyone else?"

"A few tourists. We get tourists all year long, but especially for the dole and bonfire nights. There are some in the village who count them more a nuisance, but I like having them here. Not only for the money they bring in, but 'cause I like folks."

"I bet you've encountered some interesting persons. Many unusual tales of where they've been, where they're going to."

Evan nodded. "Lots of folks tell me their hopes for the future, where they'd like to live, what they'd like to do. We aren't so much different as the media tries to make us out to be. We all want a good job, nice nest egg to retire on. But I will be glad when this bloody dole is over with and the village can return to normal. We've enough to worry us with the bonfire and mischief nights. Though it was comfortin' to see you, miss, on duty. Ta."

I nodded while Graham replied that sometimes it did seem that the stars were at odds with human endeavors.

"Right," Graham said suddenly, standing up. "I don't mean to keep you up till opening time tomorrow. I have the schedule now, thank you."

"Uh, Mr. Graham? You find this lunatic. If you need my help, I'll gladly throw in with your lads. But you find him. Killing some bloke who only wanted to see his friends again, have a bit of fun on his holiday... Gives the village a bad name, doesn't it? You catch him, Mr. Graham."

Graham said we would, and moved toward the door. "You're free to go to bed, if you wish, Mr. Greene. Only, I'd be obliged if you'd leave the pub unlocked. My team hasn't quite finished setting up yet."

"Not to worry. I'll give you a key, and you can turn the latch when you're all ready. How's that?"

Graham thanked the publican and followed him to his office, leaving me to close my notebook.

It was in the dark of the night that it happened. That's how the mystery books phrase it. It was certainly dark, and it was certainly scary. Even now, long after it's over.

I had planned to rise at an early hour, full of determination to shine like the sun. On opening my eyes, I saw it.

A straw dummy, smaller but similar to the one Ramona had made for the bonfire, was hanging from the room's ceiling light fixture. My first thought was that I had effigies on the brain, that even in this short time I was overworked. But the sensation lasted a mere second as, fascinated and repulsed, the form revolved. Morning sunlight, barely tinted yellow and above the eastern horizon, threw one side of the straw figure into relief while the opposite side hid in darkness. It rotated from a scrap of rope tied to the light fixture, the other end looped around the Guy's neck. The knot seemed drawn tighter than need be, for the fabric denoting its neck and face were gathered firmly, producing folds that hid the painted smile. Stray strands of straw littered my comforter and marked a trail to the door.

But what pushed it past absurdity was the fact that my jacket was draped over the Guy's shoulders and my police badge was pinned to its shirt. Which also meant that someone had rifled my shoulder bag.

I looked around the room for other signs of indignities. All was as I had left it on retiring to bed. After sitting there in fright for some time, I eased out of bed.

Normally I would have run over to Margo's room, but the urge to guard the crime scene—if I could label it that—nudged me into phoning. I tapped her number into my mobile phone and prayed I wasn't making a mistake.

"It's not so much the effigy, Margo." My teeth still chattered as I sat cross-legged on the window seat. Margo had conned a robe and slippers and now sat in my room, staring at the suspended dummy. "It's the idea that someone—" I couldn't say it.

"I know." Margo finished my sentence and idea. "Someone got into your room. Also not so comforting to know he wanted you to understand he wished it was you hanging there."

"He could have killed me," I whispered, staring at the Guy.

"Sure. But he didn't. He wanted to scare you. To warn you."

"Warn me about what? What've I done?"

"Nothing. Everything. You're a cop. Part of the investigation team that's poking into everyone's lives. You might have heard something, seen something. Something supposedly insignificant, but immensely important. The Guy proves that. Anyway, this jerk means business, that's for dead cert. If it were just some kid out for a lark, he might just have put a goldfish in your bathroom glass. But hanging the Guy, now..." Margo forced me to take another sip of tea. "Who've you been talking to? That might get us somewhere."

"Not many people so far. Evan—"

"He's got duplicate keys. He could let himself in and out easily enough. Who else?"

"Talbot."

"Old crazy brain? He's nutty enough to, but how would he get in?"

"Graham asked Evan to leave the pub unlocked last night so we could finish setting up. Talbot could have sneaked in, I guess."

"The kind of thought that warms you all over and makes you glad you're part of the human race." Margo pushed the teacup up to my lips. "Okay. We've got a maniac hiding in the closet till you're all tucked in. Next."

"Graham and I talked to Arthur at the hall."

"The refined ones fool you. You think they've got too much class or breeding to kill, and they're the ones who turn out to be Jack the Ripper."

"He knew where we were staying," I confessed, hating to think a gentleman would resort to such a base act.

"That's in his favor."

"His favor?"

"As a suspect. I'm learning, too, you know. This will help my career immensely if I can solve this. Anyone else you talk to?"

"Almost everyone at the bonfire before the murder. Uncle Gilbert— Oh! At the Manor house he wandered into the room as Graham and I were talking to Arthur. But he was awfully drunk."

"He has to sober up sometime. Could it be an act?"

"I talked to Derek, too. You don't suppose whoever this is got me confused with someone else, do you?"

"Who? You don't exactly look like Graham."

"I wasn't thinking of Graham," I said slowly, concentrating on her hair.

"Well, our hair's not the same color, if that's your suggestion. You're a brilliant coppery color. I'm brunette, or haven't you noticed."

"Perhaps my intruder didn't. It was dark."

"Well." Margo took my empty cup. "It's unnerving but at least you're alive. Remember that. You going to tell Graham?"

"No."

"Wouldn't he consider that withholding evidence or something equally rank-busting?

After all, this could be a clue."

"Steve?"

"Two Guys, two…uh, victims…"

She refrained from calling us 'corpses,' at least. I dug my fingers into the back of my stiff neck. Only one day into the case and it was already getting complicated. "You're probably right, Margo. But we can't spare the manpower for this. We're thin on the ground already." I wanted to add that that was the reason I'd been assigned Guy Fawkes duty, but thought discretion the better part of friendship. "Besides, it's pretty trivial when compared with Steve's murder."

Margo stared at me. I knew she was thinking the same thing I was: it wouldn't be so trivial if I ended up like Steve.

Her voice picked up speed and rose in pitch. "But if it's linked to Steve's case and it happens to contain the one lead element we need and you don't inform Graham and he finds out about it later and learns you're the culprit that had the clue—"

I wrinkled up my nose. Of course Margo was right, and I could have been busted back to constable. Or suspended, I guess. But this was personal. Two years ago during a case I'd asked for help with a personal matter. All that it had gained me was the scorn of my A.C. and the enmity of my colleagues. While outright name-calling had not been their forte, those who cared enough smirked or dropped hints as to my courage—personal as well as professional. Some even dropped want ads. I had learned, painful as it had been, not to air personal difficulties. Anyway, I was also reluctant to admit to a certain male that I ran with my tail between my legs at the first sign of trouble. So let Graham demote me. At least I'll go out fighting. "No, Margo. I won't tell Graham or anyone else."

"Too bad. Here we've got a fingerprint chap who could dust for latents, a video team, a team of specialists who could set up a cunning little trap, and we can't use any of them. What a waste."

Margo got up and hugged me. "Please, Bren, don't worry. There are two of us, and we're gonna keep our eyes open. We're both trained, intelligent cops."

"That should strike terror in any perpetrator's heart."

"I can stand watch tonight, if you'd like."

I shook my head, thanking her, and mustered up a smile. "Feminine wiles have worked wonders before, haven't they?"

"Don't worry, Bren, we'll catch him."

She gave a thumbs-up as she left my bedroom, but I wasn't at all sure I had her confidence.

9

Despite the shaky start to my day, I dressed and forced the incident to the back of my mind. Margo was right; with two of us thinking about this, we could capture the joker without Graham's help.

A few sparrows were chirping, searching out their breakfast on the stone patio of the pub. I threw them my crumbled granola bar and watched from the doorway. One sparrow, larger than many in his group, grabbed a sultana and flew off quickly with his prize. I zipped up my down jacket, shoved my hands into my trousers pockets, and wandered down the road, curious to see the village. The chill of the previous night still hung in the air.

Upper Kingsleigh was laid out along three roads that comprised the letter H. Talbot Tanner's cottage snuggled near the top of the eastern road, his house nearly swallowed by the woods. Faint rustlings murmured from the underbrush while a chorus of chirps squawked overhead from the obscure gloom. The world was waking. A hill rose along the left side of the road, harboring church, churchyard, and residential cottages farther south of the church. The expected duck pond and village green sprawled along the southern side of the connecting road, an assortment of shops facing its verdant calm. A few hearty ducks dotted the pond's surface, plunging into the cold gray water only to emerge in a chorus of quacking and flapping wings. On the right-hand western road, opposite Talbot's cottage in distance and station, the manor house consumed its acreage, its turrets and limestone proclaiming everything Talbot would never have. The village pub and post office faced each other at the intersection of the shorter cross street and this long, winding road. More cottages trickled down the western road until the woods finally reclaimed the land and melted into the craggy Derbyshire dales.

I had been walking for several minutes down a road of sleepy houses half surrounded by the deepness of woods and lingering darkness. Aromas of fried eggs and sausages, brewing coffee and hot toast drifted into the day. I was thinking of returning to the pub for my own breakfast when I heard voices. Pausing at the front drive of an ivy-smothered house, I noticed the residential nameplate. Ivy Dell. It belonged to Ramona VanDyke. Another early bird, I thought, wandering down the driveway to the back garden where the voices came from.

Talbot Tanner was straightening up from a wood-bundling chore to drag his shirtsleeve beneath his nose. He eyed the debris, then Ramona, a shapely blonde in her early forties. She seemed to have recovered from last evening's shock, though her wrist would take a bit longer to recover. She'd hit her lower arm against the ladder when she fell last night. Now it was cradled in a makeshift sling. The lilac print clashed with her teal blouse.

"Should've had this garden taken care of long ago, afore it got to be such a mess," Talbot was saying.

The large rectangle of near-wild garden had indeed lost itself in the woods behind it. Vines, bracken and stinging nettle inched into cultivated territory. Ramona gazed at the invasive plants, shook her head, and apologized for being too busy to garden properly.

Muttering that people had their own priorities in life, Talbot tackled the litter contributed by the trees. He gestured impatiently toward the huge bundles of branches and sawn up limbs dotting the garden like trussed haystacks.

It was then that he saw me. Making some unpleasant remark about losing his breakfast, he showed me his backside as he stooped down to tie up some sticks. Ramona greeted me and asked who I was.

"A bleedin' copper," Talbot grunted before I could reply. "So, ring up your solicitor, Ramona, afore she totes you over her shoulder and throws you in the nick!" His laugh disturbed the birds in the trees, for they flew up, chattering in annoyance and lighted in a grassy patch across the road.

When I explained the reason for my early call, Ramona asked if I could wait a minute while Talbot finished up. Just as happy to get Talbot out of my life, I told them to go ahead.

Talbot grumbled under his breath and applied himself to his chore. "If you call me afore you get so many castoffs, it wouldn't take me so long." He made a final knot in the rope corralling a particularly large group of limbs.

"It sneaked up on me, Talbot. I didn't realize how many branches were down until I started weeding the other day. Then, too, that rainstorm brought more down. Too bad we couldn't get to this before the fire. You could've used it last night."

"Might've if I'd had 'em earlier." He bent over a bundle and opened his pocketknife, visually inspected the blade as though he could discern its sharpness. He ran his thumb along the sharp edge, then started sawing on the rope. Seconds later it gave a satisfying 'thwack' as the knife sliced through the fibers. Talbot snapped the knife closed, dropped it into his trouser pocket, and slowly coiled up the unused portion of rope. "Have to come back for it all," he muttered, draping the rope over his shoulder. "When you said branches, I didn't know how much you were talkin' about."

He watched Ramona dig into her pocket and extract several pound coins. In greedy anticipation, his tongue leisurely ran across the roughened skin of his lips. He took the money without a word of thanks. "I'll be back for the lot. Can't say when, exactly. Have to see what I'm doin' the rest of the week." The coins clinked as he shoved them into his pocket. "Anything else you want? That tree'll need some lookin' after soon. Top her off so she won't have all those long branches beggin' to come down." He pointed toward a patriarchal oak. "I can do it pretty cheap. Halfords want some work in their back garden, too. I can do it all on the same day. Save myself a trip and give you a good price, since I'll be right across the road."

"I'll have to see, Talbot."

Talbot tugged at the knot of the bundle.

"Don't want no accidents," he said, tucking the rope's end into the tangle of branches. He ignored me as he passed, coiling the leftover rope around his left shoulder.

"I've had enough accidents, Lord knows." Ramona lifted her slinged arm as though she was a bird with a broken wing. "Besides spraining my wrist, I've a huge bruise on my arm. I didn't know bruises could hurt like this."

"Not too painful, I hope." I said.

"Not the way I'm doped up. God, that damned corpse and then my arm. If I'm not taking codeine for the pain, I'm downing Mogadon for the jitters. But it makes me sleep."

I thought she wouldn't be on the Mogadon for long. After giving my condolences I asked if she had a few minutes to answer some questions about last night.

While Talbot leisurely backed his truck out of the driveway, I followed Ramona into her house. Could either of them have rigged up the effigy in my room? Talbot certainly could; he was already on my list of Prime Suspects. But Ramona was doubtful, with her sprained wrist. Still, people have moved grand pianos single-handedly in a time of stress. I put her on my list of Doubtfuls.

"Is the kitchen all right?" She pulled out a chair for me before seating herself at the table. "Liam, my son, is still sleeping. He's here for a few days. He and his band played at the bonfire last evening and I think they made a night of it afterwards. They— He didn't get in until late."

I told her the kitchen was fine and asked her about the evening.

"Things are always so much clearer in hindsight, aren't they? I shouldn't have asked Arthur to let the boys perform, but Liam wanted to." She glanced down, picking at the corner of the tablecloth. "I think it was mainly hometown pride. He's been away in America to attend university and he graduated this past May. Since then, he and his group have been playing around the area. Nothing big yet, but he has hopes." She looked up and gave me a weak smile. "He knows it's a difficult field to break into, but he has talent and he's stubborn."

"He's got the dream of Youth, which also works in his favor."

Ramona nodded and her smile strengthened. "I've heard some complaints from residents that they didn't like the Guy hung so early. I can understand that, but Liam's band had that song they'd written, and they needed the effigy as a visual prop."

"Did he hang it?"

"He and one or two members of the band. They did it after Arthur agreed to their performance." She frowned and her voice dropped in pitch. "Art wasn't keen on the band playing. I know that. But he did it to please me. We're to be married soon and I think he didn't want to have a squabble concerning my son dangling over our heads when we start our life together."

"So, Liam returned to his village to play for his friends."

"Yes, but it was more than that, as I said. He'd been four years in America and he was enthralled with American football. They have these half-time shows that the university schools put on, right on the football field. Costumes, music, moving around into various designs. He loved it and wanted to bring that excitement to the village, called it modernizing the Bonfire Night tradition. And, too, he thought it might become an annual thing and bring in more tourists."

"Which would help village economy. Was this financial idea his, or did he hear you and Mr. Catchpool talking about his difficulties with his bed-and-breakfast venture?"

"Oh, I'm sure it was Liam's. I don't think he has even seen Arthur since he's been back." She glanced at the open kitchen doorway, as though she expected him to enter the room at that moment.

"How long will Liam be here in Upper Kingsleigh?"

"You want to talk to him?"

Again, she glanced nervously at the doorway.

"Yes. He may be noticed something about the Guy when he hung it."

"Oh." She seemed to relax and sank back into her chair. "I think he'll be here until the weekend. He has nothing pressing that I know of."

"What about the members of his group?"

"I'm not certain. I believe they're here for the next few days, at least. They're somewhere in the village. The pub or a B and B. I'll ask Liam."

"That would be helpful, thanks." I grabbed my shoulder bag and got up. "Please tell Liam I'll catch him up sometime today." Ten minutes later I was walking back to The Broken Loaf, wondering if Liam or a band member had switched the victim's body with the Guy.

Even though my stomach prompted me to return to the pub for breakfast, I decided to question Mason Conway, owner of the village gift shop. It was next to the pub, but more importantly, I was determined to impress

Graham with my initiative.

The shop looked more like a cube of scarlet Virginia creeper and green ivy than a man-made building, for its gray limestone was disappearing beneath the foliage. Rhododendrons—decades old—fanned out from the foundation, while crimson chrysanthemums dotted the greenery at its base. A gray flagstone path, free of autumn's dregs, meandered from the road to the red door proclaiming 'Conway Gifts' overhead in white, Old English lettering.

Mason Conway was sweeping the front step as I walked up, calling out 'good morning' in a puff of white vapor. The sun had just touched the shop's tile roof, transforming the dew into sequins. A bullfinch perched on the gutter, alternately eyeing us and singing into the cool air. A nearby bush seemed to respond in kind. Love song or territorial war? The bird seemed undisturbed by either prospect, for he leisurely drank from the water in the bottom of the gutter.

I stopped, trying to discern if it was a female or male bullfinch. In the dim light I couldn't make out the coloring clearly, which would announce its sex to me. But I did know that quiet warble. Bullfinch sightings were rare, a red alert posted for them. Last time I checked their breeding pairs were down to 190,000. Unlike the wrens I'd seen earlier, which were upwards of seven million pairs. A pity, for this bird was beautiful, with its red chest and belly, black wings and cap, and white rump. Yet this bullfinch sat on a gift shop roof as though it was the most ordinary occurrence in the world. Reluctantly I tore myself away from the bird, hoping I would sight it later.

Mason seemed less interested in the bird than in knowing who was at his shop so early. I introduced myself and explained my errand. He nodded, setting his broom aside, and opened the door.

It was a classic gift shop, offering the tourist the typical knitted apparel, jewelry, post cards, and mugs, and a small offering of emergency tourist essentials. It also offered the less typical pottery, watercolor paintings and embroidered place mats. A balance of predictable, indispensable, and refinement.

"I haven't been here all that long." Mason exchanged his nylon jacket for a wool blazer. He was soft, pink and round like an overripe peach, his cheeks flushed from his custodial duty. We sat in the back room—a catchall for received shipments, returned items and pre-posted packages, and a dispensary for quick meals—the electric kettle heating water for our tea, a tabby cat rubbing against my legs. Mason paused at a small mirror hung near the sink and pulled a leaf from his hair. It was brunet with streaks of white. He tossed the leaf into the rubbish bin, then cleared a space on the wooden tabletop. He spread a checkered tablecloth on it, and pulled out two mugs proclaiming 'Buxton.' It threw me momentarily. I had quite expected something more general, such as Derbyshire. But Upper Kingsleigh people can be tourists, too. I eyed the biscuit tin on top of the small fridge, wishing he would offer them. Unfortunately, his mind wasn't on our stomachs.

"You have a nice shop, Mr. Conway."

"Thank you. I'm holding my own, so far."

"And it's just you working?"

"I have help in the afternoons, when business picks up. And in the summer, when tourist trade is high."

"And you've been here..."

"Four years. I bought it when I was made

redundant."

I accepted the hot tea and added two lumps of sugar. "Oh? I'm sorry. It must have been hard for you. What were you in?"

"Accounting. All of a sudden they had too many accountants. They hadn't hired on new staff in years, had no loss of clients, no deduction in business. Just too many accountants. I was the first out the door."

There was an awkward silence in which I heard the electric kettle murmuring and the cat purring. I counted the seconds between purrs and the drip of water from the spigot. The droplets echoed as they hit the water in the saucepan. Domestic, safe sounds that comforted in an upsetting world. "I thought the shop a safe venture," Mason said, as though reading my thoughts. "It's hard when you reach a certain age. Employers look at you, see only the wrinkles and age spots and broadening waistline. And then calculate the years till you'll retire. You, as a person with a brain, vanish. They forget you're just as capable as you were yesterday and the day before. Yet suddenly you're too stupid to do anything."

I felt self-conscious about my relative youth, and tried to hide my unblemished hands. I made some inane remark about knowing a lot of people who were in that situation.

"I'm not so old. I'm just fifty-nine, for God's sake!"

I refrained from saying that was my parents' ages. There are times when consoling banter is out of place.

"I tried for months to get another job. During that time my wife became seriously ill and eventually died. My friends worried about my own health because I was depressed. They urged me to make a drastic change, so I thought I'd go into business for myself. It's something my wife and I had talked about as one of the 'some day' things." He sighed, staring into his tea. "It's worked out well so far."

Until this murder, I thought. And with the threat of Upper Kingsleigh losing more tourists, what would that do to his trade and future?

"I was late to the bonfire," he said after I had asked about Sunday evening. "I arrived just as the vicar was finishing his speech and handing off the torch. I try to miss the opening shenanigans. Not because I don't like my neighbors or am anti-social. It's just that I'm uncomfortable around Talbot."

I asked if he always felt like that.

"No. Just around dole and bonfire time, when Talbot grouses about the dole money."

"He does tend to rabbit on about the subject, from what I understand."

"It's not so much the continuous complaining. It's Talbot's talk about the war. It hits too close to home for me. I had my own tough times. I was an orphan."

An emphatic ringing of the shop's overhead doorbell pulled him from him chair. "Now, who on earth..."

"Want me to see?"

"I'll yell if I need you. Early for a burglar, don't you think?"

I agreed, and stood up, looking around for a weapon. A set of not-so-stealthy footsteps approached and moments later Byron MacKinnon walked into the back room.

Mason grinned, and I sat down, releasing the paring knife. Greetings were exchanged. Byron sat at the table while Mason refilled the kettle and turned it on.

"Didn't mean to interrupt." Byron gave me the once-over. "Mason usually has the shop open by now and I normally stop by for a cuppa. If this is a bad time or is official business—"

"Not at all," I said, thinking I could check the men off my interview list at the same time. "Tea and a chat. A nice way to start the day." I bent over to pet the cat. He was entwining himself around my legs, as though he expected me to feed him.

"Darjeeling today." Mason handed Byron one of the Buxton mugs.

"Do you know what Arthur's done? Thanks, Mason." Byron accepted the cup of tea and poured a great deal of cream into it. He stirred it, clinking the spoon against the cup's sides. The clinking increased in volume and tempo as he explained. "Another couple wanted to leave this morning. Halfway into their stay and they want to leave. Of course, Art rang up Mr. Graham to see if it was all right. Which it was. Just 'Keep me informed of your whereabouts' and off they went. Sorry." His clinking slowed briefly as he looked at me, only to return to tempo and volume when he continued. "They must be low on the suspect list if he lets them go."

I looked at them, again mentally calculating if they could have rigged up the Guy, or even why they would have done it.

"Poor Arthur," Mason said. "Is he dispirited by all this?"

"He's not exactly dancing through daisies, but to look at him, he's fine. It wasn't his fault Steve was murdered."

"I better see the Halfords when I close up." He scribbled 'Kris' on the flap of a convenient cardboard box.

"The bloody thing is," Byron said, the spoon

falling onto the saucer, "Arthur's refunded their money!"

Mason blinked, either at the volume or at the meaning. "He always was a gentleman, Byron. You can tell breeding without a coat of arms painted on everything."

"Has he ever made refunds before?" I asked.

"Oh, a few people have canceled a trip and have received their money back." His voice returned to a more normal volume. "But that's once or twice a year. And certainly not at the rate they're wanting to leave now."

"How many guests are at the manor? Are any members of Liam VanDyke's band staying there?"

"Three of them are," Byron said. "Liam's at home. But as far as plain tourists, we had booked nearly a dozen rooms, singles and doubles."

I agreed that the reservations would bring in a sizable chunk of cash.

"You're damned right about that! And with Arthur returning everything, even after expenses—"

"Hope he won't get burnt," Mason said.

A silence settled on the group, now somber. Mason got up and poured his tea into the sink, muttering it wasn't to his liking. Byron shoved his cup from him with such violence that the remaining liquid in the cup sloshed into the saucer.

Mason turned and leaned against the edge of the worktop. "I'm amazed people are leaving. People are such voyeurs these days. Court telly and tell-all talk shows, things on the news I never would've imagined seeing. I would've thought this would induce the crowds instead of reducing them."

"Maybe it will." Byron's eyes brightened.

He smiled as though he could see the reservations piling up. "But right now it's a repellant. When you're too close to it, when you've been in the fray, it's frightening. Especially if you think you're the next victim."

"There are many types of victims. We may all end up as victims before this is over. How long you people planning on being here?" He leaned forward, as though challenging me to answer correctly.

I told him we wouldn't leave until we had secured an arrest of the guilty party.

"And how long's that?"

"Mason!" Bryon stood up and took a step forward. "What kind of question is that? The sergeant—"

"The sergeant knows what kind of question it is. It's one from a concerned citizen, one who doesn't want the police traipsing around, scaring away tourists. What the hell's wrong with that?"

I assured Mason it was all right and that we were working as efficiently and swiftly as possible.

"I should damn well hope so. You can't expect tourists to hang about all week until you lot get out of their way. Blocking everything they've come to see..."

"They may come later. It's just like the curious to want to see Where It Was Done."

"And take away a piece of the scene?" Byron said. "Gruesome souvenirs."

"Let's hope they still want less grisly ones," Mason muttered.

I asked Byron if he thought any more tourists would leave the manor.

"I haven't a feel for it yet. Last night I wouldn't have thought this would happen, but this morning..." He shrugged. "There may be a lifeline in this morass. This is one of our busiest times of the year. The three-day events are getting very popular. And we do an awful lot at Christmas—mummers and the Merrie Olde England bit with feasts in the manor's dining room, carols on authentic instruments. That sort of thing."

"Byron spares no detail to make it accurate," Mason said, reclaiming his chair. "Ropes of holly and ivy festoon the walls, candles everywhere, pine logs in the open fireplaces. Gives you the thought he's lived it before."

"And the boars head?" I already felt Elizabethan.

"Complete with apple in the mouth. Well, thanks for the tea, Mason. I must be off. I've got Evan's books to balance." Byron got up and stretched.

"Time for the day to start already?" Mason glanced at the clock. "Seems like the sergeant just had her tea."

I glanced again at the biscuit tin and stood up, thanking them for the information.

Mason walked us to the door. "Well, I'm sorry for Arthur losing some of his business, but don't worry about what hasn't happened, Byron. I was just licking my own wounds before you arrived. It's natural for Arthur to play Good Samaritan. That's his character. But Arthur's got a beautiful establishment, and the village has a lot going for it. I just hope we can weather any storm that may blow up."

I glanced around her shop again, noting the handmade sweaters and tams, the homemade biscuits and breads, the paintings and photographs of local scenes. A lot of local talent had their hopes and money tied up in the Conway Gift Shop. If it died it would take more than Mason with it.

"It can't drive everyone away." Byron forced cheer into his voice. "There'll be tourists."

But tourists gawking at what, I wondered as I extracted myself from the cat's tail and left the shop.

10

Monday morning's drowsiness was punctured by a peal of church bells announcing the nine o'clock hour and nudging the idler into activity.

I've never been a steady churchgoer but either the bells or last night's event pulled me up the path.

The vicar of St. Michael's church was evidently one of the few who had kept to his normal weekday schedule, for he waved—cheery and freshly scrubbed—when I called out his good morning.

Lyle Jacoby was short, pudgy, and practically bald. More like a monk than English vicar, I thought, noting the fringe of pale hair that shone halo-like in the sun. Steady, clear eyes, devoid of the puffiness or redness that spoke of the few hours' grabbed sleep, gazed frankly back at me. Most likely stayed till the wee hours comforting the Halfords, I thought.

"I'd no idea when you'd be coming, miss," Lyle sang out after I introduced myself. "I figured you would find me wherever I was, so I went about my usual offices. Though that could change abruptly."

"How are the Halfords?" I asked. "I assume you've been rather busy with them."

Lyle nodded slowly, supporting the unspoken acquiescence and his dejection at the same time. "They both reminded me last night of little children. So terribly sad, this tragedy. Such a shock. Reunited with their friend after forty years of believing him dead, then to have him die like that, so quickly, so horribly." He shook his head and turned to face the approximate direction of Halfords' house. "I don't know which of them is the more upset. Kris, now, I'd expect to grieve, being as how she was engaged to Mr. Pedersen. But Derek— Well, not that men can't mourn. It's such a silly, self-destructive trait we've harnessed men with over the years, this machoism, being stoic and brave and keeping grief hidden. Asinine, if I am allowed any say in the matter. However, Derek had a healthy cry last night. I don't know who was holding up whom when I got there; they were so shocked and overcome. I let them talk. Seemed the best thing. You know, the shoulder and ear that only hear and don't judge. They needed that more than any phrases I could give them about resurrection and heaven."

"Sometimes," I said, "it's best just to be present and listen. Nothing wrong with being a shoulder or ear for an evening." A commiserate heart and a servile ear.

"I suppose so." Lyle went on, sounding uncertain it was all right. We'd been walking along the High Street, gravitating without conscious effort toward the church.

In the center of the early morning sky, the square tower of St. Michael's pushed its way out of the dimness, the rosy rays of sun tingeing the church's ancient limestone walls. The same limestone dotted the churchyard in tombstones and memorial crosses, their ages evident from weather-washed engraving or angle of leaning.

The same cross shape was reflected in the building itself, solid, unmovable, an anchor of centuries of hope. It seemed to rise from the very ground that supported its massive weight. Clumps of chrysanthemum, sage and bare-branched wintersweet decorated its foundation, mixing with cast-off pine needles and dried, fallen leaves. The dregs of summer, I thought, my fingers suddenly aching to rake up the floral debris and set the perennials and rhododendrons in order. As if on sentry duty, a flock of rooks suddenly rose from their perch on the church tower, screeching into the morning.

"You have a beautiful church, Vicar," I said, noting the sunlight capping the top of the gargoyle above the door. It was a perfect waterspout, its gapping mouth appearing ready to devour anyone wandering too close. All that stood that danger were the rooks that nested there.

"Thank you," Lyle said quickly, as though he had just seen the church. "Lovely building, if I am permitted to agree without sounding boastful, though it was built before I ever arrived. Do you know religious architecture well? No? Ah, then, I must point out some of the nicer features to you. The core of the building undoubtedly is early medieval, though a magnificent rood and screen were added late in the 16th century. Probably by a wealthy merchant. Upper Kingsleigh and its environs benefited from various industries as they rose and fell. Wool trade, taking the waters, milling, coal mining. As the wealth accumulated in pockets, it slowly trickled into the church. But we've had the devil of a time of late reinstating the church to its proper condition. Honestly! What those Victorian architects destroyed when they 'restored' the altars and gallery! But we've got it put to rights now. You must see our parclose screen, Sergeant."

I murmured I would love to, but thought I'd not have the chance. Lyle bubbled on. "Magnificent carving! But here we are, now. Climb's getting a bit longer each morning. But that's old age for you. Now, then."

Lyle bent to remove a damp leaf from the top of his shoe before following us through the lychgate. Its squeak mingled with the shrieks of the retreating birds. It also startled me, for I snapped my head toward the sound, expecting another Guy magically dancing before my eyes.

"It's a shame this has happened to them." Unmindful of my unease, Lyle lapsed into a recital of the couples' volunteer involvement in the village. "But you've come about Steve Pedersen, and you want to ask me something about it. That's right, isn't it?" He cocked his head, blinking as the sunlight fell across his face.

Reminds me of a pigeon, with those eyes, that wisp of hair looking like a ruffled, misplaced feather, and those pudgy cheeks undulating as he breathes.

"Unfortunately, yes. There are some things I need to ask if you have several minutes."

"Is it secret? I mean, do we need to go inside, or would it be all right over here? So few nice autumn days left to us. I like to grab them as they come." Lyle indicated a secluded section of the churchyard and led the way when I agreed that area would do nicely.

Autumn had splashed its colors on the deciduous vegetation, giving the somber, solid graveyard a spark of life. Across the tombs, gold, yellow and bronze leaves, like offered coins, shone with the morning's dew. Like Derek's bag of gold, I found myself fantasizing. My shoe crushed a fallen twig of pine. I drew in a lungful of the sharp scent, wanting this time in the sun to last.

"I suppose," the vicar continued once we stopped at an ancient grave and I'd asked my first question, "I shan't be able to forget this particular Bonfire Night, no matter how I try."

"That's the bane of any tragedy. It stays in our minds and picks at our souls for more years than we can imagine."

"One of the thousands of things that form us. Well, where do I begin? Talbot was there, as you know, Sergeant, guarding his stack of wood as much as he was adding to it."

I asked if there was trouble with pilfering.

"Hardly any trouble to speak of. Though that was why you were here, no doubt. Keeping an eye out for firecrackers. Some villages have more than their share of idiots, if you'll excuse me for saying so. But honestly, if these people would only stop to think about what could so easily happen by their disregard for safety. So many small children about. Why there aren't more accidents from fireworks and such is beyond me. Perhaps our quota of idiots has taken residence in other villages."

I wanted to say that Upper Kingsleigh had two candidates for the role right now, but satisfied myself instead with a noncommittal safety statistic.

"I don't know. I've given up trying to sort it out. Talbot, I'm sorry to say, was as upset this year over the graveside dole as he usually is. He latched on to poor Kris when she came up. Then he poured his anger onto Derek. Uncle Gilbert—

he's Arthur's uncle, do you know?—maneuvered Talbot out of the way, and I did the same with the Americans who are staying up at the Manor. I was thoroughly embarrassed by the entire scene. And it was a scene. Talbot carrying on like a right berk, confronting Kris and Derek as if they had anything to do with a ceremony instigated one century ago! And then the tourists had to witness Talbot's antics. If I've told him once, I've told him a thousand times that there's nothing the Halfords or Arthur can do without any proof from Talbot."

"If Talbot is so persistent about his claim, why hasn't he brought forward proof?"

"There's a small problem. You see, Talbot was born in Cornwall in 1953. He lived in the west country for the first ten years of his life."

The vicar paused to let the significance of the date settle into my brain. 1963 saw one of Britain's worst winters. Cold, snow with six foot deep drifts, disastrous spring thaw, floods, buildings and belongings and legal documents destroyed.

"Poor Talbot. His proof sinks into a watery grave."

"You may well say that," Lyle agreed. "I feel sorry for him if he really is the lawful claimant. Well, he could use the money, there's no question."

"So just why does Talbot think he's entitled? I understood the dole went to Derek because he's grandson to the original dole recipient, the crippled grandfather."

"Men get crippled in all sorts of ways. If they're not crippled in the flesh, they're crippled in the spirit or mind. Or in the purse. And some have the misfortune to be crippled all ways."

I nodded. I was still struggling from the

effects of my tyrannical father. "He and Talbot aren't brothers, are they?"

"That is doubtful, but..." Lyle looked at us, as if wondering how many village secrets to divulge. "This time of year Talbot yammers on constantly about how he would be able to prove his claim if only Derek's dad were alive. He swears he was adopted. Yes, you may well look incredulous, miss. Without the legal papers, anyone can venture a guess as to its validity. But he asserts the dole through rightful inheritance."

I shook my head, all sorts of scenarios filling my mind.

Lyle nodded. "Now you can understand the intensity and duration of his row with Arthur and Derek."

"Do you think this row was serious enough for Steve to get involved in since he was a close friend of the Halfords?"

Lyle denied the suggestion, but he quickly explained his answer. "Talbot flares up like this for two or three days each year, then forgets all this foolishness about being included in the dole, and goes on with his routine as though he had never heard of the ceremony."

"But Steve, being a stranger, wouldn't know that it was normal for these brief temper displays. He'd assume it was serious, and he might interfere, thinking he was doing a noble thing by defending his friends against Talbot." I can see it, strangely enough, the confrontation focusing in my mind, the heated exchange of words ringing in my ears. Just the sort of thing a former soldier would do, especially one who was still in the throes of bliss with rediscovering a cherished friendship.

"Perhaps." Lyle admitted it reluctantly, as though not wanting to give any false hope or steer us to the wrong conclusion. "But unless Talbot can tell you, we won't know. Besides, I don't recall if Steve actually saw any confrontation. Dear me, my mind is becoming so hopeless lately. Advent, you know. There's so much to do in the next few weeks before it starts. But I do know that Tom Oldendorf was spared one distasteful scene last night." Lyle nearly whispered, looking around the churchyard. "Gilbert. Disgraceful! I won't mince words, miss. He was drunk. Why Arthur can't keep him in tow is beyond my comprehension."

I muttered that it was difficult to keep one's relatives or loved ones in line at times. I only knew from the gossip circulating in Buxton's police station that Graham was the victim of a broken engagement. Some say he had never gotten over it.

"Now that I've mentioned Gilbert, I must tell you something about the fire last night."

"Do you know something about that, sir?"

"It may or may not be pertinent to your investigation, miss, but at approximately half past four, I observed Gilbert loitering by the oak. The one near the stage."

"Was Mr. Catchpool cognizant of his surroundings? Did he seem to know what he was doing, what was going on around him?"

"If you mean was Gilbert in his usual addled state, I regret to say yes. But that didn't appear to hamper his fascination or attention to the rope. He was at the tree, near the stage and the rope."

"Was Gilbert actually doing anything to the rope, or fussing about with the Guy? Did he look as though he were trying to hide something, however nonchalantly he might have loitered?"

Lyle shook his head, looking uncomfortable.

"I only know for certain that since the deceased was found at the end of a rope and Gilbert Catchpool was at the other end of it, as it were, you might be interested."

"I am. Thank you. The fire area, now… I understand Steve Pedersen checked the bonfire earlier for firecrackers, and that Talbot helped him. If so, it must have been before I arrived on duty. I never saw him."

"I can only repeat that Talbot is the person you need to interrogate on that subject," Lyle said. "I don't know what went on between him and Arthur, or him and Steve Pedersen. Or if anything went on at all. I wasn't there. I hadn't any idea until you said something. But personally, I find it rather far-fetched that Talbot would kill this American, temper tantrum or no. He didn't know the man. What motive did he have?"

That, I silently agreed, is what we're trying to ascertain.

"No. Talbot may be a bit funny about this dole business, but he's not violent. I bet he's just as saddened over this man's death, as are we all. Derek loved Steve Pedersen as a brother."

Brother. I recalled the recent photograph Derek had shown me. Loved as a brother, no doubt, but the two men also looked like brothers.

11

As is usual on the 'day after,' the village's bonfire circle lay in disorder and inelegance. Graham stood at the edge of the brutal scene, visually taking in dozens of burnt, untasted potatoes among the cold, charred wood and ashes. Merry-making and death, laughter and fear shoved together, the lightness of one relinquishing its segment of the evening for the petrifying horror of the latter. His eyes turned to the table on which the glasses sat glazed in lingering frost until thawed by the emaciated sun, everything neatly corralled within the confining circle of plastic police tape.

"There's something offensive about it, Taylor." Graham shook his head, muttering about the waste of time, effort, money, and human life. I'd grabbed a quick breakfast at the bakery, then joined him at the green. His hair was rumpled slightly from the breeze darting over the common—the only ripple in his professional appearance of grey suit, maroon shirt, and tie. "The innocence of a homely scene like this dragged into a murder investigation. The scarring will break open for many of Upper Kingsleigh's folk next Bonfire Night. Perhaps for me, too."

"Sir?" His declaration caught me off guard.

Before he could explain, Tom Oldendorf wandered up to the fire area, his steps slowing as he approached us. Her white hair was carefully combed though his cheeks and chin showed he'd not shaved this morning. He was a different person from the joker who'd listened to Byron's narration of the Guy Fawkes history earlier yesterday.

"Morning," Tom uttered, pushing his low-slung camera out of his way and blowing on his hand before offering it. He spoke with a slight southern accent. The wool jacket he wore reeked of newness and nearly matched the cotton baseball cap angled back on his head. A tuft of hair poked out of the area above the cap's adjustable strap. "I saw you standing here, and I guessed you're from the police. I…saw *you* yesterday, miss." He nodded his head at me by way of introduction. "I'm Tom Oldendorf."

Graham shook hands, introduced us, and added that we appreciated Tom's thoughtfulness.

"I thought I might as well save you a trip. You'll want to question me, I expect."

"You knew the victim, then?"

I unobtrusively opened my notebook and sat on a bale of straw.

Tom managed to look embarrassed and inquisitive at the same time. "'Course I knew him. I used to be related to him. He was married to my sister."

Graham tried to recover his astonishment as gracefully as possible. "Divorce, might I ask?"

"She died." Tom's response rang through the still morning air with the sharpness of a rifle shot. He let his voice match his anger. "She died four years ago, and it was Steve's fault. I don't care what the doctor's report says. Steve's to blame."

"Accident?"

"Only accident was that damned idiot of a doctor. She had a history of hypochondria before she was married, so when she complained of feeling bad we tended not to believe her. She went to doctor after doctor and got conflicting reports. Steve wouldn't believe the ones suggesting stomach cancer. She died of it." Tom seemed almost triumphant to prove everyone wrong. He wiped his nose, then apologized. "Sorry for my outburst. Her death's still raw. I'm trying to forgive, but it's hard."

Aside from blaming Steve, Tom seemed to blame himself. Perhaps he thinks he should have known his sister's diagnosis. I hoped he'd find peace.

"I'm amazed you and Steve took a holiday together."

"I didn't want to come at first. I was afraid I'd get into as argument with Steve. Usually I can swallow my anger, but I do have a temper. Aside from being connected by marriage, we really did like each other once. That's why I thought this trip would be good for both of us, to see if we could patch up the contention."

Contentions, I thought, are unfortunately part of many relationships.

"And did you?" They certainly had looked happy enough during Byron's talk.

His cheeks flooded in embarrassment. "I think we would have. We only just got here a few days ago. We didn't have much time to sort things out. Steve was intent on contacting his college friends and delivering a family heirloom to Kris. He got kind of wrapped up in that. He stayed with them until—" He broke off, his face reddening deeper. It took several moments before he could continue. "I was content to prowl about the village. I love photography, so I didn't mind waiting for the real start of our vacation until Steve had finished with the Halfords. We were both pretty excited about seeing the Lake District." He stared toward the western horizon, as if he could see the area. "I can't believe it. I mean, things don't happen like this to people you know. It's always strangers. No one harms ordinary guys."

I wanted to tell him we investigate ordinary guys' deaths all the time.

"How did Steve seem?" Graham asked. "Nervous, agitated?"

"No different from usual. Just glad to be here and happy he found his friends. Though, he was kind of worried."

"Yes? Why was that?"

Tom shrugged. "Sunday he heard about the Guy Fawkes celebration, about there possibly being firecrackers planted in the fire. He was afraid of sudden, loud noises, afraid they would trigger memories of the war. He got flashbacks quite often from ordinary, everyday things— planes, helicopters, car backfires. That sort of thing."

"I can understand that." I remembered similar stories from veterans. "It must be a nightmare to live with."

"We searched Sunday morning. I met up with him in the bar. Pub. Sorry. Takes a while to get my tongue and brain coordinated with your English. We didn't find anything, but I think he felt better that we looked. Everybody here kept telling him there wouldn't be anything like fireworks, but he wanted to make sure. Especially since that rock group wanted to use the effigy in their act and were staged beside the bonfire. We thought they might've put firecrackers in it so there'd be explosions or pyrotechnics during their act. You know how some groups do, anything wild and rowdy and loud. But, as I said, there weren't any at that time, so we felt better. Then you came on duty, miss. I saw you and I told Steve."

"I hope that relieved his anxiety."

Tom cleared his throat. "He said so, but I don't know if he really believed it. I strolled around the area late afternoon. I wanted one final check, in case some kid had crammed a firecracker into the torch. There was nothing obvious."

"And when did you and he part?" Graham asked. "Were you with him until tea, or until he returned to the Halfords?"

"I didn't look at my watch, if that's what you're after."

"An idea would be helpful."

"Before tea time. I don't know where Steve headed. I expected to see him at the fire, but I really didn't think anything strange about it when he didn't show up. He must've had second thoughts about it. He probably thought it would be safer not to attend, just in case."

"I suppose someone saw him after four o'clock."

"Not just his killer?"

"Hopefully not. So you didn't see him after that."

Tom picked up a rock and looked at it carefully. "The man from the pub and a bunch of people were here. I didn't really think so many would show up in so small a village, but they do say it's a famous three-day event here. Steve could've been here and we missed seeing him. Maybe the vicar saw him. He got around a lot. He was down here before the fire started and took me on a tour of his church. Nice guy. Not at all what I expected. You aren't either, if you don't mind my saying so."

Graham let the obvious question pass.

"Hell of a way for a marriage to end." Tom grabbed a rock and threw it at a tree as he walked away.

"Oldendorf's statement." Graham's gaze followed the man until he disappeared into the bakery.

"Which one, sir?"

"Hell of a way for a marriage to end." He slowly repeated it verbatim. The words, so filled with anger when Tom had uttered them, now sounded heart breaking and regretful with Graham's rendition, as though he had experienced the pain of the tragedy. "That talk about the wife's death bothered me more than I realized. Sorry." The corners of his mouth lifted slightly, as though he was forcing a smile.

I mumbled I understood, which I didn't, and wondered why Tom's simple statement had evoked such an intense reaction in Graham. Office rumors were rife with hints at his failed engagement, but nothing was whispered about a wife. Did she occupy an earlier corner of his life, one that was still raw with his loss?

Graham glanced at his watch and swore. I was spared making a response as dear Uncle Gilbert and Talbot converged near us at the fire circle. Either not caring or thinking we couldn't hear, Gilbert hailed Talbot, chattered about the pleasant morning and previous afternoon almost as though he were describing a saunter through the Dales.

Seems like he's ready for one, I thought, taking in Gilbert's emphatic wristwatch, sunglasses and sturdy shoes. So where are we off to, then?

Graham, sensing the meeting could be important, motioned me to accompany him back to the pub. He signaled to Margo, who was standing in the pub's doorway. I glanced back at the fire area. If Graham wanted Margo to stroll around and eavesdrop, she might be the perfect candidate. She hadn't had much to do with the villagers yet. And she looked innocent, like a tourist.

She wandered off, zigzagging toward the circle, nonchalantly consulting a guidebook and searching her purse. We watched her perch on a bale of straw within several yards of Talbot and Gilbert before we went inside.

Quarter of an hour later, the men had separated and Margo was reading to us from her shorthand notes. They were scribbled, I noted with amusement, inside her guidebook.

Talbot: "What the hell do you want now?"

Gilbert: "Got no time to chat?"

Talbot: "I got things to do."

Gilbert: "Well, here you are, then. I just wanted to do my boy a favor, Tal, that's all. Just a bit of a favor. How'd you like a bit of help snagging the lovely Ramona?"

Talbot: "What are you on about?"

Gilbert: "I shouldn't have thought it needed any clarifying, but if needs must. I'm worried about your future, Tal. You don't look too well off to me. You could do with a bit of help in the money department, I don't doubt. Ramona's got plenty of her own, never mind her shaky alliance with my nephew. Now's the time, Tal. Strike before she marries Arthur. If there's one thing I've learned in my seventy-two years, it's the value of offense."

Margo looked up from her notes as a telephone rang. A constable grabbed it, held his hand over the receiver, and looked hopefully at us. I mouthed 'Who is it?' When the constable pointed heavenward, I screwed up my mouth. It was Detective Superintendent Simcock. Probably checking up on Graham's progress. I shook my head and held up my hand, fingers spread. The constable nodded and returned to the phone. Margo, who had witnessed this pantomime, said, "I couldn't quite hear what Talbot answered, Mr. Graham. He turned away from me. All I really heard was a belch."

"In keeping with his character, at any rate," Graham said.

"Then Gilbert said something that I also couldn't catch, being as he turned in the same direction as Talbot. Some agitated conversation ensued, during which Talbot sniffed, wiped his nose on his shirtsleeve, and crammed the cigarette he was smoking back into his mouth. He gestured in the direction of Ramona's house, which caused him to turn again toward me. I could easily hear them again. Talbot said, "Why should you worry about my future? You've never done much for me in the past, only comin' 'round to see me every few years. 'Sides, it's all taken care of. I've already seen to my future security. It's past the plannin' stage, even, and through no help of yours, Dad." Margo lowered her voice to a more conversational tone. "Talbot was very emphatic about calling Gilbert 'Dad.' And Gilbert seemed happy. He smiled."

"About what? The Dad part or Talbot's information?"

"That's open to interpretation, sir."

"Gilbert could certainly be a father. He's seventy-two."

"Talbot's fifty-four, I believe."

I did some quick mental math. "Gilbert would've been eighteen when Talbot was born."

Graham ran his fingers through his hair, sighing heavily. "It's been known to happen, yes."

Margo looked at me, probably wondering this was about. She said rather quickly. "After that bit of conversation, Talbot said his partner has already seen to his part, then he walked off. I'll type up these notes for you, sir."

"Thank you, Lynch. So what was that about? Are Talbot and Gilbert related, do you think?"

"I thought Talbot was related to Derek," I said.

"I'd hate to see his family tree. Branches kind of intertwined and tangled."

"They're both a little squirrelly, but who will turn out to be the nut?"

"I'd rather be the nut off the tree than the poor sap." Graham frowned and inhaled deeply.

"Just how successful were we in all this? What have we really learned?"

"Aside from us not being Tom's idea of English police detectives, you mean?"

"What's he want, sir? Deerstalker hat, or monocle and manservant?"

"Most likely a crossword sticking out of one jacket pocket, and a bottle of Samuel Smith jammed into the other. You may ask him if you feel so inclined. Only, I'd wait a bit. He's had a nasty eighteen hours, what with the murder, us and Upper Kingsleigh's dear vicar tarnishing his images."

"What's wrong with the vicar, then?"

"Suffers from the same malaise as we do. Uncooperative costume or personality, or something like that. Sorry, I don't mean to sound uncaring."

I muttered that Tom should leave his prejudices and preconceived notions behind, and maybe he'd not only learn something but also have a better time on holiday.

"I think he'd have had a better time if he hadn't gone on holiday with Steve Pedersen. I doubt his first taste of Old Blighty is exactly his cup of tea."

"The Super rang up just now."

"What's he want? No, don't tell me. A miracle."

He reached for the phone and I excused myself, disappeared for a few minutes and returned with two mugs of tea. "Everything all right?"

"Heavenly." Graham hung up the phone. "He just asked if we'd had any luck with tracing the jacket found on Steve."

"Speaking of which, Ramona was in charge of the effigy's clothing. She got the cast-offs this year from Arthur. Do anything for you?"

"Convenient, keeping it in the family like that."

"Sir?"

"She snags Arthur and gets a suit of clothes for the effigy all in one transaction."

"Yes, sir. Anyway, Ramona wasn't at Friday's dole. She was still in Buxton, doing her weekly grocery."

"Small world, Taylor."

"She works in the Crescent, at the visitor's center."

Graham nudged the handle of his mug,

rotating it three hundred sixty degrees before replying. "I've probably seen her a hundred times, and I don't even know her."

"Quite a striking woman. Blonde, figure reminiscent of the 1950s. Curves," I answered in response to Graham's confusion. "Very nice figure, if that doesn't make me sound envious." I sucked in my stomach, and thought again that I should lose fifteen pounds.

"I think you can safely voice your opinion of the lady without my spreading gossip."

I announced my gratitude. "In her early forties, I'd judge. A widow. Local gossip has it she's after Arthur for his money."

"And you found out all this before our walk this morning? You have been busy, Taylor. Who else have you been talking to? I'd bet my undernourished pay packet the desirable widow didn't tell you all that."

"No, sir. Well, I have been walking about a bit this morning, listening. Did you know Kris Halford's the product of an English father and American mother? One of the few British-American marriages to have endured over here, I'll warrant. What is it—our climate, food, culture differences? Why do most mixed marriages fizzle?"

"I'll leave that to psychologists. You're a wonder of eclectic information."

"I also talked to Mason Conway, owner of the gift shop." I related my conversation, trying to keep the pride out of my voice, hoping he would realize I hadn't been assigned the duty.

"I repeat with all awe, you have been busy."

I shrugged, trying to keep my pleasure from showing. "I guess they don't mind talking to a woman."

"The motherly attitude? You don't in the

least look matronly."

"Thank you, sir. It must be my face, then."

"Either that, or you're a born gossip. You're a gem, Taylor. I'm glad you're with us and not the *Sun*."

I muttered that I'd probably be paid better by the publication.

"Then let's applaud your devotion to detection, and distaste for wealth. We'll file that with the rest of the pertinent info."

"Our Ramona remembers Tom and Steve in Buxton's visitor's center. She recommended Catchpool Manor and even phoned the reservation through for them."

"We could assume she was feathering her fiancé's nest, but I'd like to believe she's more honest than that would indicate. There's nothing wrong with suggesting the manor house. It's handy to the festivities, grand, and probably just what the Americans were looking for. Don't they have this thing about staying in castles and such?"

"Catchpool Manor's quite popular. Even Chesterfield and such places push it to their tourists."

"It *is* in the books. Well." Graham sighed and stretched. "Ramona likes to dabble in straw and old clothes, does she? She probably likes amateur theatrics, too. Does she actually make and hang the effigy?"

I slowly flipped through my notebook to the desired information. "Arthur did that. He volunteered to make it this year. Normally she does it. Arthur usually drops the clothes at her house, and she then lets her artistic juices flow and creates the Guy. It's probably not so hard to get it over to the fire circle when it's finished." I mentally judged the weight and length of the dummy. "And the band members most likely had no problem lifting it. Just tie the rope around its waist, run it up the back beneath the jacket, loop it around the neck to simulate a noose, and Bob's your uncle."

"Then the rockers position it in the spotlight, as it were, beside their stage." Graham tossed his pen at the mug. A sharp ping indicated he'd hit his target. "Only this year, of all years, Arthur makes it. Tell me, Taylor, could Arthur have dressed Steve up in place of Mr. Guy Fawkes and let his future stepson hang it?"

"A very fascinating idea."

12

Graham's fingers drummed on the outside of his mug. I could imagine he was good at playing his keyboard instrument. His fingers moved quickly and easily. I wanted to hear him, wanted us to be in his flat, having tea, talking music, playing duets. I tried to recall something my brother had told me of the Baroque musicians, something that would impress Graham so he would see me as something human instead of a police badge. But all I could remember was the tidbit of Bach and his twenty children. So I sat, feeling another chance of developing a friendship had passed, hating myself for my stupidity.

After many moments, Graham broke the silence. "I wonder how we can find out if Arthur had opportunity. Did Steve disappear some time close to the effigy's delivery?"

The crisp flip of pages soared over the incessant tapping, like a descant to a bass continuo. My pen jabbed at the note page. "The two don't jive, sir. The effigy was originally delivered and hanged Thursday morning around ten o'clock. Arthur, perhaps to impress his girlfriend with the size of his muscle, lugged it out of the car himself, and brought it to the fire circle. And Steve—"

"Steve Pedersen was still walking around very un-effigy-like until teatime on Sunday. Damn." Graham muttered the oath rather than hurling it at someone specific. "I hate to waste great theories. Damn." He repeated the word, more as a feeling of loss than of anger.

I gave him time to sip his tea. "It's a bad case. I mean, here Kris sees her ex-fiancé after forty years, and then, in the next minute you might say, she sees him hanging there in front of her. Not a pleasant thing to remember. It would almost make her wish he's stayed in America, and spared her and Derek any brief pleasure they might have had with their reunion."

"I wonder, Taylor, if Kris married Derek because the two men looked alike. Well, there *is* a similar appearance about them, like relatives."

"You mean like being proposed to on the rebound? It wouldn't be quite the same as true love."

"It wouldn't. Still, if you have a fixation about someone, and that person's out of reach, you might grab at the available person because there's a resemblance."

"And you think Derek offered that option to Kris?"

"Yes, but it was probably not a conscious thing on her part. I wish I had a photo of the three of them in their rowdy university days. I just bring this supposition to you now because it struck me that there is marked sameness to the men. Same height, give or take an inch, same hair color and build. Could the one have been mistaken for the other?"

"But why would Arthur try to kill Derek?" I

said, jumping in on Graham's idea. "That's what you're leading up to, isn't it, asking about Arthur making the dummy and such? If it's mistaken identity, there's the problem of motive. And I, for one, would think it obvious. I mean, wouldn't the finger point to Arthur as substituting the corpse for the effigy if he's the one who made the thing? And he can't have needed the money that badly, if you're thinking along the lines of him stopping the yearly dole. Three hundred pounds is a lot of money to the average person, which Derek certainly is, and Arthur certainly isn't. Why kill someone just to put an end to that payment? After all, Arthur's lord of the manor."

Graham smiled. "I've known country squires, landed gentry who weren't as well off as the title and house would imply. Besides, what's Derek good for, another thirty or forty years? That's thirty years of dishing out £300. Arthur could do a lot with £9,000."

I mumbled that most people could. "Maybe his fiancée nagged him into it. I don't mean she came right out and told Arthur to kill Derek, but in a roundabout way. You know, when Arthur and Ramona were discussing their marriage, say. She sighs prettily and says she sure wishes they could replace the draperies in the drawing room, or wouldn't it be fun to have matching pink Jaguars and mink driving gloves."

"A woman's point of view, Taylor. Well, that's a nice little job of work for you. Find out the financial status of those involved."

"Yes, sir." I knew what I was in for. Maybe I could pawn it off on one of the constables.

The noises of the incident room had quieted to a background rumble of ringing phones, clacking computer keys, and conversational buzz. The door banged as someone left; a metal chair scraped across the floor. Someone was complaining about the weather forecast and wishing he had warmer socks. Graham leaned back in his chair and stretched. The morning was nearly bumping into afternoon and, if I knew him, he would be feeling we weren't progressing very quickly.

"So, Taylor, what did you think of the vicar seeing our Uncle Gilbert near the bonfire?"

"Do you think Lyle could've misinterpreted what he saw?"

"Anyone can assume, and it was dark, way past sunset." Graham pushed the mug across the table.

"At least he's trying to help. It makes a nice change of pace."

Graham smiled. "You always try to see both sides of a situation. It's wonderful to have such law-abiding citizens, yes. They'll point out a possible murderer but they won't actually lower themselves to slander by saying he's drunk. So what've we got, then?"

We bent over our notebooks, conferring and sorting through possible motives until I insisted on lunch.

When I tried to interview him after lunch, I discovered Uncle Gilbert had forsaken the whiskey bottle Monday afternoon for his lithium salts. It was his normal antidote for the attacks of manic-depression that cyclically claimed him. He was not altogether good at remembering to take his medicine. And right now he was not good at remembering much about the previous evening. He'd taken a nap after downing a substantial liquid lunch, but now sat on the edge of his bed, his feet dangling over the side, his body in rumpled shirt and trousers, and half-listened to his nephew. It was obviously still too early to think. Besides it probably hurt his head.

"You bleeding berk!" Arthur yelled. "You're looking at a murder charge!"

Gilbert blinked stupidly at Arthur, hearing the words and the wrath behind them, yet not comprehending what he had done to warrant such an outburst. He asked again whom he had murdered.

"That American tourist," Arthur snapped, forgetting I hovered in the open doorway just behind him. "You were more awake when you went out this morning than you are now. Snap out of it!"

Uncle Gilbert sagged against the pockmarked headboard, the pillow puffing out on each side of him like whipped cream oozing from a cream puff. His eyes tried to determine from his nephew's face what his ears couldn't, for he stared at Arthur. "Don't yell at me, laddie. I'm under a lot of stress. I'll forget to take my medicine." He didn't have to enumerate what that might cause. Evidently they both knew.

"*You're* under stress? Hell, what about *me*? What about this nose-above-water establishment? If many more guests check out and the business should fold—"

Gilbert groaned and pulled the sheet up to his neck. His fingers gripped the fabric as though he needed the tactile assurance that he and Arthur weren't players in one of his alcoholic nightmares. He squinted at Arthur, who was pacing the floor and coaxing all types of groans and creaks from the wooden floorboards. Yet there was something surreal about the scene, something Max Ernst might paint.

Arthur stopped his pacing and turned to me. "Honestly, Sergeant, the man's more of a nuisance than he's worth at times. But what can I do? He's family and I love him."

I said I'd known many similar situations.

Arthur glared again at his uncle, evidently short on sympathy. "Where were you last night? The Sergeant wants to know. And so do I. I didn't see you all yesterday afternoon, and you weren't at evening tea. Byron said you were at the bonfire. Where'd you go afterwards? I didn't hear you come in."

Gilbert pulled the sheet tighter, shielding himself from Arthur's verbal battery. "Art, why all the questions? Slow down, slow down! Where was I, when did I come home... What's so important? Why did you wake me from my nap? I need my sleep."

"You need your sleep like you need another drink."

The sarcasm failed to make an impression. Instead, Gilbert blinked again. "Who's that behind you?" He evidently saw me for the first time. "Ramona? Come in, Dear. Such a bold one you are, coming into my bedroom."

"That's not Ramona. That's Sergeant Taylor. Police! C.I.D. And what's so important is that Steve Pedersen was murdered." He tried conveying the problem by loudness where logic failed. "You made an ass of yourself last night, confessing you had killed Steve. The Sergeant, here, heard you. Now she wants to question you."

Either volume or repetition finally won over. Gilbert sat up, letting the sheet fall from his chest, and stared open-mouthed. He screwed up his eyes, as though willing his mind to sort through the confusion. "The fire. Yes. I remember. There was Talbot and the vicar, and a tall, trim man taking tea. Right?" Arthur swore. Gilbert took that as encouragement and went on. "Were we talking over your wedding, Art? That'd explain the vicar. But that tall chap— Is he an antiques dealer? But there's something about the woods, isn't there? Did I kill someone in the woods?" Gilbert rubbed his eyes, opening them to look at Arthur's bright crimson face. A hint of saliva ebbed from a corner of Gilbert's mouth as he squeaked out his disbelief.

"Can't remember?" Arthur strode up to the bed, grabbed Gilbert's shirt, and shook him till the mattress springs squealed. "I'm not surprised, considering the whiskey and brandy you put away earlier yesterday. It's another typical day, isn't it, with you not recalling a thing. Is this police officer going to accept that? Will she overlook your convenient faulty memory, whisper consoling things about your mental illness, or figure it's all an inept attempt at an alibi, that you really did kill that man?" He had finished his speech in a fury of sound, and pushed his uncle back against the headboard. He paid no attention to Gilbert's wailing of innocence; the slam of the door behind us punctuated his opinion.

13

After my sojourn at the manor house, I wandered down the road, enjoying the autumn afternoon and trying to make sense of the scene I'd just witnessed. Not that there probably was much, considering Uncle Gilbert's condition. But it was something to think on.

I met Margo as she emerged from the gift shop. I waved at her and we walked to the pub.

"A note came in from the CSI lads, Bren. Did you read it?"

"No. Did it just arrive?"

"Yeah, fifteen minutes ago or so. A hair was found on Steve's shirt, which seemed odd because it didn't match his hair color."

I shrugged. "Peculiar, perhaps, but Ramona got the clothes from Arthur. It could be one of his."

"Logical."

"All the same, it's an example of how well the tech officers do their job."

"I'll give them that. But all that gear they don... At least I didn't have to put on one of those space suits you and Graham had on last night,"

Margo said, referring to her eavesdropping of Gilbert and Talbot. "God, if there's anything that camouflages my figure—"

"Margo." I interrupted her tirade on fashion. "Have you ever taken any acting classes?"

She stopped to throw the last bit of her sandwich at a group of sparrows, watching them peck at the bread and ham. "No. At least no RADA stuff. Strictly amateur in the church hall. Charades and things. Why?"

"I don't suppose someone could put on an act every time you see him, pretending to be inebriated."

"Why? Who's pretending?"

"Uncle Gilbert. Gilbert Catchpool." I explained as she straightened up from watching the feeding frenzy.

"Don't blame me, blame the booze and my genes?"

I found myself looking at her, wishing I had her genes. Even ten years ago, the age Margo is now, I didn't look that good. I never had a great figure. It was lying somewhere beneath the two stone of baby fat I euphemistically called my weight problem. And my shorter stature tended to make me look dumpy in a way Margo never would experience. I ran my fingers through my short-cropped hair. That was one of my good features. It was red and glowed like a new penny. I was proud of my blue eyes, too. At least genes had handed me something nice.

"Bren?" Margo called me from my contemplation. "Did you hear me? Why would he pretend to be drunk?"

"The only thing I can think of is he doesn't want to be questioned about something. He's using it as a shield."

"Are you getting any information from him?"

I shook my head and showed her a blank notebook page.

"Works damned well, I'd say."

"And Sir Lancelot only had a shield of heavy metal."

I figured it was late enough that Liam VanDyke should be up, so I returned to Ramona's house. She evidently had gone to work or was doing errands, for Liam was the only one home. We sat in the kitchen, I occupying the same chair I had earlier, and he sipped his coffee.

"All I did was ask Mum if Art would let us move the straw effigy to the stage." Liam looked more tired than irritated at my presence. His chestnut hair held streaks of bright blue and green, which matched the dominant colors of the rose tattoo on his neck. A heavy silver chain and ring were the extent of the jewelry he wore. On looking at him when he opened the door I expected a gruff, rude individual, but he spoke in a soft, low voice and had impeccable manners.

"When was this?" I opened my notebook and waited, hoping for a break in the case.

"Thursday afternoon. My group arrived by then and I'd scouted out the bonfire area earlier that day. The Guy had been delivered and lay on the ground, waiting for Bonfire Night. I thought it would be a smashing visual for our new song, so I asked Art if we could use it in our gig."

"Use it how?"

"I wanted it propped upright at a mike, like it was singing. Art didn't want it moved around that much. I suppose it was fragile, like the straw would fall out. He suggested we hoist it early so it would be hanging while we performed." He took a gulp of coffee and shrugged. "I was disappointed, but that was better than nothing, so we strung it up. He indicated which tree bough they usually use. Luckily, it was right next to the stage, so it was nearly as good as I'd planned. The audience couldn't help but see it while we sang, it was practically hovering above the stage."

"Who actually hanged it?"

"Josh and I. Art gave us permission just before teatime, so Josh and I trotted down to the fire area and strung up the effigy. It looked good in the lantern light Sunday."

I replied that I'd seen it. "How long were you and Josh at the bonfire area?"

Liam rubbed his forehead, as though he needed to fully wake up to think. "Not long. I'd say fifteen or twenty minutes. We looked at the space for a bit, discussed the best place for it, like closer to the tree trunk or farther out on the bough. Then we raised the effigy. The rope was already there, so all we had to do was throw it over the limb and hoist the Guy off the ground. It didn't take us very long."

"Was anyone there when you arrived?"

"Not a soul."

"How about when you left? Had anyone arrived or was anyone approaching the area?"

"No. Unless someone was in the wood and coming up that way, then I wouldn't have seen the bloke, being behind us. But no one was around. Just Josh, me and Mr. Guy."

"Your mother says you got the idea for the Bonfire Night performance from American football."

"Yeah. It's a real show at half time." He shook his head, as though arguing with someone. "This burg is so out of date. They've been doing things the same way for centuries. It's time they stepped into the twenty-first century and lived in the present instead of wallowing in the past."

"You feel your entertainment accomplishes that."

"Sure. If not us, some group doing the same thing. If they want to bring more money into the village they need to give the tourists something to see. People want a show, a spectacle, something exciting. The villagers can keep the hanging, but they need to update it with some dazzle. I mean, firecrackers and bonfires are okay, but you've got to put on a real show if you want to swell the tourist numbers." He looked at me for my reaction.

"Some people like the tradition the way it is."

"There are other villages that do it the way it is, year in and year out. I tried to tell Art that this is progress and would solve a bunch of financial problems for everyone here."

"What did he say to that?"

"Not much. He gave me the old evasive answer about needing to think about it and not wanting to step on anyone's toes. Personally, I think Mum needs to talk to him again. She'll make him see this is best for the village."

I made a noncommittal remark, then asked if he had noticed anything wrong with the Guy.

Liam drained the last of his coffee and refilled the mug. "No. It just looked like all the other straw dummies I'd seen growing up there. Old clothes stuffed with straw or wads of newspaper. What was wrong with it?"

"The substitution of the corpse."

"Yeah. Hell of a thing to happen." His thumb rubbed the back of his ring and he looked thoughtful. "Sorry I can't help, but Josh and I didn't notice anything particularly odd. It looked like the Guy, felt like the Guy, behaved like the Guy. Which means it was uncooperative when we tried to move it and it was damned cumbersome. We'd have noticed if it was unusually heavy."

"Are you sure?"

"Certainly, miss. The rest of the group was back in the B and B. We had a few days before the performance so there was nothing to unpack. A raised platform had been constructed for us, leaving nothing for us to do. We hanged the Guy, and I told Josh to make sure they were all at my mum's for rehearsal that evening. Josh returned to the B and B and I went home. It was that simple."

I was glad it'd been simple for them, but I wished it'd prove simple for us.

The rest of the band members were just sitting down to their late lunches at the manor house when I walked in. I talked to each boy separately in a sitting room Arthur let me use. Either everyone had rehearsed an agreed-upon story or they told the truth. Nothing varied in each telling but the words. I thanked them and left, feeling dejected.

I returned to the pub's private barroom. A few of the constables were back from their afternoon investigations and entered computer data or made the myriad of telephone calls needed in a murder inquiry. Graham was at a computer, conferring with a constable, obviously pleased. He equated the hum of efficient work with progress. And he hated to think that a killer would get away with murder.

"I suppose it's too early for anything medical." He said it to no one in particular, then consulted his watch. "I'd like to know if the postmortem examination differs from last night's cursory report. Oh, hello, Taylor. How'd it go with our favorite relative?"

I told him he didn't want to know, and slumped into a chair.

"So, what we've got so far... It doesn't matter right now if Steve was bludgeoned or hanged. For the moment, let's abandon the line assuming Steve is the intended victim and concentrate on the mistaken identity theme. It makes more sense to focus on a local, anyway. There are all those years of village living that give your neighbor reason to wish you dead."

"And opportunities to do it."

"If you're agreeable to my suggestion, Taylor, who'd want to kill Derek? You may consider the dole or not, as you wish."

"Well, I'd say most likely it's Talbot."

"Even if he can't substantiate his claim, aren't there any friends who would've known him, someone who could prove his family line? Never mind the flooding disaster. Someone must be able to speak for him. What is he?"

"Fifty-four. Prime of life these days."

"Uncle Gilbert's seventy-two. Forgetting the fatherhood theory for the moment, if Gilbert knew Talbot, he's got eighteen years on him. He could have known Talbot when Talbot was growing up."

"Either one could have babysat the other," I said, thinking they were both infantile.

"But who'd watch the babysitter?" He grinned, easing the tension of our session.

"Some older relative would certainly help Talbot's case for inheritance. Family photo album ought to be somewhere. They didn't all live in the southwest, did they?"

"Since you've turned the mere act of gossiping into a higher art, Taylor, would you mind seeing if you can ferret out something along that line?"

"Now?" I gazed fondly at Graham's coffee mug.

"I know you just returned from battle, but if you wouldn't mind."

I stood up, then paused for a question. "I'm not betting either way on anyone. But as much as Talbot screams 'real motive' to me, I've got to ask if a fifty –four-year-old man isn't a bit old for this sort of game."

"You mean murder? "

"No, sir. Proving he was adopted. That was more than a half century ago."

"Some people are never too old for greed, Taylor."

The computer printer at the next table began spitting out paper and Graham walked over to it. "This might be the postmortem report. Hold on, Taylor."

In response to Graham's inquiry, a constable looked up from the huge monitor before him. "Nothing from Buxton or Ripley, sir," he said, referring to Constabulary headquarters. "But I've finished entering all the names. And the current notes from the other constables. I'll type up yours and Sergeant Taylor's if you'd like."

"Thank you."

The officer nodded, then sympathetically uttered that some cases were worse than others.

"Any time you want to show off your Questioning 101 technique, you can have a go at Uncle Gilbert. Or Talbot."

The man shook his head, punching a computer key. "I've seen him. *And* heard him. I'd hate to be up against Talbot on a bad day."

Graham, his eyes still fixed on the page before him, casually asked why.

"Oh, sorry, sir. I thought you'd read all the notes on the Pedersen case."

A slow blush crept over Graham's face. He explained he'd had a late night and had only returned from questioning some people and conferring with me.

"Well, sir, Talbot Tanner almost killed a man a bit over twenty years ago."

14

The constable averted his eyes from Graham's astonished face as the room grew quieter. Everyone had abandoned any semblance of work to stare at Graham. It wasn't often he did a cock-up of anything.

"Killed a man?" exclaimed Graham after he found his voice. "Are you certain?"

"Yes, sir. In 1993. I can print it out for you."

Graham thanked the officer, but said he would read it in detail later. "Who got into a dust-up with Talbot? Don't tell me Derek. I don't think I could take that just now."

"No, sir. Byron MacKinnon."

"Arthur Catchpool's secretary?" I said.

"Yes. The only thing that saved Byron, evidently, was the vicar."

A hurried thank you just squeaked out of Graham's mouth before he tossed me my jacket and we left the pub.

Luckily for Graham's blood pressure, Lyle was at the church, bending over a letter he was laboriously composing in his cramped office. The space felt more like a cave than a room, with its towers of books and parish registries, stacks of papers, and boxes of candle stubs smothering every conceivable flat surface. I wondered if he even saw the mess.

Lyle looked up as we entered. Clearly curious as to the identity of my cohort, he glanced at Graham before welcoming us and indicating two chairs. He stammered his apologies when he realized they were impossible to use as seating, and rose from his desk, picked up the pile of books that hid one chair seat, and told me to sit.

"I'm delighted you dropped by." The clergyman turned slightly, trying to find a depository for his armful.

Graham introduced himself as he took the books from Lyle and set them gently on the floor. He cleared his own chair, winking at me. "I hope we haven't come at an inconvenient time."

"No, no." Lyle reclaimed his seat behind the desk, looking relieved that the books had found a temporary home and that his composition chore was delayed. "It's nothing that can't wait. I find these letters difficult to compose. What can one say after the first sentence expressing sorrow for a death?"

"You're writing to the Halfords?"

The vicar nodded, sighing loudly and pushing the pen away from the paper. "I was with them last night, of course, but I always think it nice to follow up with a note expressing my understanding of their grief. I try to offer comfort, and to remind them of our Lord's love and the certainty that Mr. Pedersen's' in heaven. But sometimes..." Lyle shrugged his shoulders, indicating the difficulty of such an epistle. "It's my duty, as it is with every caring human being, don't you think? Where would we be if we didn't care for each other?"

Graham refrained from saying the obvious. In a way, ours was a strange job, combining the extremes of uncaring and caring. Uncaring, self-centered people broke laws—robbed, assaulted, killed. Caring, respectful people became witnesses, comforted the victims. We dealt with both. And Graham had too, as a minister. He had merely changed clothes and rules.

Graham coughed, and remarked instead that it was very kind of Lyle to give his support.

"I'm only doing what I want to do. I need to help."

"Well, perhaps you can help us for a moment. I was told you know something of a tiff involving Byron MacKinnon and Talbot Tanner a few years back. 1993, I believe it was."

I did some hasty mental arithmetic, eyed the pudgy, short man, and wondered how he could have stopped a fight involving that leviathan. Even now, the handyman wasn't exactly in his dotage. Like David confronting Goliath without the slingshot. "It was a case of attempted murder," I said, nudging Lyle's memory. "Assault with a hammer."

"You're referring to Talbot's little trouble?" The vicar rubbed a pudgy hand across his chin. "Yes, I remember it, though I must confess I'd nearly forgotten. I haven't dredged that up in ages. What do you want to know about?"

"Any particulars you may remember about the event. The reason for the altercation, the outcome…that sort of thing."

"I don't suppose I'd be doing anything unethical in relaying the story." He eyed Graham as though judging the man's honesty.

"I shouldn't think it's anything like revealing a confession," Graham replied. "I'm conducting a murder investigation, sir, and one of the usual dull bits of routine is the sorting out of pertinent and impertinent facts. This may or may not have anything to do with Steve's murder, and if it hasn't, I'll forget it. But if there's a link between Talbot's rash behavior with Byron, and anything with Steve, it'd be useful to know. If one of the men told you something in confidence, you may leave that out. I'm not asking for a baring of the soul. I just want the bones of the fight. Who started it, how it was resolved..."

"Yes." The vicar, now released from guilt, readily gave the information. "If you say it was 1993, it was 1993. I'll accept that. I'm not much good on dates. But I do remember the altercation. It was this same time of year as now. Is that what brought it into the open?"

"May I venture a guess, and ask if the Catchpool dole sparked it?"

"Yes, that blasted dole. I swear I don't know if it's more of a blessing or a curse. The money helps the Halfords, I'm certain, but the discomfort that comes with it may be more a bane." He shook his head, no doubt recalling previous trouble with Talbot. "Not only for the Halfords when Talbot's in one of his moods, but also for the poor man himself. He can't be a happy person if he's always so agitated over this dole business. But you asked about the fight. I'm afraid I'm inclined to ramble.

"Anyway, Talbot was going on and on about his rightful fortune, and Byron called Talbot a liar, I'm afraid. Such a nasty scene. That was bad enough, but then Byron suggested Talbot leave the village because no one liked him, which wasn't true. I do! Byron said Talbot had no real job, just the few odd ones he got from Arthur, me, and some of the villagers who felt sorry for him and had a few pence to direct his way. We've been remarkably successful in keeping him employed and fed. Anyway, Byron got angrier and angrier at Talbot, finally boasted that when he—Byron—married Kris Alton— Oh, that's Kris Halford's maiden name, by the way. Byron bragged that when he married Kris, Talbot had better not be poking around the manor house."

"Implying Talbot shouldn't be expecting any odd jobs from that direction," I asked. "Did Byron oversee such things?"

Lyle nodded, his eyes blinking again like a pigeon. "Yes. Byron had the key to the till, as it were. He's a powerful man, Byron MacKinnon, in his way. He does a myriad of jobs as Arthur's secretary, among which is controlling the running of a good portion of the estate, though what right he had to say that to Talbot, I can't fathom."

"I can't read any other meaning into it at the moment," I said, marveling at the vicar's memory.

"Exactly. Well, Talbot, who has always liked Kris and made no secret about it, snapped. It was the first he'd heard of Kris' engagement, I suppose. Talbot was holding a hammer and swung it at Byron's head. He succeeded in knocking him to the ground, whereby he kicked him in the ribs, still trying for Byron's head with that hammer. A truly nasty scene!"

"Where was all this?"

"Just outside in the churchyard. Talbot had just finished with some chores I'd given him, and Byron came strolling up the walk to talk to me. Byron had innocently asked where I was and Talbot inquired why he wanted to know. Byron, of course, said it was none of Talbot's business, and it worsened from there."

"That's why no one else was around to help you stop the fight," Graham said. "And why he had the hammer. Unfortunate."

"I tell you, I don't know how I got the two men separated. 'Course, I wasn't yet into my fifties." He shook his head.

"Did Byron marry Kris? I know she's married to Derek now, but with divorce so prevalent—"

"No. They got as far as the engagement and that was it. It was probably some pre-wedding tiff about child rearing or mothers-in-law. All too common, these fallouts. But isn't it better to get that all sorted out before you need it? Of course, you'll want to ask Byron or Kris the reasons. I don't reveal more than the obvious or what is common village knowledge."

Which constantly surprises me, I wanted to say.

Graham thanked the vicar and we left to see if Byron's intended was awake and ready for a game of Do You Remember?

Sounds of everyday life washed over the village as Graham and I drove to the Halfords'. Not for the first time I thought how odd life was: we were investigating a murder, yet wet laundry flapped from clothes lines, women shopped at the butcher's for tonight's mince or lamb or chicken, the baker's shop displayed fruit flans and iced buns in its window. Farmers from the outlying granges stopped at the pub for a quick pint before heading home. Children playing in the schoolyard laughed and played at kickball or tag. People unconcerned about the murder, cocooned in their world and ignoring us as long as we didn't intrude on their comfort zones.

Kris Halford had been one of these people. Now, cradled in a blue comforter, she was lying on the living room sofa when we entered her home. Her dark eyes stared at me from beneath reddened, swollen eyelids, and a box of tissues near the sofa suggested her interminable crying. She pushed a coil of limp brunette hair behind her ear, making a semblance of caring. Graham took a chair opposite her while I sat on the end of the sofa.

"Yes, I suppose I am better." Kris dabbed at a tear with the damp tissue. "If you can call a numbed head better. All I see is Steve. Him sitting here, so happy to be with us. Him at the pub where we had dinner Saturday night. Him walking up to us at the bonfire."

Just as well Derek shelved the photograph for a while, I thought, noticing its absence from the tabletop. She remembers readily enough without that visual aid.

"I won't apologize. I'm going through hell, and if anyone can't see that and sympathize with me—"

Graham nodded. "I'm neither impatient nor condemning you, Mrs. Halford. Unfortunately, I have questions concerning Steve's death, and you, also unfortunately, are part of the tragedy. If you'd rather we return at some later time..."

Kris waved her hand, stopping his rising from the chair. "Please stay. I'm just lying here. I'm all right. Derek's at the office. I couldn't see him staying home for me. Besides, either Arthur, Byron, or Lyle stop by every few hours to see how I am, warm up some soup, bring me something, or make me a cuppa."

I said it would be hard to beat help like that.

Kris nodded. "Besides, I wasn't good for anything except having a lie in and a cry. It was silly of Derek to take a day off for that. If you want to talk to him again, he won't be home till six or so."

Graham assured her that he could catch up

with Derek later, but that right now he wanted to ask her a few questions if she was up to it.

"I haven't done a thing all day. I'm living on hot chocolate and tea. Plenty of nutrition there."

I gazed at the array of mugs littering the tables, their interiors circled with dried chocolate froth or bits of tealeaves.

Kris, following my gaze, asked if we would like tea or coffee. "I can do a no-brainer like that."

I looked at Graham, who shook his head. I declined, also, but said, "If you'd like a cup—"

"Thanks, Miss, but I'm full to the gills. I'm either experiencing a caffeine buzz, or your surgeon's pills still have a hold of me. Mogadon, I think. Great sleeping pill. I'm out in twenty minutes and sleep like the dead."

I averted my eyes as she reddened. In the silence I heard a cat mew outside.

"I must admit I rather enjoy the hot chocolate. I haven't had any in ages, but Derek insisted last night. He said it'd make me sleep. Something about hot milk..." Her hand fell limply to her lap and she laughed. "God, as if I needed hot milk to top off the pill. Funny. While we're working we say we'd love a day of just doing nothing. And here I am, doing nothing, only it's not the relaxation I wanted. Do people really know what it's like, how hellishly boring doing nothing is?" Her eyes sought Graham's for a gesture of understanding, asking no response. "Why Steve, of all people? Can you tell me that, Mr. Graham?" She held the empty mug, almost like a caress.

"Are you sure I can't get you anything? I'm quite handy in the kitchen. I've been known to make soufflés, even."

"You've got my husband beat." Kris grabbed a tissue and dabbed at her nose. "He knows his way around the tinned soups and such, and even makes the occasional sandwich or heats up a scone. But you and the Sergeant don't want to know about our domestic bliss."

"I understand Talbot, Evan, and Lyle were at the bonfire. But we don't know about Steve's involvement. I know this is painful, Mrs. Halford, but do you know if he changed his mind about attending the event? It would help us in our investigation if you could talk about it."

"My husband and I didn't see Steve after tea. We had it early, around half three, I should think. I wanted to help Evan in the pub. He needed to get down to the green while it was still early." She broke off, fighting down a sob. "Steve left after the meal. He said he wanted to check the torch and lanterns for firecrackers."

Graham glanced at me and I nodded.

"Derek and I were surprised we didn't see him at the fire, though after a while we assumed he was somewhere in the crowd watching the foolery, or he had figured there would be firecrackers after all so he felt safer skipping the fire."

"I understand that the reason Steve came to Upper Kingsleigh, apart from renewing his friendships with you and your husband, was to bring you a family heirloom."

"Gran's ring." Kris waved her hand at Graham so the opal winked with fiery colors. "It's one of those family jokes that you don't quite expect to mature. Gran promised me this ring, then before she got around to giving it to me, it got mislaid. I thought that was the end of that. But Mom wrote to tell me she'd discovered it quite by accident one day when she was going through some of Gran's things, and would see I'd get it. Mom lives in the States."

"It must be wonderful to have it," I said.

"Yes. I assumed it would come with my Christmas parcel. I never dreamed it would be hand delivered. And by Steve."

"More trustworthy than the mail," Graham said. "How did Steve get the honor? He knew your mother, I take it."

"He had looked her up when he got discharged from hospital, after he returned from Viet Nam. He was trying to find me, so he contacted her. That's when he found out I had returned to England on our graduation from university, that I had married Derek. Mom gave him my address."

"And his arrival was a surprise?" I asked.

"That's like Jonah saying 'What fish?' After I got over the shock, I was elated. Steve came laden with other family mementos besides the ring— Dad's scouting paraphernalia, Gran's favorite doll, some duplicate photos that Mom had assembled into an album and labeled for me. Some were from my university days, and there were family snaps of holidays and such. God, it brings back the memories. Birthdays, Thanksgiving, Fourth of July..."

Graham nodded. "Fourth of July. Of course. Their holiday with fireworks. Is it usual for Upper Kingsleigh to use fireworks during Guy Fawkes Night? I thought they were generally outlawed these days." He looked at me as though wondering why headquarters had assigned me bonfire duty. I hoped he was finally noticing my potential.

"If you're trying to get the names of any criminals, I can't tell you. And I mean can't, not won't. We've never had them, but Steve had no way of knowing that. There's always the odd chance that some child might think it funny to poke a firecracker into the tower of wood, even with your officer on guard. They do use them on Mischief Night, however. And, frankly, I'm surprised that rock band did use them at their performance."

"Did you think they would?"

"I had no way of knowing. But some groups do. It's supposed to make it an Experience, I suppose. I was upset Liam VanDyke's group did and was worried about Steve. That band was bad enough without the explosion of the firecrackers."

"You didn't like their music?"

Kris frowned. "I don't mean that, Chief Inspector. I meant having them play at all was a bad idea. It destroyed the tradition. Why Arthur ever allowed—" She broke off and took a breath. "It might've been better if there had been firecrackers in the bonfire. At least that would've been in keeping with our custom."

"Yet in all your years living here..."

"Nothing. We follow the speed limit, adhere as closely as we can to the Ten Commandments, stand patiently in queue at the post office window. We're a law-abiding village, on the whole. Except when it comes to murder." She banged the mug onto the table, her eyes glaring at him, not because she held him responsible for her friend's death, but because he was handy.

Graham said nothing, and I wondered if we should leave. Before I could suggest it, Graham asked if her marriage to Derek was her first.

Kris' knuckles grew white as she twisted the edge of her comforter. "It's none of your business, Chief Inspector, as far as I can see. I shouldn't be surprised if you ask me next to see my bank statement."

"I apologize if I've offended you. But there's a good reason behind all my apparent poking and sniffing about. I was informed today that you'd been engaged to Byron MacKinnon."

Kris' eyes shone through her tears with an intensity that startled me. It was as though she glowed with the rage fueling her grief. "It's true. I'm sorry. I shouldn't have gone off like that. It's just that the past's not as buried as I thought, is it? That's what makes it hard. After I'd lost him to the war, as we supposed, Byron walked out on me. Derek was my last chance for happiness. I wasn't getting any younger. What a moronic phrase, but it's true! If Derek hadn't come along offering love and security, ignoring the faults of my aging body and personality... It sounds like I accepted him for something other than love, and that's absurd. I'm clinging to Derek with every fiber in my body. If anything ever happens to him, if he's ever taken from me..." The narrative had cost her. She leaned her head against the back of the sofa, shut her eyes, and choked down a deep sob. "You've found your niche in the C.I.D., Mr. Graham. You've done a first-rate job of ferreting out the little dramatic bits of village life, the sordid or just plain embarrassing secrets most of us have and most of us pray will be forgotten."

"If you think I'm impertinent or being just plain nosy, I'm sorry. I assure you I'm just gathering facts at the moment. I don't go to bed and gloat over people's misfortunes or think about methods of blackmail. That's not as flip as it may sound. I've been accused of both. I only ask because it may give me an insight into Byron's or Talbot's behavior or emotional stability. It may come in handy, or it may not. And if it doesn't—" He shrugged.

"In one ear and out the other?"

"Precisely. I can't be bothered remembering trivial bits. Cases get too complicated too quickly for me to retain such pieces of remarkably exciting information such as what Talbot has for breakfast."

Kris laughed suddenly and released her hold of the comforter. "I wouldn't dream of asking you, either. But I don't think I can tell you details of Byron's and my engagement. You must ask him. He ended it. Tell him I sent you, if you need to break down his reluctance."

We uttered our thanks for her help and let ourselves out while Graham echoed Kris' general opinion that Upper Kingsleigh was a respectable village except for murder and greed.

15

Fortified with afternoon tea, I parked my car at Catchpool Manor but stood momentarily, mesmerized by the magnificence of the house. The late afternoon sun shone halo-like behind it, casting blue shadows into the eastern woods. I recalled the brochure's text, and mentally checked its accuracy against what I had seen. 'Catchpool Manor, predominant and well positioned in the picturesque Derbyshire village of Upper Kingsleigh. Exposed oak beams, gourmet meals, en suite facilities, peaceful flower gardens.' But there was more than this simple declaration. A curving, tree-framed driveway from the main road from the village eventually led to an immense lawn, which lay like a green tablecloth under the building's limestone grandeur. That same green color accented the northern side of the house with its walled rose garden and head-high boxwood maze. A confusion of oriel windows, strapwork, and sharply pointed gables welcomed callers to their own slice of England. Sunlight and shadow played against the far western window, re-enforcing many speculations that perhaps ghosts did walk the corridors after midnight. This November afternoon, however, the ancient walls harbored only a handful of tourists eager to explore the halls and surrounding hills.

Ramona was leaving the house and heading toward her car when I walked over. She still wore the arm sling, but she kept her wrist—wrapped in gauge dressing—close to her body. I said I was glad she was making progress and able to drive.

"Thanks, but I confine myself to local jaunts only. I'm still on the pain pills but I hope not for long. I detest taking any type of medication."

I asked if she could spare me a minute for a question and she nodded. She tossed her shoulder bag onto the car seat and leaned against the closed door.

"I understand you procure the clothing for the Guy from villagers, is that right?"

She looked slightly startled at the question, perhaps expecting to be asked about time and alibis and witnesses, but she replied readily enough. "Yes. Some years I go around, asking for castoffs, but sometimes people drop them off at my place or at the manor house. This year I had to knock on doors to get donations."

"Did you get many?"

"Not really. I got a pair of boy's jeans from one villager. Those weren't really the right size for the Guy, so Arthur had to come up with things. He offered me two shirts, a hat, and a pair of adult-sized trousers. I chose the hat, one shirt and the adult trousers. Oh, and he also supplied the jacket."

"Would you remember who donated the boy's jeans?"

She blinked, clearly confused. "You're serious?"

"I thought you might recall the giver, since

you had so few offerings."

She gave me the name, saying she didn't understand but hoped it would help with the investigation.

I thanked her and waited until she drove off before I walked to the front door.

I sat in Arthur's study, my notebook on my knees, wondering if Uncle Gilbert would stagger in, if he had sobered up.

"I assumed you or the inspector would be around for this story." Arthur cradled his teacup on his lap. "Talbot seems to attract attention, whatever the year or circumstance. Even if it's ancient history, I suppose you must delve into it. We can't keep much private in a village. Not that anyone cares about Talbot's claim but the Halfords. It's just an annoyance at times, the way he goes on and on about it. Still, it's the type of thing that could yield so much to an investigation, isn't it?"

"Depends, sir, on how the investigation proceeds. If there's nothing to it, we forget it and get on with another line."

"Waste of time, wouldn't it be?"

"Both the chief inspector and I have wasted a good deal of time through our careers. I wouldn't let that worry you."

"I won't. I'm just intrigued with the policeman's job. Err, woman's."

I figured he was confused about being politically correct. I let it pass. "It has its moments."

Angling farther back into the chair, Arthur nodded. "Well, Talbot was born in 1953, and survived the West Country flooding ten years later. Fortunately, he was living with an aunt at the time. Farther north, where it wasn't as bad."

"Parents killed in an accident?"

"Yes. A car crash. This aunt took Talbot in, gave him a home and such until he was adopted. It was a bit of a long process. There was no thought of adoption when Talbot first came to his aunt, of course. She was all for doing her duty by her brother's child from some sort of misplaced family loyalty, but she couldn't quite swing the financial end of it. Plus, I don't think the two of them exactly hit it off."

"Bit of an odd man out, was he?" Uncaring home life, lack of understanding, and associations with hooligans tainted many a child. It was nice that Talbot had straightened out.

"Probably, knowing Talbot. He has a shingle loose, at any rate. I can't see him fitting in with most normal households, which is assuming this aunt had a normal household."

"There's no accounting for some folks' lifestyles."

"No, there isn't. And I wonder how some of them survive in society. Well, all I know is that Talbot was living with his aunt from '63 until he was adopted. I hesitate to say 1965, but that seems right."

"From what I understand, the flood destroyed a lot of village and town records and papers."

"Yes, including adoption papers. So Talbot's out of luck there. His aunt was confirmed dead years ago. I checked. I thought I'd help out the fellow, at least put a stop to his annual whine. But I can't prove his adoption, though privately I believe it happened."

"Would you happen to know the name of Talbot's alleged adoptive parents?" I looked up from my note taking, holding my breath.

"Certainly. He made no secret about it. He

flaunted it, in fact. The only trouble, as I said, he couldn't prove a thing. Talbot always swore that his adoptive father was Peter Halford, Derek's father."

I asked if anyone else knew of the supposed relationship.

"I should think anyone older than forty would. It's no secret at all. Peter Halford always called Talbot son, but then he called all the boys in the village son. Derek insists it was just an affectionate nickname his dad used for all the lads, Talbot included. The older Halford was keen on children. I always thought it a shame he only had one. But it does seem reasonable that Halford would adopt Talbot. He and Talbot's dad were chums as lads. I've often heard Derek's dad talk of Talbot's parents."

"I suppose Peter Halford—"

"Dead, I'm afraid. Died in 1978. Just before Kris' dad in 1979. He had a heart attack. But that doesn't help with this adoption puzzle, does it?"

Nothing would help, I thought, except the official paper from the adoption service. "He left nothing with his estate papers? No inclusion of Talbot in the will? I would've thought, if Peter Halford adopted Talbot—"

"If he left anything, Derek never found it or mentioned it."

He wouldn't if he destroyed it, I wanted to say. "There's no family solicitor who can help sort through this?"

"I don't suppose that would do any good if the original papers are gone."

I murmured that it seemed to be problems at every turn. "So, Talbot became fixed on this legal son-and-heir bit."

"If only they would've let Tal alone. If only people would let others just live. Tal's not a bad chap, really. He does good work, doesn't ask for much out of life."

"Just every third of November at dole time he goes crackers."

Arthur nodded. "And him being older than Derek by four years, well, you see why it's important. If he was legally adopted, he'd be the elder son and entitled to the dole."

"So there's no proof to Talbot's claim. None that anyone has ever found to date, at least."

"I'm hoping to set up something for him without his knowing of it. A bit of annual income."

"How will he receive that without being suspicious of a handout?"

"That's my legal team's worry. But I've talked it over with Ramona, and she's in favor of it."

I thought that was democratic, including the fiancée in the financial arrangements. "Speaking of Ramona, I saw her as she was leaving. Her wrist must be some better if she's driving about."

"Yes, it *is* good, isn't it? Of course, she's limited in what she can do, but it's the pain that's the problem at the moment. I've been insisting she be faithful in taking her pills. You don't know Ramona, miss. She can be very stubborn."

"Even when it comes to medication?"

"If the problem's painful enough, she'll take it. I was there Sunday evening. And Byron or I will go down tonight with dinner. I tried to get her to move into one of the guest rooms for a few days..." He trailed off. I knew he was thinking of the vacated rooms from the tourists.

"That would be a help," I agreed.

"She won't have it. She says it would look bad."

"It's nice to see someone still worries about

proprieties."

"Yes, well, we do. And, I think it's partly due to her son being at her place for the week. Have you met Liam?"

"Superficially at the bonfire and later at Ramona's."

Arthur exhaled and shook his head. "That was a big mistake, I admit. I shouldn't have let his group play. But Ramona wanted the village to hear him."

"Sort of a local-lad-does-good thing?"

"I suppose. But I'm paying the price right now. People ringing me up, cornering me in the village and on the lane. I haven't heard one person thanking me for the music. It's all been complaints."

"How unfortunate."

"Isn't it! Talbot's upset, but of course he would do. Anything out of custom annoys him. Byron isn't too thrilled even today with the group. And then there's Mason Conway. What an earful I got from him!"

Thinking I'd be here until tonight if I stayed to hear the full list of disgruntled residents, I thanked Arthur for his time and took my leave, wondering if the adoption mess would ever get sorted out.

"I tell you, sir," I said as Graham and I compared notes in the incident room. My tea momentarily forgotten, I stroked my necklace as I tried to put sense to the mountain of growing information. "I'm amazed at these villagers. If I lived here and had to put up with Talbot's constant haranguing, I don't know if I wouldn't be moved to do something about it."

Graham paused with his cup to his lips. "That's a bit thick, Taylor. You, of all people, talking like that. Where's that famous compassion?"

"Stretched thin, I'm afraid. Anyway, I found out Kris Alton Halford's dad died in 1979, if that's of any interest to you."

"Popular year. Also the year of the quick engagement and subsequent breaking of same between her and Byron MacKinnon."

"Do you think the two incidents are connected?"

"I don't know. It's tempting to put too much weight on it. 1979. What month did Mr. Alton die?"

"December. I checked it through the computer to substantiate Arthur's story. It was a wintry road accident."

"Bad way to go." Graham closed his eyes, then rubbed them. "Life for our two love birds was certainly fine in November. That's when the perpetual row came up and Talbot got the news of the forthcoming wedding."

"So what happened to break it off, then?"

"I couldn't get a clue from Kris. Shall we try the unlucky groom?"

"Might as well. You haven't talked to him yet."

"We must rectify that, Taylor. He'll feel left out."

"So, how many rooms, then, you figure?"

Graham came to such an abrupt halt outside Byron's office that I bumped into him. He held his finger to his lips and inclined his head toward the door. It was nearly closed, yet left an inch for the skilled listener to sidle up to and listen. Which is what we did, I stooping somewhat to accommodate Graham's tall frame. His chest was against my back and I could feel his warmth. We must have looked ridiculous, but I loved it. I'd never been so close to him.

"I'll know more when we get the plan finalized."

"And when'll that be?"

There was a scraping of a chair, as though one of the talkers was getting to his feet. I recognized the voices. Talbot and Byron. They seemed like strange bedfellows, but perhaps not. We had yet to deduce the topic of their conversation.

Byron said something that I couldn't hear. He had moved away, possibly turned his back to us. Graham leaned closer to the door. I felt his breath on the back of my neck.

Talbot said, "Fine. Just so you keep me up to date. I don't like surprises."

"You sound as though you don't trust me. Is that a way for partners to start out?"

Talbot's verbal reply was inaudible, but I did hear his belch. "And converting it will take—"

"Now you sound like a ruddy banker."

"Well, when there's this much at stake…"

"You leave it to me, Talbot."

"That's just what I have to do for the moment, don't I? I'll feel better when I can actually get my hands into it."

Another verbal exchange that was muffled by a moved chair followed this, then two sets of footsteps growing louder and evidently coming toward the door. Graham and I stood up. He motioned me to the opposite side while he then took a large step backwards. I raised my fist as though about to knock. It was not the first time I wished I had some Royal Academy dramatic classes under my belt. When Byron opened the door he saw what appeared to be two police officers just walking up to his office.

"I'll see you later, Talbot," Byron said after recovering from his initial jolt.

Talbot mumbled something just audible about never knowing what will turn up on your doorstep and being careful what you step into. He sniffed as though there was a putrid aroma somewhere, and left. Byron then held open the door for us.

Looking like a patient who's been given bad news by his doctor, Byron took us into his office, and asked us to excuse the mess. It consisted of a camera, sketch ideas for ads, and the usual letters, books and brochures of a tourist-oriented business, yet harbored more papers than I had expected. Either business is so good he can't keep up with his paperwork or the man's heart's not in the business. He belongs to the landscape and the breed of nature-linked ancient Scot, I thought on seeing him again, taking in his ginger-colored hair and mustache. Remarkably like overgrown patches of heather on a craggy mound.

"I'm afraid you've caught me at a rather bad moment." Byron cleared a space on his desk.

I could believe that. Did he suspect we had overheard his conversation or was he referring to his work?

He jammed his personal checkbook into a drawer, wadded up a paper nearly black with mathematical calculations, and tossed it at a full waste bin. The sheet glanced off the edge of the can and rolled beneath the desk. "Sorting through my accounts," he explained.

"If we've come at an inopportune time," Graham began, only to be waved off by Byron, who said it was all right.

"No time's really good when it's got to do with murder."

"Murder does seem to take up a bit of everyone's time," I agreed.

Graham asked about the car crash involving Kris' dad.

Byron seemed mesmerized by my notetaking. "December 1979, perhaps? I can't remember. Sorry, but there you are. If you give me a day or so, I might recall it." He played with his watchband, then rushed on as Graham coughed. "Well, it was a hell of a winter, even at that early stage, wasn't it? George Alton and I had been debating about the trip to Edinburgh. But since he had cleared his calendar and sort of made up his mind, we went. I used to do a lot of driving for Mr. Alton. I wasn't his 'driver,' or anything like that. It's just that I was in my thirties then, needed a bit of extra cash, and had the time."

"I understand Kris had gone briefly to America in the mid-seventies. When did she return?"

"Oh, must have been May 1979. I started driving Mr. Alton about, quite sporadically at first. He and his wife had gone over to America just before Kris' graduation. Something about seeing where her mum had grown up. Illinois, I think. They made quite a holiday of it for several months. Well, you would, wouldn't you, going all that way?"

"Was Mr. Alton banned from driving?" I wondered about the circumstances that warranted a chauffeur.

"You mean had he any restrictions on his license? No. He simply didn't like making long trips or driving at night. I didn't mind, so I ended up with the job. We liked each other well enough. I liked Kris, too. Well, to this day I don't know what went wrong. I was driving, and must have hit a patch of ice. The car skidded. I couldn't control it, no matter how I steered it. God, I still hear it, the brakes squealing, the crash against the stone wall, the screams. Anyway, I couldn't go through with the marriage after I had killed her dad, could I?" He asked the question as though he were challenging our morals.

"But it wasn't deliberate," Graham said.

"No. And Kris knew that, but I couldn't have her look at me each day and be reminded of the accident, or her dad. So I broke it off and walked out of her life. Literally. I left the village."

Uncomfortable with Byron's emotions, I looked at Graham, mouthing my request to leave. He shook his head. "When and why did you come back, Mr. MacKinnon?"

The secretary's hand dropped to his lap. He raised his head, squinting at Graham and looking as though he had just awakened and was bothered by the light. "1981. When I heard she had married Derek. I knew it was safe for me, for us. I still love her, though."

It was then that Graham nodded and we quietly left the room.

We interrupted our return from the manor house to pause beside the burnt-out bonfire. The police tape still fluttered in the breeze, the dregs of Bonfire Night still sat mutely where they had been left. The dole and Guy Fawkes: two ceremonies dealing with long-ago deaths. The first ceremony honored a death, reverently recalling personal passions of a loved family member. The second ceremony ridiculed a death, transforming an ancient tragedy into a mocking entertainment and social festivity. Amazing, I thought, staring at the charred potatoes, their blackened skins barely discernible in the ebony mess of the fire and the fading afternoon light. Two events two days apart, illustrating the two sides of human nature.

A gust of wind whipped up a handful of ashes and dust, mixing them into an eddy that peppered the air. "Dust to dust, ashes to ashes," Graham said. He rubbed his nose. The aroma was not pleasant. It stank of spent wood, old ashes and dry earth. "How many hundreds of fires, Taylor, have been enjoyed without any tragedies?"

I was unsure if he wanted an answer, but he kicked at a potato, just tinged gray from the fire. A fly buzzed off at the interruption to its feeding and faded into the deeply coloring sky. "Burnt potatoes and burnt chestnuts," Graham sniffed. "Burnt offerings to Revelry and in merry memory of Mr. Fawkes. Burnt offerings, sacrifices that are ignored or go to no avail. The broken hearts are still there, for all the efforts. Remember, remember the 5th of November. Damn."

Graham picked up the potato, flicked off an annoying ant, and threw it at the gallows tree. There was a satisfying splat as the potato hit its mark. He turned and hurried down the road, his shadow momentarily obliterating the few potatoes scattered in the grass.

I took the scenic route back to the pub. Not that it was difficult to find, for any walk in the village proved a picture post card vista.

Taking the eastern road, I walked past Talbot's house, entered the woods, then turned toward Arthur's castle. The climb had been steady, yet not tiring, and I emerged from the woods into the open greenery. Rather like a woman gone mad with cosmetics, sunset splashed its lavenders, blues and vermilions across the leaden sky. A hint of crimson glowed along the western horizon where the sun hovered, its base nestled firmly on the hazy hill. On the summit of Ashmoor Pike the trees stretched like black lace across the lowest edge of the sky.

I paused to pick a crocus, the *crocus sativus* of saffron fame, astonished to find the fragile purple flower still in bloom. Yet, it was sheltered somewhat from the cold, northern wind. So I picked it, thinking I would admire it more in my room tonight than anyone else would do in passing along the road. Twirling it slowly against my thumb and index finger, I felt the stiffness of the stem. I peered into the cup, looking at the small stamen. I decided to sketch it as a last offering of autumnal joy before winter swept all delicate beauty from the land. I should have left it alone, then perhaps I wouldn't have been so preoccupied with my find.

I might have seen him, but I didn't. On turning toward the village, I heard "Hey! Job Cop!" It was the ridiculous, taunting nickname he had created for me in police class. I had colored when he had whined it—anything to demean or make it arduous on me, the sole woman. Mark had laughed at his cleverness in inventing the nickname. By now, though, The Job had disintegrated into TJ, and most of my colleagues had forgotten its history.

I know I blushed. He always unnerved me. I hated myself for it. Of course I couldn't pretend not to have heard or seen him. I held my flower in front of me, as though it was a banner leading me into battle, and smiled.

"Hello, Mark. You having a busy day?"

A foot taller than I, he towered above me, which added to my anguish, for I was forever looking up at him. His muscles were obvious and contributed to part of his cockiness. The other ingredient was his premature gray hair, which he wore down to his collar. It was thick and curled becomingly, I had to admit. It also complemented his gray eyes.

"Not as busy as some." He noticed that I had been intent on his face. He flashed his white, even teeth at me. "You got your walk in this morning before dashing about with The Vic. Congrats."

I stiffened, upset he had been watching me, despising his use of Graham's nickname. The way Mark said it gave the name an indecent, offensive quality.

"Is that all you could find, one lone pansy?" He reached out and I clutched it closer. His laughter held a mocking that reminded me of class. "Still learning about the birds and the bees? Is that why you're still single, darling? Any time you want to learn under my tutelage instead of Graham's—"

"You're certainly working hard." I needed to change the subject.

"Don't worry. I'm earning my pay. But you're up earlier than I was. Did you find anything interesting?"

"Haven't you got anything better to do, Mark? We're investigating a murder, or don't you remember?"

"Some of us have time for pansies, I see. Does The Vic know about your passion?"

"What's it got to do with Graham?" I felt my heart rate increasing and my jaw muscle tensing. "I'm not taking time off. I'm going to the incident room to make my report, if you have to know. If you'd apply the same energy to your work—"

"Hey, you don't have to explain anything to me, Brenna. I'm a sergeant, just like you. Equals.

Just don't work so long in the woods that you can't get your beauty sleep tonight, not that you have to worry about that. And if you don't feel like sleeping— Well, you know where to find me." He smiled, touched the crocus and walked down the lane, but not before calling out his room number.

I stood there for some time, trying to control my temper. Mark Salt was a good cop. He had been near the top of our class, but he was at the bottom in emotional development.

After he'd had a five-minute head start, I tucked the crocus into my jacket and walked back to the pub.

"He was just being his usual jerk self," Margo said when I had found her at the pub. I was looking for Graham, but he was out somewhere. Margo was at a laptop, typing faster than I thought human fingers were capable. She seemed to be drowning in a sea of papers and sticky notes. I refrained from looking at the table Graham and I usually occupied, afraid I'd find messages from Simcock or notes from Graham telling me to take another statement from Talbot or work with Mark on something. I shuddered, thinking I'd rather endure a root canal procedure without Novocain. "You're letting him get to you, which is what he wants," Margo said when I finished telling her about my encounter with Mark. Luckily, he wasn't in the room. She looked up from the monitor. "It doesn't mean a thing, Bren. He's flexing his muscles."

"He didn't lay a hand on me, Margo."

"His badgering muscles. Follow the conversation, girl."

"I wish I could believe you. I saw him talking to Evan this afternoon."

"So? I talked to Evan. Does that condemn me to having hung the Guy in your room?"

"No, but he could've gotten the key to my room from Evan, said he needed it for the investigation."

Margo shook her head. "Evan would've sent him to Graham for a key. He's not dumb, Bren."

"You don't know how much the average person fears the police, Margo. They're even afraid to talk to us. If we say something, they believe us; they obey us. We have an incredible amount of power."

"It's the uniform."

"What uniform? We're plain clothes cops."

"See? We need jeans and sweatshirts. They evoke friendliness."

I groaned, rolling my eyes heavenward. "Big help. I still think it's Mark. He's devious. He can wheedle."

"He never tries to wheedle me. I wish he would. Don't you think he's handsome?"

"*He* thinks he's handsome."

"You're afraid to admit it, Bren. You know, men don't joke with women they don't like."

"Do you know the difference between joking and harassment, Margo?"

"He's trying to impress you, make himself bigger than life in your eyes. You know…macho copper who saves the day and the heroine. I think he's just trying too hard. Cut him some slack for that. If you got to know him, he'll probably ease off on the maleness."

"I don't know if I want to get to know him."

"Why don't you turn the tables, Bren, and instigate something? You might get a date."

"I might get sick. Oh. Gotta run. There's Graham."

Margo whispered 'Give The Vic my love' as

I headed for the door.

16

Graham and I had no trouble finding a table that Monday evening at The Broken Loaf. And evidently Evan had no trouble in the kitchen, for he returned with our dinner orders just as Graham was draining the last of his beer.

"You'll be wanting the other half of that drink?" Evan nodded at Graham's empty pint.

I gave my glass to the publican, but Graham said he'd wait a bit.

"I'm glad to see we're not the only diners tonight. Murder hasn't put them off." He leaned back, chewing a forkful of ham, and looked around the room.

The public bar area mimicked the décor of the private bar, where we had set up the incident room. Photos of village events, framed articles from the local newspaper, and children's drawings covered the emerald green-flocked wallpaper. Mahogany tables and chairs sat on a well-washed flagstone floor. An open fireplace large enough to roast an ox consumed a good portion of the wall opposite the bar, while someone's collection of royal and political commemorative china plates commandeered the wall before us. Staring at the names and pictures was a great time killer while waiting for your meal.

Byron sat at a nearby table, his voice low as he talked to Ramona. This time there was no door to hide behind or constable who could sit unobtrusively by to take shorthand notes. We chalked it up to the failure that occurs periodically. Besides, they wouldn't be talking about their part in the murder with us so close. But I glanced at them periodically, as though that would heighten my auditory senses. They both looked as though they had come directly from their jobs, for they were dressed in dark suits. Byron occasionally stroked his tie—a brightly colored yellow and green stripe—and glanced around the room. Was he afraid to be seen with Ramona, or did he have some work to do for Arthur?

We finished our meal in silence, which annoyed me. I'd exhausted all conversation in the topics I kept for social occasions, and even ventured into more personal material in my attempt to become close to Graham. When I finished relating my brother's concert tour agenda—thinking the piano close cousin to the harpsichord and, therefore, of some interest to Graham—I sat stupidly, feeling my face warm. He'd nodded and made polite responses during my account but offered no similar response. Now he sat gazing over my shoulder, his mind obviously elsewhere, and I felt the chance to develop a relationship fading.

I folded my napkin and laid it on the table, ready to call the evening a failure, but stopped as Graham gestured toward Tom Oldendorf, who was walking around the room, stopping periodically to examine something. "He must want a lot of memories of Upper Kingsleigh, the way he's snapping away." Another flash from his camera illuminated the room. "What's he saying? Did you catch it? Don't be obvious about it, Taylor."

Graham, angling his thin frame in his chair so he could stretch out his long legs without entangling them in the maze of table and chair legs, appeared not only to be disinterested in his surroundings but also having a bit of a kip. If he'd had a hat, it would've been pulled over his eyes. But even without it, he looked completely off duty and relaxed, his arms folded across his chest, his chin nestled in the collar of his shirt. It was an attitude he employed often, and it usually helped glean startling bits of information. This time, the noise of too many conversations and the distance between tables prevented him from hearing anything.

Byron got up, threw several pound coins on the table, and finished the last of his beer. Ramona grabbed the tail of his tie and pulled him down so their faces nearly touched, leaning in our direction as she tried to make herself heard above the din.

"Dear, you want to get back to your place, put your feet up and have a beer. I've never seen you like this."

Byron shook off her grasp and straightened up, running his hand through his hair. The gingery strands stood away from his pale skin, giving him the air of a hedgehog. He said something in reply but I couldn't catch it.

Obviously Ramona could, for she said, "Think nothing of it. You trot back to Art like the good employee you are. And I'll guard my tongue, so that worry's ended. After all, if I haven't said anything in all these years, your secrets are safe, darling. You and Derek have a good evening."

Ramona's smile broadened as he left the pub.

"Hear that?" Graham asked, watching Ramona join Tom at another table.

"Yes, sir. What's the little secret Byron's afraid of?"

"It's a secret, Taylor."

I nodded and wondered how many secrets Upper Kingsleigh's residents harbored. Minutes later, Graham pulled in his legs, threw his napkin on the table, and stood up. He glanced down at me. "I think we'll do the Public Servant bit and help Tom with his holiday budget."

I murmured it seemed the friendly thing to do.

Tom had just finished taking a photo of the scared tabletop when Graham walked up to him. Tom was seated with several tourists from the B and B. Graham nodded to everyone, then asked Tom how the holiday was going.

"Oh, uh, fine." Tom seemed to consider the battery charge window on his camera. "I've about had it, though. What with Steve and traipsing around today, I'm thinking of calling it an early night. Are you anywhere closer to solving the murder, or don't you let on?"

"I don't think you'd be happy with anything other than the name of the murderer, would you?" Graham smiled pleasantly. "Things are developing, let's just say."

Tom sat down abruptly, cradling the camera on his lap. He extracted the memory card and tightened his fingers around it. Graham seemed unusually interested in Tom's procedure. "Did you take other photos than this group tonight? I remember you had your camera when we met at the bonfire today."

Tom shoved the card into his jacket pocket. "Sure. I'm partial to architecture and landscape, though. You know, church, gravestones, Haddon Hall. Why? Have I done something wrong? If I've been a nuisance to someone..."

"So you've been about the village and photographed parts of it, then?" Graham's voice remained calm, but I could see the faintest tensing of his jaw muscle.

Tom nodded, his attention torn between his camera, Graham, and me.

"I know I'm a hell of a nuisance, but would you mind telling me what you snapped of the village? It's an odd request, but I wouldn't be so insistent if it weren't important." He stood in front of Tom, non-threatening, his dark gray suit and cranberry-hued shirt as foreign to Tom's impression of a policeman as Graham's manner was.

Tom swallowed repeatedly. "I've just been taking shots like any other tourist. A dozen or so during the bonfire, some during the dole ceremony, parts of the village, including a close-up of the church tower. I got it with my telephoto."

"Excuse me for asking what must appear to be an odd question, but did you take any of the effigy before Bonfire Night?"

"Yeah. I was down at the fire area that afternoon."

"Would you mind terribly if I borrowed all your memory cards, looked at your photos, and then returned the cards to you?"

"Well, I—"

"It's a strange request, I know. But I have a reason for it."

Tom shrugged, extracted the card from his pocket, and dropped it into Graham's outstretched hand. I already had the receipt written out and into Tom's hand before he said 'yes.' "You want the other memory stick, too?" He dug into his camera bag. Moments later the second card lay alongside the first. "Just these two." Nothing followed Tom's declaration but a sincere thank you and the transferring of the cards to Graham's pocket.

"He seems to have recovered from his brother-in-law's death quite rapidly," I observed as we paused in the vestibule connecting the two bar rooms. "He must have an iron constitution."

"He certainly displayed more anger than grief at the fire circle," Graham agreed.

"Maybe that's why he came on holiday with Steve. He wasn't particularly friendly or unfriendly with him, so he's not all that broken up over his death. Anyway, women show their emotions more easily."

Graham pulled the memory cards from his pocket, threw one to me, and wrapped his long fingers about the remaining one. "This just might have something on it. I'm not going to let this slip past us. Even at my age I learn from past mistakes."

Your age, I wanted to say. You're all of forty-one. Trim, healthy, good looking, mentally and physically able to beat most of us in B Division.

Graham pushed open the door to the incident room, noted the startled looks of the constables who were clustered around a single computer, and walked briskly over to a table. I followed, hoping I could find an opportunity to instigate a personal conversation.

There were two new messages from

Simcock, received this evening eighteen minutes apart, stuck to the front of the case folder. Both were marked 'Urgent.' Both asked the same question: had we learned anything more about MacKinnon's 1979 road accident? Ignoring the notes, Graham idly flicked the memory stick along the tabletop, as though it were some bizarre rugby game. The card crashed into the case folder—thick with typed notes, statements and photographs—and I picked it up. I knew Graham had seen Simcock's messages, yet chose to ignore them for the moment. Which was fine with me; Graham was easier to work with when he wasn't reeling from the Super's impatience. I placed the card gently by Graham's hand. Granted there's very little leeway for mistakes in murder cases, but he's too hard on himself. He's got to be perfect, solve it as fast as he can. Like he's trying to prove himself all over again, make up for those five years of demotion. I let the card inch back and forth a few times before my hand slapped onto it, quieting it.

Graham's head jerked up from his concentration, and he looked around for the constable. "Byrd!"

An energetic 'Here, sir!' echoed off the walls. Chair legs scraped across flagstone, and the steady tempo of hard soles tapped out the path to his superior officer. There was a sharper tap as Byrd came to a stop at Graham's side and snapped to attention. Then the room returned to that quiet that settles on a space when people are comfortable with each other and their duties. Graham scooped up the two memory cards and handed them to the P.C. "I want you to take these to the station. Get them developed and printed on photo paper. Glossy. And have them back here tomorrow—early."

"Yes, sir" cracked into the stillness as the man accepted the cards.

"Two sizes of prints—our standard working size, and 4x5 for the owner. Got that? Oh, and if the pathology report's ready, bring that, too, please. *And* the knife. Don't forget the knife, Byrd. That should do it."

"Very good, sir." The door opened and closed quickly, and the constable was on his way to Buxton.

"That knife'll be dusted by now. I want to dangle it in front of a few people's eyes, see if anyone recognizes it. Not that anyone will. Is there a universal motto I'm not aware of, Taylor?"

"Besides Mum's the word?"

"Unless it's *Forsan et haec olim meminisse juvabit.*" Graham smiled, glanced at his watch, then echoed 'Perhaps this too will be a pleasure to look back on one day.' "Do you feel like putting in an hour or so before we catch a final pint?"

"That's fine, sir."

"Right."

We sat down, shoving the case folder and Simcock's messages farther down the table, pretending we didn't see them. Graham grabbed a pen and the notes still lying in the printer tray, and laid a blank sheet of paper in front of us. He seemed happier now that he had dealt with Simcock.

"Most all the villagers have been interviewed about the clothing donations," Graham said, glancing at a page in his notebook. "No discrepancies have been found between their statements and the list Ramona gave you."

"It's nice to find a truthful person. What about the hair found on the jacket?"

"The color doesn't match that on the body."

"It's not a wig, I assume."

"Steve sported only a hat and a few wisps of straw on his head. And it's a human hair, Taylor. Nice try."

I said I was trying to cover all angles, including dog or cat hair.

Graham murmured his appreciation of my thought process and yawned.

"The more we get into this thing, sir," I said, tapping my notebook, "the more these villagers get all intermingled and show up in each other's stories."

"Like a massive Celtic knot. Are you thinking of our favorite year, then?"

"Not just 1979. Several years involving the entire village. Byron nobly gave up Kris but still loves her. Kris was engaged to Steve. Talbot was adopted, if you care to believe it, by Derek's father, only he can't prove it. And Arthur's great-granddaddy runs over Derek's granddaddy and starts this whole miserable dole and its consequences. We need more than a computer to sort all this out. We need a crystal ball."

"It could come in handy, but let's spare the Derbyshire taxpayers the additional expense and try our brains first."

I mumbled something about it being a definite disadvantage, but jotted down ideas readily enough when Graham started talking through things.

"You mentioned Steve and Talbot. Would your credibility extend to Talbot killing Steve by mistake, if strangling is his preferred or first attack?"

"I don't quite follow you, sir."

"Think back to that entertaining bit about the attempted murder twenty years ago, Taylor. If Talbot lunged at Byron, ready to strike and kick the life out of him back then, would Talbot also just as easily have struck Steve now?"

"It's obvious he didn't die from the knife wound. He'd hardly have to wash his clothes for all the blood that was on them. It was part of their tradition, using a knife to affix a note to the effigy, remember."

"So, what's the motive?"

"I told you we needed that crystal ball." The minutes ticked away as we considered our suspects and motives. Finally, almost apologizing for interrupting our contemplation, I said, "Could Byron stage the murder in his desire to kill Derek?"

"For what gain? The only tango those two ever did, as far as we know, was for Derek to take over as Kris' fiancé. And that was certainly nothing personal. Derek stepped into the matrimonial picture after Kris' dad was killed in that car accident."

"People harbor grudges for ages, sir."

"What grudge? Byron was driving. He lost out on marriage, not Derek. He's the one who left the village."

"True. And I doubt it was a suicide attempt. He wouldn't be certain he'd die, in the first place. And why would he take Kris' dad with him?"

"That's a bit far-fetched, Taylor. The man came back and in twenty-two years hasn't killed himself."

"If anybody deserved to be dead, it should be Derek."

"Meaning, with him out of the way, Arthur could keep his money?"

"Yes, sir. Arthur and Ramona would probably vote for that." I added that I meant that only as an economic measure, that the couple probably liked Derek a great deal and wouldn't mean him any personal harm.

"But someone might have." Graham stared at his mess of mind-mapped notes, the arrows, cartoons and boxed-off words remarkably accurate in portraying the condition of our thinking at the moment. He hummed a snatch of a Gilbert and Sullivan song, and grinned when I joined him on 'Spite of ye all, he is free—he is free! Whom do ye ward? Pretty warders are ye...'

I sighed heavily, evoking fond memories of the operetta. "One of my favorites, *Yeomen of the Guard*. I played Dame Carruthers." I smoothed the fabric on my trousers, hoping he wouldn't say something about matronly type casting. "I still remember all the lyrics. 'The screw may twist and the rack may turn, and men may bleed and—'"

Graham looked at me with a new admiration, I thought. "I didn't know you sang, Taylor. What a deep, secret pool of talents you hide."

"Yes, sir." All through dinner I'd wanted a conversational topic that would develop a personal relationship, and now that I'd found it, I was embarrassed.

"And where was this? I would have come if I'd have known. Next time, tell me."

I could feel the heat flooding my cheeks and I hated myself for being so self-conscious. "The church hall. A few years ago, I think."

Graham grinned, squeezing my hand. "I bet the tower was never kept in better tune than by you."

I was hoping he would say something further, something more personal, mentioning my singing voice, but he had dropped the subject and was once again focused on murder. Fanning through my papers, I said, "Do you have the timetable handy, sir? I can't seem to place my copy. Thanks. Was our Good Arthur alone long enough to slip down to the green and waylay Steve?"

"Well, if Arthur traipsed down to the village green for some nefarious purpose, mum's the word from him." He closed his eyes briefly and stretched, the stress of the case and the long days catching up with him. "I don't know. I think I've had it. I can't seem to think any more."

"You've been chasing the clock hands fairly steadily, sir. Pity the overtime pay's a thing of the past."

"Nothing more than a fond memory." He yawned after he had given his opinion of the constabulary policy. "We ignore the clock and plug along. Well, I, for one, am having a damned hard go this evening. What say we give it another quarter hour before surrendering to our beds?" He folded back the top page of his notebook. "Let's look long and hard at these flittings by our key personnel. Motive aside for the moment, it seems to all hang on opportunity."

I nodded, but thought of the Guy that had been hanging in my bedroom. Who had had the opportunity to fix up that?

"Very little time to accomplish anything," Graham continued after he had closed his eyes. "We've got the vicar, Talbot, and Tom Oldendorf at the bonfire area at quarter past six or so, with the place literally crawling with people from then on."

"It had to have been done earlier. They put it up well in advance of the bonfire."

"Right. That rock concert affair. When did they hoist the Guy?"

I told him what Liam and the band members had said.

"And we don't know if anyone came along after Liam and Josh left. That might've been a perfect opportunity to substitute Steve for the effigy, except he was walking around very much alive that afternoon. Damn."

"Of course, there were snatches of quarter and half hours throughout the day when the substitution could've happened, sir."

"Right. I don't fault you, Taylor. You had to have a few breaks while on duty. No one can expect you to stand there for that length of time." He said it by way of an apology, to let me know he didn't hold me responsible if the substitution had been done while I was powdering my nose.

I thanked him but felt embarrassed by the calls of nature. "It wouldn't take long to make the switch if he had Steve all dressed for the occasion."

"So it still comes down to after teatime on Sunday."

"And motive, too, sir. I doubt if Liam or his group knew Steve, so why would they kill him?"

"Maybe it goes back to what still riles the villagers."

"The rock concert itself?"

Graham nodded and stared at his page of notes. "Maybe Steve knew about Guy Fawkes Day and wanted to experience the real thing. Maybe he got perturbed when Liam starts setting up for the rock concert, and they exchange words. Maybe words led to anger and violence."

"And Liam or a band member tops Steve in anger." I paused, considering the scenario. "I don't know. It sounds a bit thin. But anything can happen if someone's disappointment leads to anger."

"It could've happened the other way, too, Taylor. Steve, being full of the American ideals of freedom of speech, defended Liam's rock concert when a villager spoke against it. Steve could've become protective about Liam's right to perform, especially since he had permission, and he got into a fight with the tradition-loving resident." He eyed me. "What's that do for you?"

"Plausible, sir. But we're back to proving it."

"Certainly, but we've got somewhere to start. Anyway, in those quarters of an hour or so when you were not all-eyes on the stack of wood, we've a bunch of tourists and villagers alone and at loose ends, waiting for the bonfire to begin, probably quite available to commit the crime."

"Alone." I turned the word and the meaning around in my mind. "I know our time constraint is awful, but do you suppose our murderer could have had an accomplice?"

"Nothing would surprise me. What I wouldn't give right now for a stone-chiseled tablet of everyone's whereabouts. Where's Moses when we need him?"

17

"So, did anything happen last night?" Margo asked, on coming into my room Tuesday morning. She looked at my ceiling fixture, expecting the Guy still hanging there. I didn't tell her, but it had taken all my nerve to get close to it so I could take it down.

"What do you consider 'happen'?" I busied myself with brushing my hair.

Margo laid both hands on my shoulders and turned me toward her. My resolve, so steady earlier, crumbled on the confrontation, and I felt tears forming . "More importantly," she said, her gaze drilling into my eyes as though she was Mesmer, "how do you label it, if it happened? Was it anything gross and indecent?" She headed toward the bathroom, seeing nothing obvious in the room itself. I pulled her back.

"It's not in there."

"So something did happen. A note? A phone call?"

"That I could deal with." I grabbed a tissue. Even now, eight hours after I discovered it, I was still angry.

"For God's sake, Bren, what happened?"

I walked to the wastepaper bin, reached in and removed the brochures and tourist info supplied by the pub. Then I held the can so Margo could see the dead bird inside. A string secured a wilted mum to the bird's chest. For once Margo had nothing to say. I placed the bin on the floor and slowly tossed in the papers.

I looked around, aware of the flowered curtains and coverlet, the fireplace and over-sized cushions and rocker, yet searching for some clue to the intruder.

In the silence I could hear the sounds of the pub waking: the creaks of the wooden floor, the phone in the bar area ringing, the scratchings of a wind-tossed tree branch at my window. It wasn't until I heard a bird singing outside the window that I cried.

"Bren, dear, it's all right." Margo came over, smothered me in a hug that spoke of her anger and concern and sorrow. We stood like that for several minutes, my head on her shoulder, dampening her blouse with my tears, and her voice floating in my ear.

When I finally lifted my head, I said, "It's not me, Margo. I swear I'm not crying for me. It's the sparrow. Why would anyone harm such a defenseless creature that never did anything?"

Margo held me at arm's length, searching my eyes for some hint to my emotional stability. "It's not the bird, Bren." I must have looked astonished, because she hurried on. "Listen to me. Think like a cop, Bren. You're letting your emotions get in the way. And that's just what this berk wants. You're not using your brain. You're forgetting everything you ever learned of police work."

"But how does he know about me and

birds?"

"Maybe he doesn't. Maybe it's just a coincidence. It's not the bird; I'm trying to get through to you. It's the message."

I gazed at the cloudy sky, at the patchwork of sun and shadow sweeping the land, before I could find my words. "He wants me dead? Like the bird?"

"Or he's trying to scare you off this case."

We sat on the bed while Margo rattled off suppositions. They were probably good bits of wisdom, though I can't recall any; I was too emotional over the bird.

"So how is he getting in here?"

Margo's foot tapped the wastepaper bin. "I'm not half so concerned about that as I am about his messages. This was left in your bathroom sometime yesterday, then, and you found it—"

"Around eleven o'clock, when I was getting ready for bed."

Graham's door opened and closed. She waited for his footsteps to fade before asking, "Does he know? Have you told him?"

"If I haven't said anything about the Guy in my room, you think I'm going to mention a dead bird? I told you—"

"I know what you told me. But this thing's not just about a dummy anymore, Bren. It's escalating. And in a frightening way. I think you should at least tell one of the lads."

I must have grabbed Margo's hand rather tightly, for she yelled and asked what was the matter. I apologized and reminded her about Mark Salt.

"You can't suspect him, Bren. Really?"

"Just the sort of thing he'd do. Birds, flowers, nature. He might use my passions, as he calls it, to make me nervous."

"And hopefully propel you into his arms."

"Or his bed," I added.

"Just like him, the berk. 'I'm scared, Mark. Help me!' Men!" She exhaled loudly and stood up, her eyes hardened. "Well, whoever is getting in here at least isn't harming you. Remember that. He's had opportunity."

"You don't think it's more of a practical joke, do you, Margo, instead of the warning off the case?"

"Now that could definitely be Mister Detective God's-Gift-to-Women Mark Salt."

I suddenly felt better thinking along that line. It would be just like Mark to first use a piece from the case, then something personally associated with me, as a big joke. Perhaps he even wanted me to confide in him. What had he said yesterday?

"Well." Margo's hand gripped the doorknob. "It's a damned shame we can't use some of our equipment to catch Mister Funny Man. What a waste. Come on." She opened the door and stepped into the hall. "You'll feel better after breakfast."

"Not necessarily." I indicated Talbot at the end of the hall. The handyman had a large canister, into which he was dumping trash from people's rooms. I thought about ducking back into my room before he saw me, but then reasoned I'd have a face-to-face confrontation when he tapped on the room to get my wastepaper bin. I stepped into the hall and quietly shut the door.

Fortune was not smiling on me that morning. Perhaps it couldn't break through the clouds. Talbot turned to knock at the next door in his procession, saw me, and called out. "Leave yer door open, will ya? I know you've got somethin' ya wanna get rid of." He shuffled down the hall, his eyes fixed on me rather like a snake staring down a rabbit. I stepped aside as he approached and opened the door. As he passed I could smell the cigarette odor of his clothes and breath. I turned my head to avoid the aroma.

When he had tipped the waste bin contents into his canister, he shoved the can into my hand. "You're lookin' at me like I was gonna steal it. Here. Now you've got it again you can sleep safe." He bent over, butt angled toward me, conveniently picking up something off the carpet so he could show his opinion of me.

Margo called impatiently from the top of the landing, wondering what was taking me so long. I put the can back, shut the door, and tucked the key into the zippered section of my shoulder bag. In turning to go, I rattled the doorknob once more. It was locked.

"Go and fill yer belly, then," Talbot said, on straightening up. "We can't have you fainting from hunger. Ya might hit yer head and get concussed. And then you'd be in hospital. What would we do then?" He ambled down the hall, rapping on the next door. Getting no response, he moved to the next. I noticed, on the door opening, that he could talk civilly when he wanted to.

Tea had just been poured the second time that morning when Constable Byrd dashed into the incident room. Thinking he wanted a hot drink after his drive up from Buxton, I held out a mug. He shook his head, and looked around. Seeing Graham at the far end of the room, he walked over waving a folder that looked very much like the pathology report.

The morning was well advanced. Shops

were open, the Royal Mail van was on its rounds, and motorists were pumping petrol at the service station. The baker's shop discharged a handful of customers, all of whom hurried away with bags or boxes. I imagined the glass cases with their array of bread and biscuits and wished for a pastry or a plate of digestives: something nice for our mid-morning break. Instead, we had a tin of stale pretzels. Graham put down his cup, his attention peeled from the pathology report to Byrd's impish face.

Opening his clenched fingers to reveal a camera's memory card, the constable watched Graham's confusion as he glanced from it to the processed photographs. The computerized report fell haphazardly to the table, momentarily forgotten. "No, sir," Byrd said, handing the photos to Graham. "I didn't overlook it. I just received it from Tom Oldendorf."

"Tom? I thought he gave us the memory sticks last night."

"Nice bit of timing, actually. I was coming, he was going." Then as though thinking he had better put it in officialese for his superior, Byrd reiterated, "Upon proceeding toward the village from my duties in Buxton, I observed the aforementioned subject motoring at a speed I considered in excess of the posted limit. Needing to reprimand him for the speed violation, I detained him. To make certain, as it were."

"Yes. Right." Graham's thumb and forefinger dented the edge of the photographs. "What, exactly, was Tom doing on the road with this memory card? Can you tell me in twenty-five words or less?"

"Yes, sir. Taking it to Buxton to be developed. That was his story, anyway."

"You didn't believe him?" I said, enjoying

the verbal tennis game.

"He didn't give me any particular reason not to." Byrd eyed the pretzels. "Tom overlooked it yesterday when you asked for his memory cards, Mr. Graham. He thought he'd given you all of them, but when he was hanging up his jacket..."

"So, his conscience bothered him." Graham tossed the photographs onto the table.

"Yes, sir. He also gave me another story. This one's about Gilbert Catchpool. As pertains to the murder. He wanted you to know that Gilbert has an affinity for knives, that he has a small collection at the manor. In particular that kukri thing that the British troops used during the Second World War."

"And how does Tom know this? Was he in Gilbert's room?"

"No, sir. He saw the knives in a glass case in the entrance hall. Near the B and B section," he added. "He remarked on them, and Arthur said his uncle had accumulated them."

Graham eyed me, and said slowly, "Interesting, but it doesn't get us anywhere. If it's so prominent, most anyone could've helped themselves to a knife."

"Yes, sir." His message delivered, Byrd remained at attention.

"Too bad it wasn't a kukri sticking out of Steve," I said. "We would have had our smoking gun."

"Tom would have told you himself," Byrd added, "but to tell the truth, I think he's a bit frightened of you, sir."

And the friendly bobby offered more comfort during the investigative storm than Graham does, I deduced. There's a fine between appearing official and stern. I had been intimidated on our first meeting, seeing only the stern. I still was at times, as I'd confessed to Margo. But as we continued working together, I was seeing other parts of him, for there was also the man who liked to joke.

Graham tapped his index finger against his lips, then slapped his hands onto the tabletop. The cushioning of the p.m. report muffled the crack. "So he thinks we should concentrate on Uncle Gilbert. Is there any other reason than his assumption Gilbert could hit a gnat at one hundred metres with a knitting needle, provided he's ever sober?"

Byrd shrugged, relating that he only knew what he was told.

"Gilbert had no motive as far as we've been able to discern. He didn't even know the American. And I can't see a seventy-two-year old man strangling a healthy specimen like Steve Pedersen, even if Steve was knocked out. Manual strangulation takes more strength than I'd assume Gilbert has. But I hate to speculate, and I've been wrong before."

"Knives aside, I'd like to know why Tom's memory card wasn't with the lot bestowed on us yesterday."

"He could have shot it all today, I suppose."

"Then why not trot up to us with card in-hand and tell us?" Graham said. "Why sneak out of the village at such a break-neck pace? Whatever his devious scheme, let's hope you've thwarted him, Byrd. Would you mind? As soon as you get your breath and a cuppa, back you go to Buxton." He thanked Byrd, who muttered that it was his pleasure, and held out the tin of pretzels to him. Looking simultaneously astonished and pleased, Byrd took a handful, thanked Graham, and left.

The pathologist's report was the one substantial element in the confusion facing us. Graham read the confirming details and smiled as he mentioned the high points. "It wasn't hanging that did in Steve. Death due to hemorrhaging, as if you need to be told, Taylor. Fractures of the skull...subdural hematoma...pupil dilated—indicating acute pressure on the injured side of the brain—numerous bruises to the left side of the body: waist, ribs, jaw and neck...cracked ribs, also on the left side..." Graham tossed me the report. "The weapon was your classic blunt instrument, though wider than Talbot's ancient hammer. It could be a rock, I suppose. The place is littered with them, with the creek so handy."

"This bruising on the left side of the torso..."

Graham eyed me, waiting for me to finish my thought. He leaned against the edge of the table, his arms folded across his chest, his eyes bright with interest. It was a common pose when he let me think things through. A teacher observing his pupil. I rambled on. "If Steve had merely fallen, as the bruises and cuts to the knees and palm indicate, I don't see how he could have sustained the bruising to the waist, ribs and jaw. Bruising there suggests a fight. How can anyone fall forward on his knees and come up with bruises on his left side?"

"And barring your personal demonstration, Taylor, I'm inclined to agree. What does the left side bruising suggest?"

I took a deep breath and swiftly ran through a short, mental prayer. "He was involved in a fight before death."

"From a right-handed bloke standing in front of him. Or a left-handed bloke standing behind him, as Mr. Holmes might have said in his day. Do you think it odd that even a right-handed person wouldn't have landed a punch with his left hand on Steve's right side?"

I nodded slowly, the strenuous fight scene shimmering before my eyes quickly shifting into a different scenario. "He was attacked while he was down."

Graham nodded, his hand moving to his rib cage. "This area would be exposed if Steve lay on the ground from his fall. A couple of energetic kicks would produce the bruising and cracked ribs."

I grimaced, not liking the image of the dirty fighting I conjured up. "And the bruises on the jaw and neck?"

"Fist fight, I should think." He made a fist and slowly, accurately aimed for the left side of my jaw, stopping so close that I could just feel his knuckles. He dropped his arm. "Lights out, and Steve's down on his knees."

"Where does the rock come into it? The report states a rock or something equally convex, hard and smooth fractured his skull."

"When Steve was trying to get up, perhaps it was applied then. It's as good a time as any, though our killer didn't really need it. From the depth of the bruises and the broken skin..." Graham stared at me, the humor gone now from his eyes. "What a lot of power he'd need to fracture Steve's skull."

And, I thought, not really seeing the photographs, the berk who had such free access to my room seemed to thrive on power. In my mind I again saw the Guy hung from the ceiling, the wren's limp head flopping as I picked it up from the bathroom basin. Someone's in love with the strength of his hands.

"All this information doesn't do much for us in terms of a solution.. What's that get us?"

My eyes widened as he voiced what I had just envisioned. "Nothing much, except it's easier to string up a victim if he's dead first. Is there anything on the knife?"

The knife, printed and analyzed to death by the police laboratory technicians, revealed blood on the shaft near the wooden handle and smears on the blade. It must've arrived safely, for I hadn't heard any swearing or threats of demotion from Graham. It also was now housed for easier viewing in a plastic bag, which Graham held up to the light.

"'The smiler with the knife under the cloak,' Taylor," Graham mused, half aloud.

"Beg pardon, sir?" I wondered what he had quoted and what he meant.

"Chaucer." He smoothed out a wrinkle in the plastic to see the knife edge better. It was four inches long and angled into the wooden handle when not in use. Graham tried to depress the latch at the upper edge of the handle. He struggled with the rusty mechanism, pushing on the blade to force it home. The blade resolutely refused to surrender its outward position. "This thing's as stiff as I feel some mornings."

"It's a scout knife, isn't it?"

"An old scout, to be sure. It probably dates back to my youthful days."

"It might have done, but not likely. Weren't the knives removed from sale for a bit in the late '60s or so, on account of all those accidents the lads were having with them?"

"So we've got a more current knife—is that what you're hinting at?"

"Or older, sir, though there are other ways besides the flow of years that would rust a knife."

"Such as the flow of water. That's a careless sort of scout, leaving his equipment outside to be rained on. Well, it's a nice task for our energetic constables, then, seeing who's been a scout among the villagers."

Margo would welcome the job of work. She'd relish anything that would get her noticed by Graham and promote her to an actual name.

"Speaking of smilers," Graham said, "do you think that's how it was done? It would have had to be a smiler, someone who wouldn't upset Steve, who could murder him without unduly warning him, don't you think? Otherwise there's the risk he would have given one hell of a fight."

"He'd scream his head off and alert someone. Plus, there might be all those hard-to-explain scratches and bruises on the murderer's body."

"Came at him nonchalantly, all friendly."

"Who's more friendly, if it comes to that, and familiar to him than his former brother-in-law?"

"Arthur Catchpool, Derek Halford, Kris Halford." Graham turned the bag slowly, noting every inch of the knife. "Strange thing, this knife. Why use it?"

"You said yourself that it was just for dressing, that he was strangled and the knife used as part of their annual dramatics. But if you wanted a knife, you'd use a letter opener, say, or a carver. Those are more common types."

"Or use a Stanley knife."

I nodded. Most households had one, just as they had a saw, hammer and stepladder.

"Well, we'll dangle it in front of a few eyes and see if we can cut through more than mat board. Anything develop from those?" Graham set down the knife and gestured toward the packet of photographs.

"They're nice, but not exactly startling.

Nothing to hang a case or a corpse on. What were
you hoping to find?"

"Something hinting to our murder. These
don't prove a thing. They can't even prove the
time when they were taken, let alone the day. The
date range is too large." He lowered his head,
peering at the purple shadows that stretched
across Tom's snippets of captured landscape.
Mumbling in disgust, he waved the photographs
at a convenient constable. "Would you mind,
Constable? Take these out to the corresponding
areas in the village this afternoon and see if the
shadows line up. Thanks." He waited until the
officer returned to her computer before saying, "I
want to check up on the lay of the land as much
as on Tom. Not that I don't doubt his veracity as a
photographer or a tourist, but... That lens of his,
Taylor..."

"Telephoto."

"Maybe his roving eye caught some elusive
detail of the crime scene before it got eradicated.
We'll know with his weekend snaps."

Graham seemed to focus on the day
outside—crisp, sunny and smelling of fallen
leaves. Layers of clouds, gray tinged on their
bellies, crawled across the sky from the west. The
air held the scent of approaching rain. Inside the
room it was quiet, some of the constables
grabbing a bite to eat, others working at
computers. I took a deep breath, pulled a folded
piece of paper from my pocket, and spoke
Graham's name. He looked at me, momentarily
lost in his thoughts. I held the paper toward him
and asked if he would like to see the chart of
suspects and motives I had drawn up.

He gazed at it for several minutes, his pen
making tic marks beside several of the columns,
then looked at me. His eyes were brilliant and

held no sign of mockery. "I'm impressed, Taylor. When did you do this?"

"Uh, late last night." I refrained from mentioning it was because I couldn't sleep. I glanced at Mark, who had just entered the room. He caught my stare and pursed his lips in a kiss. I turned back to Graham, hoping I hadn't reddened.

"First class work, really excellent. Do you have time to go over this?" He pulled out a chair for me and I sat beside him, not across the table as I usually did. We talked of Uncle Gilbert mistaking Steve for Derek. "To benefit from the extra money Arthur would get when the dole stopped," Graham read. We talked of Arthur mistaking Steve for Derek. "Same motive," Graham read, then smiled at my brief analysis. We talked of Ramona mistaking Steve for Derek. "Ditto," Graham read again, then laughed.

I hated the idea of a murderess, not because I thought Ramona such an outstanding woman as that I thought women above such emotions. They were the keepers of the hearth, the soul of the home, the giver of life. For a woman to taint that centuries-long gift was disgraceful. I knew women killed; there have been many famous murderers among the sex. But it still turned my stomach. And I couldn't see Ramona, independent as she was, murdering Steve.

Graham seemed to read my thoughts. "I don't know, Taylor. No matter how liberated she is, I don't think she could kill him and get away without a scratch. She'd have to know jujitsu or something. Does she know jujitsu?"

"Do we know her sprained wrist is legitimate, sir?"

"Your idea being she's hiding a telltale scratch, received in her fight with Steve?"

I nodded.

Graham exhaled slowly, as he did when considering something he deemed important. "Very well could do. I'm impressed you take nothing as obvious, Taylor. It could easily be window dressing, set up to fool us."

"I suppose there was an attending physician?"

"Why not find out? Ask the populace. If no one recalls the fall..."

"We unwrap her wrist. But is there any reason why Steve would be killed for his own sake?" I said, rather glad that Graham had seen the value in my suggestion about Ramona's sprain.

"What's your chart say?" He turned to it, not as a joke, but to see how I had reasoned it all out. He may have been impressed by the hours I put into it, but I was impressed he was taking me seriously. Graham read aloud, "Derek. Although Kris was originally engaged to Steve, she seems earnestly in love with Derek, who also welcomed Steve." He looked up, supplying his own observation. "And if we're considering broken hearts as fuel, Taylor, Tom has had plenty of time to murder Steve. Why would he risk it in a locality he didn't know?"

"If his anger or hatred over his sister's death got the better of him, he'd lash out."

"What else?" He read my chart again. "What's this last column say? I can't make it out— Oh, symbolism." This time his eyebrow was raised when he looked at me. I knew at the time I wrote it that it would be questioned, but I had to put it down.

"Yes, sir. Whoever killed Steve would be taking a huge chance by dressing him up as the Guy. Why stage the murder like that? Why not leave the body in the woods or wherever? It'd be a lot easier. All that time spent replacing the effigy with the body is just asking for discovery. There has to be a reason it was rigged up." I waited for what seemed a century for Graham to speak.

He had been focused again on life outside the pub window, watching the residents, tourists, and police mingling and going about their own lives. Finally, he said in a barely audible voice, "All the world's a stage, Taylor, and we had a highly significant stage Sunday evening. But who was the intended audience?"

18

Graham had asked me that afternoon to interview a few of the suspects while he busied himself with hearing Tom's new story about the photographs. I needed my notebook, which was in my room. My bedroom door was locked, I noted on jiggling the knob. Good. One less thing to worry about. When I entered my room I found out just how wrong I was.

My bed was strewn with photographs of me: me at the village pond, me walking to Arthur's, me standing at the pub door, me talking to Margo. I might have been merely annoyed if it weren't for the nooses. In each photo a noose was carefully drawn around my neck.

I don't know how long I stood there unable to release my stare from the atrocity. I do remember my mouth had gone dry and my heart was beating as though I'd just run a marathon race up Mount Everest. I tried to put the outrage down but I couldn't control my fingers. My hand shook violently. The knock on the door restored what little sanity I had left. I stuffed the photographs under the pillow and yelled, "Come in." It was Mark.

I didn't know whether to laugh, cry, attack, or hug him. I opted for asking what he wanted.

"Nothing more than the usual." He seated himself beside me on the bed and smoothed out a wrinkle in the coverlet and leaned back.

Angling my body against the pillow, I told him I had only come up to get my notebook, that Graham needed me. Which wasn't completely a lie, but I needed to get rid of Mark. I figured Graham's name would do it.

"What if I need you, Brenna?"

"I know what you need, Mark, and it's a cold shower. Now, out."

"Is that any way to talk to a friend?"

"I didn't know you were one."

"A colleague, at least."

"There are all types of colleagues, Mark. Consider me a long-distance one. Now, out!"

"I just thought you'd have a minute or two. I saw you come upstairs."

"I didn't see you in the incident room." I felt rather paranoid now that I knew someone was watching me. Whoever had taken those photos had a good quality camera and had taken them with a telephoto lens. If not, I would've seen the photographer.

"'Course not. I was in the public bar. Just walking out when I saw you on the stairs." He was staring at my nightgown, which was thrown over the back of the chair. I grabbed it and stuffed it under the coverlet. He laughed, one large, roar that editorialized my prudishness.

"Can't you take a joke, Brenna?"

I buried my fingers into the bedding, not knowing how to respond. Barely finding my voice, I stared at him. "Joke? You mean this whole thing—"

I exhaled, rather too loudly and quickly, for he added a bit softer, "A guy can always hope you'll come around. Would flowers do it?" He looked around for the lone crocus. "What do you like besides pansies? A dozen or two roses? It would be worth it if you'd come willingly." He patted the bedding before standing up. "Well, if Graham calls, you must obey." He leaned against the doorjamb, his gray eyes traveling the length of my body. "You know, Bren, this is a compliment. A lot of women would love to be in your shoes. Or out of them."

I slammed the door, distrusting my voice.

But he was right. Margo would like to be asked. Well, I wasn't going to tell her about this.

The sun wandered over the village, peeking from rifts in the graying clouds, throwing the lower valley into gold, orange and ochre hues. The church spire of St. Michael's caught and held the light, the yellow rays nearly igniting the brass cross. I averted my eyes, not so much from the painful splendor as to keep my footing along the uneven cinder pathway. I walked slowly, quietly, as I imagined a native American walking so as not to make a sound. I started out resolutely enough, but as I entered the shady path, my determination quavered. Partway up the path I turned suddenly, thinking someone lurked behind me. No one. Only waving tree branches and a frightened grey squirrel. A twig snapped and I froze. No one appeared. I walked as noiselessly as I could, determined to hear my prankster approach if he was following me. I emerged from the shady path, having met no one, and having succeeded in fraying my already tense nerves.

I found the vicar seated on a wooden bench, his black shirt silhouetted against the near-whiteness of the old tombstones. Lyle smiled at my approach and stood up. Assuring the clergyman that I was only there for a few minutes, I suggested he resume his seat.

"It's a peaceful time of day," Lyle observed, his eyes on the western horizon. "Lovely to take a breath and review where one's been. The Journey's rough at times, don't you think?" The vicar, speaking in ecclesiastical terms, took my affirmation of my cinder-strewn stroll as relating to something higher. "I assume you didn't climb this hill to listen to the sparrows, Sergeant. To what do I owe this visit?"

I explained that we needed a timetable of everyone's whereabouts from three-thirty to six o'clock on Sunday.

"I was in my study, doing a few odds and ends such as straightening my desk, dashing off a few letters. Nothing very interesting or that gives me an alibi. I assume that's what you meant. Do I need something public, something shared that proves where I was?" His cheeks bulged slightly as he grinned, the sunlight tinting the rosy flesh a pale yellow.

I nodded.

"I thought so. Pity it wasn't Saturday, because I was with Ramona and Arthur. We could confirm each other's schedules. But you'll have to take my word about Sunday afternoon."

"And what were you and the betrothed couple doing?"

"Redressing the effigy." He spoke like an actor making his entrance and stating that the theater was on fire. "Though I overstate my role somewhat. In all honesty, I wasn't physically with them. I'd just walked down to the green. They were at the edge of the fire circle, back by Talbot's pile of wood. I only saw it from across the road. Is it important?"

I thanked the vicar and walked with as much dignity as I could down the lane.

Ramona hadn't much to add to the effigy-dressing narration. I sat at her fireside, fortified with strong tea and a new felt-tip pen, adding notes to my growing collection, taking in the Victorian surroundings.

The front room of her vine-smothered cottage was itself nearly smothered. Plant cuttings in glass jars and mugs dotted windowsills. Mementos of holidays, plays and concerts consumed every available space—miniature frying pans brightly inscribed with 'Crete' or 'Wales' or 'Gibraltar,' ceramic birds, salt and pepper sets, framed tea towels and calendar pages, a post card of a gilt-haired Lady Godiva, stacks of picture travel books, a black vase from Blackpool, a tartan-draped Highlander doll, several toy sheep, a too-yellow stuffed canary holding a limp ribboned 'Souvenir of the Canary Islands' from its beak, and a mirror elaborately bordered in painted flowers. No doubt to make the beholder assume she's still in the springtime of her life. The Antipodes were equally well represented with a wooden kiwi bird, a Maori tiki and mere of greenstone, a boomerang, an Indian pearl-handled knife, and a Chinese folding fan. Normally, I was Discretion itself. But the display demanded inspecting. And while not museum quality, it was certainly museum quantity. She needs Arthur's large manor for her display, I thought. The woman must spend half her life dusting this lot.

I abandoned my tussles with a fringed pillow on the sofa as Ramona asked if my tea was all right.

"Fine, thanks, but I wish you'd let me get it. How's the wrist?"

She patted her arm. "More inconvenience than pain, right now. But I'll survive."

I said I was glad to hear it. "Did you have it seen to professionally? I ask because those injuries can swell if not properly looked to, and cause no amount of pain and trouble later on."

"A local physician saw to it, thanks. Evan phoned him up. I felt a right fool, all the fuss everyone made over me." She repositioned the sling to support her wrist better, and I asked about the effigy.

"I usually make it. But Arthur volunteered this year although it wasn't the norm for him. He had a bit of extra straw from some landscaping he's doing at the manor, from seeding the lawn. He said he'd do it, save me the expense and trip to get the straw."

"That was thoughtful of him. It was lucky for you he was seeding."

Ramona nodded. "He feels an obligation to the manor, to his father, and to his guests. He wants everything as posh as possible. He says it's worth the extra work if he gets the extra quid from it. I don't know about that, though. I must be thick as a plank. Spend money to make money... A bit of a vicious circle, isn't it?

I agreed it was like treading water to keep solvent these days, then asked about the Guy's clothing.

"What Lyle saw us doing Saturday was exchanging jackets. I did it there at the fire circle so I wouldn't track straw into my car or the house. It was a bit of a wrestle, but I did it."

"Did anyone see you or help?"

"You're thinking of alibi?" She squinted at me, as though trying to discern if she was about to be carted off to Holloway. "No one stood around and watched, if that's what you're suggesting. Arthur left. I suppose I can't ask why you're asking, not even as girl to girl?"

"Did your son cart it over to the stage from where you left it?"

"I suppose so. I didn't keep track of it. I had no reason to think someone would fool with it. But that was after I left it, obviously. Normally Talbot would hang it since he's always down there fussing over his woodpile. But of course this year he didn't."

"Because you son's group needed it."

"Yes. I've heard from several residents who enjoyed Liam's group, as well as those who thought it out of place. I admit I had misgivings about asking Arthur if they could perform, because I didn't want to drive a wedge between the residents. But Byron convinced me to talk to Arthur, and in the end the band played."

"And the premature hoisting of the Guy is the only thing out of the ordinary this year?"

"Other than Arthur changing jackets because he'd given me the wrong one."

"What jacket had he meant to give you?"

"That tan plaid thing it was wearing during the bonfire lighting. Arthur'd originally given me a tweed, but had meant to give it to Oxfam. It was still quite good, quite wearable, so he rescued it from the dummy. I didn't mind. We might as well give away the better clothing instead of watching it go to waste by the torch."

I thanked her and went to enlighten Graham.

As it turned out, Graham enlightened me. He had seen Tom Oldendorf but got nothing more than an earful of anger. "His point being,"

Graham said, "that he'd be an idiot to kill Steve over here when he could do it at home, if he wished. He told me Scotland Yard has a ninety-seven percent success rate solving their crimes."

"We don't do too badly either," I said, my pride of Derbyshire B Division rising.

"And Arthur gave us another date to figure in."

"I should have read mathematics at university."

Graham ignored me. "Talbot first appeared in the village in 1968, at the invitation of Derek's dad."

"Did it make any difference to anyone?"

"Not to hear Arthur tell it. Mr. Halford loved both Talbot and Derek equally, treated them the same. And Talbot needed a home when his aunt died, so Derek's dad took him in."

"Adopted him?"

"There's that pesky question again, Taylor. Anyway, Talbot didn't catch on to the dole business until some of the local lads explained it to him. He thought it was a bit of play-acting at first, like an outdoor pageant or charade."

"Three cheers for the local lads."

"Many people would echo your sentiments, I'm afraid. And how did you get on?"

I told him of my interviews with the vicar and Ramona, and we spent the rest of the day interviewing the other players, however minor, in this game.

That evening, we relinquished our usual late-night routine and went to bed early. It was just as well, for somewhat later my bedroom clock simultaneously announced the hour and the arrival of the rain. Midnight clattered in with a storm that threatened to peel the bark off the trees. Rain thundered along the pine-thick ridge, through the hills, down the dales. Along the pond's shoreline, wave and rain slapped the reed-wrapped rocks and cratered the smooth sand. Hat-holding blasts of wind scythed through the thickets, gleaning the pungency of moss and pine. Rain, heavier than chilled syrup, planed down plants. A cloud-splitting crack of thunder shook the pub, jolting me from my sleep.

Outside my window, the inn sign swung crazily in the wind, its screech keeping time with an annoying, banging shutter.

It was impossible to sleep. I sat up in bed, knees drawn up to my chest, the skirt of my nightgown pulled down tightly. I stared into the darkness, cringing when lightning splintered the dark.

From the room next to mine, a name, sharp as the thunder, jumped out of the silence. "Rachel."

I listened, aware I was eavesdropping but wondering if Graham was entertaining a woman. None of my business, of course. But if he was indeed sharing his bed, I was more than astonished. I was disappointed. Never mind I had secret desires to be in Rachel's place. Until I actually was there, I wanted him celibate, waiting for me—whether he knew it or not—because I was the love of his life. Of course it was ridiculous. But the emotions of love don't always allow clear thinking. I hugged my nightgown around me, remembering the ardor in his voice, and all of a sudden I wanted it to be my name instead of "Rachel" on his lips.

I could hear the name again, more muffled this time, then several seconds of silence, followed by a chair scraping across the floor, and a book or something similarly heavy thudding, as if it had fallen off the nightstand. I did not even attempt to visualize what Graham and Rachel were doing. When I heard another crash and an oath, I threw off the duvet, shrugged into my jacket, and opened the door.

The hallway was dark except for a feeble lamp at the end of the passage, marking the staircase landing. From the adjacent room, light streaked from beneath the ill-fitted door and across the floor. It was Graham's room.

I hesitated. The hall embraced the scents of wax and spent candles and winterberry. Comforting, ancestral fragrances. Had this been Graham's world, these aromas of altar trimmings and cleaning supplies? I inhaled deeply, and once again imagined him in his black robe. He had quit the pulpit, office scuttlebutt whispered, by as to why... Shrugged shoulders answered my questions. Jokes and fabricated innuendoes stung my ears. Affair with a parishioner. Rudeness to the bishop. Struggle with his conscience over church doctrine. I could believe almost any reason, for I was learning how explosive Graham's temper was, how intolerant he was of bureaucracy and pedantic superiors. And for Graham, that was stifling.

Thunder exploded overhead, and I ducked, thinking the building had exploded. There was no response from Graham's room.

I left my doorway. The floor, silent during the day, now groaned and popped with all the uproar of a 1930s gangster turf war. Tiptoeing, though lessening the cacophony, increased the coldness biting into my bare feet. I paused just outside his door, wondering if he had fallen and needed help. It seemed plausible enough, for the sounds and following curses indicated a small clash within those four walls. Yet, I was hesitant to knock. I might embarrass him if he knew I heard him. I also wondered at the protocol of a single woman, dressed in nightgown, entering a man's room. Maybe my concerns seem quaint or prudish, but Graham—no matter how long ago—remained a minister. And I didn't want to ruin my career over an indiscretion. Or confront Rachel.

Within his room it was as silent as the grave. I was about to return to my bed when a movement on the stairs drew my attention. A whispered "Brenna" made me turn to the figure. It was Margo, cringing at the cracks of thunder. I went over to her, silently amused at her death grip on the staircase's newel post.

"Is this how you keep surveillance?"

"So it's not subtle." She ducked in the lightning flash. "At least I can see your room."

As much as I wanted to, I refrained from asking what Rachel looked like. Margo must have seen her enter Graham's room. Better not add fuel to office rumors by suggesting I was interested in Graham's private life. "Why not hide under my bed?"

"My mum was frightened by a chamber pot. Let's go to your room." We ran down the hall, hoping the building would survive the attack. Inside, I lit the dresser light. I should have left us sitting in the dark. The photos of me parading as the Guy sat on the dresser, and Margo spotted them.

"This is beyond a joke, Bren. Anyone could be wandering about in the day, sure, but who would have a key to your room?"

"Take your choice. I don't think our suspect list has changed any since Monday morning. I thought it was Mark, but after talking with him, I'm not so sure."

"You talked to him again? When?"

I told her the bare bones of the afternoon's encounter, leaving out the gory details. "Now that you've got something to dream about, how about returning to your bed so I can get into mine?"

"Fine. Refuse my help. But I still say the key to all this is who has the key."

As I listened to Margo shut the door behind her, I wondered if we had a pickpocket among us.

I emerged from my room the next morning looking as ragged and tired as if I had endured an all-night work session with Graham.

I clumped downstairs to the luring aromas of fried bacon, baked scones and warm cinnamon. Mark was just leaving the pub and hadn't seen me. Graham, I was relieved to see, was alone, Rachel either slipping out at dawn or was eating at another table. I looked around the room, trying to surmise which of the several single women might be Rachel. None of them fit my idea. Perhaps I was wrong about the entire incident. After all, wouldn't Margo have said something? Cheered by Graham's restoration to his pedestal, I walked noiselessly up to the table.

His head jerked up, revealing eyes that might have stared at poker cards until the wee hours. He motioned to the vacant chair, groaned that I should know better than to sneak up on a cop, and said the coffee had certainly perked him right up.

"I assume you've finished your porridge, kippers, and eggs, and are now on to your second pot of coffee."

"I had everything but the porridge, kippers, and eggs," he muttered, kneading his eyes. "Shall I make it a double order, then?" Graham looked up as Evan came up to our table. "Perfect timing.

How about poached eggs and haddock, Taylor?"

"Haddock? You know anything remotely connected with the sea—"

"It's a cure all, Taylor. Evan—" He stopped as Evan's face lapsed into a sickly grimace.

"Sorry to bother you, Mr. Graham."

"Bother?"

"Telephone, sir. It's in my office. Byron says it sounds urgent." Stepping aside, he let Graham stand up before motioning toward the phone.

"Thank you. You might give the sergeant some tea, if you would. I'm afraid we didn't get much sleep last night."

I had barely drunk half my tea when Graham was back, extracting the car key from his pocket. "I'm afraid we won't get that glorious breakfast after all, Taylor. It was Arthur Catchpool. He's at Ramona's. She's dead."

19

Graham related the skeletal facts during the drive to the cottage. His words came haltingly as he concentrated on both the road and the death. Gravel splayed onto road-hugging plants, dusting the frosted vegetation a dull brown as he executed a sharp corner. It wasn't until he braked the car several meters from the cottage that I relinquished my life-preserving grip on the door's armrest. He was out of the car before I could unbuckle my seat belt.

We remained approximately twenty-five meters from Ramona's body so as not to contaminate the scene, yet close enough to get a preliminary view. The paper suits we needed to wear to allow up close and personal contact with Ramona would arrive with the rest of the crime team. Until then, we would have to be content with examining from afar.

Graham paced back and forth on the driveway, trying for the best view.

Ramona lay on her back, knees bent, feet tucked beneath her. Her left arm stretched out above her head as though she was in school, raising her hand. Her right elbow was bent, allowing her right hand to lie beneath the small of her back. She seemed more suited to the bedroom than to the wintry elements, for she was clothed in a matching turquoise robe and nightgown. That and the slippers appeared to be her only attire.

Frozen, I thought, my eyes traveling over the frost-stiffened fabric. Frozen in time. As though mimicking a 1950s pinup photo. The robe was open, the tie belt strung out and several feet from the body, having freed itself from the belt loops. She seemed to be barely wearing the robe, for the upper portion lay halfway down her arms, exposing her shoulders. The generous hemline of the nightgown fanned out and bunched up in one place to expose her right thigh. Like an absurd epaulet, a broken strap dangled over her right shoulder. She might have been provocative if it wasn't for the ghost-white, shocked face with its eyes staring at the sky.

She was also very wet and very frost-covered.

"For God's sake, can't you cover her up?"

Arthur's voice pleaded behind us, yet we couldn't comply. It was a travesty, the body lying unprotected, the eyes moist, the eyelashes hoary and starched. I stared at the feathered mules encasing her feet, the turquoise feathers reduced to a sodden pulp.

"She obviously hadn't intended to stay out here," Graham muttered. He turned, gazing at the end of the driveway where Arthur stood, leaning against the fence. The man was hatless and gloveless. His heavy woolen jacket was unbuttoned, as though he had loosened the restraints to stoop over Ramona. Dampness had seeped into Arthur's shoes and edges of his jeans.

"Taylor," Graham called, gazing at his watch. "It's seven-twelve. Byrd, I assume, has created a sensation at the station. I told him to get everyone back out here."

"They should be here by eight or so."

"I don't suppose the scene will change much before the video tea arrives."

"It probably won't get much warmer in three-quarters of an hour."

"It never hurts to be careful." As well as distance permitted, he pointed out the details of the immediate area surrounding Ramona's body. "Someone's knelt next to her—Arthur, I assume. See the area there, where the grass is crushed and devoid of frost? And the same marks from the driveway?"

"He got out of his car, saw her, and came over."

Graham indicated Ramona's right hand jammed behind her back. "I wish the police surgeon was here. I'd love to know if that hand position's from death throes or if she was reaching for something."

"What would she be doing out here, dressed like this?"

Graham shrugged. "The back door's open. Barely, I grant you, but it's open. I only noticed it because it is swinging slightly in the breeze."

"She was expecting to return."

He pointed to the broken nightgown strap. "She might have done that in a tussle."

"If someone else was out here, why wouldn't she have on more clothes? Sexually assaulted?"

Graham shrugged, saying that was in the realm of medical magic.

I pointed to the ground. "If another person was out here, wouldn't there be more evidence?

Besides, this patch where someone—probably Arthur—stooped can in no way be construed as a fight scene. There are less than a half dozen sole prints where he knelt and then got up again. His prints, too, go straight as an arrow back to the driveway."

In the quiet I heard Arthur's incessant stammering as he poured out his heart to a constable.

"Does he always come over for breakfast?" I asked. "He phoned you up at seven, for God's sake!"

"I don't know his habits."

"One thing's certain. He wasn't just leaving after a comfortable night out. The condition of the body screams that she's been out here for hours."

"Unless he left at midnight, say, and came back."

"Even if she kissed him good night—"

"I would have done that from the warmth of the house."

"Is it a heart attack, you think?"

He shrugged. "I suppose we should talk to Arthur."

I stared at the house, feeling ill. "Does anyone know if Liam is home?"

"He's staying there during his visit to the village, isn't he?"

I nodded and reminded him that the band members stayed at Arthur's. "There's always the phone." At least no one would have to walk through the crime scene to get to the door. "But that's not a very pleasant way to be told of a tragedy."

Graham agreed. "I dislike compromising the scene, but we need to know if Liam's there." His voice trailed off and I assumed he meant discovering if Liam was still alive.

It wouldn't be the first time we'd have attended a double murder, one victim slain inside and the other outside as she tried to escape. Except the killer caught up with Ramona, if that had happened here.

He got a pair of white paper booties from his car and stepped onto the lawn. He glanced at the body as he put them on. "I'll go in and see if he's there. It'd be helpful if you talk to Arthur in the meantime. Would you mind?" He walked across the lawn and entered the house before I could reply.

"Terrible thing," I said, walking up to Arthur. He nodded, staring at me, his red-circled eyes still moist from crying. "You found her like this?"

"Around seven. I'd just got out of the car and was walking up to the house. I saw her. Well, I didn't know it was her. I didn't realize it was a person. At first I thought it was a bit of tarp or something, perhaps blown off the bundles of sticks." He turned his head, blowing his nose.

I waited, remembering the sage advise of never rushing your witness, letting him recall and report things as he could.

"Those are my footprints, sergeant. I was walking up to the door when I saw her. I thought she'd just fallen, that I could help. When I found out, I phoned the pub. I'm afraid Byron must think me an idiot. I probably sounded hysterical."

"No one can fault you for that. Have you a key to her house?" We both knew what I meant, for there were no signs of his footprints leading from the body to her house.

"No. We aren't as modern as that. Or as immoral, however you prefer to classify it. You won't find my footprints leading to the door. I knew you were at the pub, so I used my mobile phone instead of driving to get you. It saved time."

"You didn't check to see if the door was open, then, or go to the house to see if Liam was there? I'd have thought that would be a natural thing to do. Since the door was open, and seeing how she was dressed, I'd have gone in to see if Liam knew anything. Or, seeing he was absent, I'd have phoned from the house."

"Is the door unlocked? I didn't look. One doesn't think clearly in a crisis, does one? Mobile phone's a natural reaction for me."

"So, why did you come over at such an early hour?"

Arthur made a sound somewhere between a cough and a gag. "This is going to sound awfully inane."

"Don't let that bother you, sir."

"I had a few things that needed to go to the cleaner's. Ramona did too, only with her sprained wrist, she couldn't handle all the items so I came over to get them. And although Liam's a helpful lad, I had no idea if he would do that. I don't know about band rehearsals and playing dates and such. I didn't want Ramona to rely on him and be disappointed."

I jotted down a note to check his car for the presence of the clothing.

"We talked about it over dinner last night, joked about her atrocious memory."

"How about Liam? Did he eat with you?"

Arthur shook his head. "Oh, no. He was out. I don't know where. Ramona didn't say. But I assumed he had a date with a girl, or he and his mates were at the pub. You know how it is when you're twenty-one."

I let the remark slide. "How about this morning? Did you see anything out of the ordinary? No strange car parked near the cottage, for instance?"

"Of course not. We never have any trouble in the village."

Except for a spot of murder for Guy Fawkes Day. "You didn't phone up a physician or ambulance?"

"There was no need."

"Really? I would've thought that would be the first call you'd make."

"It was obvious she was dead." He colored instantly, darkly. It was the first time he had used the word. "It was the way she was, you see. I knew just from looking at her. She was all white, her body and clothes stiff. You could tell from the frost. Frozen stiff. There was no need for a doctor. Not when she was like that."

"And when did you leave her last night?"

"How the hell should I know?" Arthur threw his car keys at a nearby tree. "Sorry. Eleven, I think. Near enough. Byron heard me return. You can ask him."

I echoed the information noncommittally, making a note of it. "Excuse me for a moment." I walked to his car, picked up and searched through the bundle of clothes on the back seat, and returned. "Very good, sir. I must ask you to remain here for a while, until Mr. Graham can see you."

Mumbling he had nothing else to do, Arthur slowly picked up his keys and walked to his car, pausing just long enough to glance at the first police contingent arriving from Buxton.

At the same time, Graham left the house and walked back across the lawn. He removed the paper booties as I asked if he'd talked to Liam. He shook his head. "No. I walked through the house, which I was loath to do, called his name, looked in every room and closet. He's not there. There's nothing circled on yesterday's calendar date and no note on the kitchen table. So, rather than risk damage to the scene, I left it at that." He glanced down the road, toward the village. "I have no idea if he had a suitcase or rucksack with him, so that got me nowhere. And his guitar could very well be at Arthur's with the rest of the band's instruments. No use lugging that to his mum's." He shook his head. "I pray he's easy to find. I'd like to get the news to him quickly."

"If you'd like me to ask around…"

"Thank you, Taylor, but this is something I need to do. I'll stay for a bit, then go into the village. That's the most likely place he'd be."

The video technician came up slowly, noting the footprints and the condition of the area. He greeted us and began to suit up.

"You want to suit up now, sir?" I asked.

Graham shook his head. "We've got a good team. They can handle it. I can view the video. But if you…"

"Not particularly."

Margo, I was pleased to see, had been assigned an active role and was stringing up the police tape to confine the scene. An officer was placing the trail of white squares up to the body and laid down a larger covering so the pathologist could work there without damaging anything on the ground. Byrd came back slowly and disappeared around the corner of the house.

"Well, I think I'll try to find Liam. I feel bad that he doesn't know about his mother." Graham pulled the car key from his pocket, then gazed at me. "If I leave, how will you get back to the pub?"

"I'm used to walking, sir. Or Margo can give me a lift.

As if hearing her name, Margo called to

Graham. "Sir, I'm having a video shot of the hemline of Ramona's nightgown so you can see it later."

"Fine, Lynch, but what's unusual about it?"

"Puckers, like she caught it on something."

"Is there anything out here that would have caused that?" He moved over a few feet so he could see the cottage's back door. "We'll get the lads to do a thorough going-over. Damn that storm. It might have wiped out more than we know."

Graham turned and nodded to a Custody Officer. They walked over to Arthur, who was leaning against his car. I could hear his yelp of indignation as Graham requested his shoes. After a brief argument, Arthur shoved them at the officer, who put them into a paper sack, folded and cellotaped it closed. Arthur slid into his car seat, talking to Graham and gesturing toward the house. An officer was measuring and photographing Arthur's footprints that led to Ramona's body. The photos, I knew, would be black-and-white and to scale. Another officer was taking samples of the grass from the print depressions, packing each specimen flat between sheets of folded newsprint. When he had collected samples from several areas in the garden, he sealed them in paper sacks. The mortuary van attendants, bored and yawning, stood at the end of the drive, talking to a constable.

"You can get me on my mobile if you need to." Graham glanced once more at the scene, as though torn between staying and hunting for Liam. "Don't hesitate."

"No, sir." I tried to show him confidence through my smile so he'd have no qualms about leaving me in charge. The quiet conversations of officers at work must have reassured him, for he nodded and strode to his car.

The pathologist came, examined the body *in situ*, and an hour or so later the mortuary van attendants left with the zipped body bag. I gave a white-faced Arthur permission to leave, and wondered if he'd destroyed anything before he'd phoned us. I'd mentally made a list of possible items when Margo called to me.

"You have something, Margo?"

"I think so."

"What?"

"When they moved Ramona—" She broke off, as if unsure how to tell me.

"What, Margo? Is there something that was beneath her?"

"Yes, on the ground under her. There's a small twist of hemp fibers."

"What's the ground like?"

She pressed her palm against the ground, feeling its condition, then said that it was wet. She backed away when an officer came over to videotape the area.

"Is that unusual?

"Shouldn't it be dry if she was out before it rained?"

"Not really. The ground would have sponged up the water," I said. "It doesn't matter if she was out here before it started or afterwards. Do you think she was groping for that piece of hemp?"

Margo shrugged, and I called to a constable, who hurried over to Margo with a pair of tweezers and a clear plastic bag.

"There's a lot of rope around this village," I said as Margo came over to me. "Enough to hang someone with, if hanging is required after we've finished."

"Hung for a sheep, hung for a lamb."

"Or lambs to the slaughter." I took the bag from Margo and stared at the encased rope fragment.

"Does this do anything for you, Bren?"

"I hate to jump to conclusions, but it sort of brings to mind another piece of rope we've seen with another recent Upper Kingsleigh death." And, I thought, another series of rope incidents that I was involved in. Three, to be exact: my personal Guy, the string tied around the wren, and the nooses drawn on my photos. So what was the connection?

Turning so she now faced the back garden and the dotting of bundled tree branches, Margo murmured, "It does indeed."

20

While Graham tried to locate Liam, I attempted to get a sober, straight answer from Uncle Gilbert. It took longer than I expected, in part due to time wasted on a strange game of hide and seek. Arthur had practically torn apart the house before finally finding his uncle in the ballroom. It was a cavernous room, as such rooms are. Satin-cushioned chairs lined its perimeter, ready for foot-weary dancers. A half dozen crystal chandeliers polka-dotted the ceiling, their rows of diamond-like pendants glittering in the morning sun. I crossed the hardwood floor, conscious of my footsteps.

Gilbert, amazingly enough, was conscious of them too, for he looked up at my approach. He was placidly sitting in the middle of the vast floor, putting together a jigsaw puzzle. Though all five hundred pieces were scattered about him, only a few dozen were assembled. And very creatively. One piece in particular buckled drastically from the forced fit. Still, I gave him credit. Both pieces were blue.

Gilbert's eyes were as bloodshot as the last

time I'd talked to him. And as unfocused. He craned his head back to study better who was standing beside him. Upon seeing me, he laughed and gestured toward the bare floor.

"Just the person I need! You must have been sent by Athena herself, sergeant."

It might have been more appropriate if Gilbert said Dionysus sent me.

"Just who I need—a copper, a 'tec to lend her great wisdom, to snoop out the errant pieces! Say you can find the missing amongst all this!" His arm flapped haphazardly in the direction of the scattered pieces. "I'm working on this tricky bit here. Need a knobby bit on the right. Blue and a funny little red stripe. If you can locate our missing member, I shall personally write a letter to your chief constable, advising him of your superior traits and recommending immediate promotion!" The puzzle piece fell to his lap as he leaned backwards in his roar of laughter.

"While you're at it, mention I need a raise."

Another blast of mirth roared over me. Suddenly serious, he said, "Wages are a hell of a thing, aren't they, sergeant? Money's gonna be the death of civilization. You see if I'm not right. The rich get richer, and the poor get—" He sniffed. "Wages, sergeant. We're all wage slaves in one form or another. Work and wage. Four-lettered words if there ever were. I, myself, for all the grandeur about me, am reduced to a wage. Yes, a wage! Supplied to me by my kind nephew. Not as regular as I should hope, nor as much as I should hope, but there you are." Without any concern for matching color or shape, he wedged a piece into an accommodating area, then hammered it flat with the side of his fist. Pleased, he looked up from his work, then frowned. "Oh, it's you. Back again? More questions?"

"I'm back, yes, but it's over a different matter."

"Different? What the hell do you mean?"

"Ramona VanDyke was found dead this morning."

For all of Uncle Gilbert's advanced alcoholic state, the news of Ramona's death appeared to sober him quickly enough. He watched the placement of my puzzle piece with no sign of awareness. His head lifted slowly until he was nearly eye-to-eye with me, his mouth dropped open, revealing yellowed teeth and an alcoholic odor. I eased backwards as Gilbert expounded his innocence. "I didn't do it! I had nothin' to do with it! I was here. Asleep. Ask Arthur."

"I'm not accusing you of anything, Mr. Catchpool."

Gilbert asked what had happened. When I had told him, he slowly shook his head. "Awful. God awful."

"When was the last time you saw her?"

"What's today?"

"Wednesday."

"Ahh, yes. Well, it'd have to be. Ramona saw Arthur for dinner, but that was last night."

"I'm asking about you, Mr. Catchpool."

"Me?" He blinked slowly. "Me and Ramona? Well, that'd have to be at the bonfire. Sunday."

"Do you know of any reason she might have been killed? Grudges, old love affairs that didn't end amicably, debts never paid..."

"Other than her short-lived marriage, I can't think of any old loves. And that left her a widowed mum with a tiny infant, so you shan't have to look for a husband."

"Married to whom?"

"Don't know. Ask Arthur. Ask Ramona.

She'd know. Can't remember."

I sighed and tried another line. "You were seen Sunday before the bonfire in the vicinity of the effigy. Are you interested in rope? Did you ask Talbot for the loan of any remnant he had, perhaps?"

"Loan of rope? What the hell are you on about? I didn't ask for any rope, then or later. Not from anyone. And I didn't buy rope, either. We've got enough about the estate. Why you asking? She wasn't hanged, was she? Rope! That's why—" His shaking hand swept uncontrollably across his mouth, trying valiantly to moisten his lips and tongue. "That's it. There was rope on her body. She was hanged or tied up. Or else you'd not be asking me about rope. Oh, God, I had nothin' to do with it. Nothin'! I swear, I swear..." He lowered his head, cradling it in his hands, and repeatedly groaned his innocence.

I left him to his suspicions and denials.

Back in the incident room, I gave Graham the particulars of the Home Office Forensic Pathologist's examination. "He said we'll get the full report when he's had a chance to full go over the body," I said. "But he learned a lot at the crime scene."

Graham settled back and let me talk from my notes.

"He couldn't get an estimate of death from body temperature."

"Frost and snow play havoc on bodies, I agree."

"Rigor mortis is largely discounted, too, for the same reason. There was no blanching of the skin. The blood had clotted. Fixed lividity won't help, either."

"How about her attire?"

"He felt it was obvious she'd been here over night. She was rained on, judging by the condition of her gown. It wouldn't get as frosty as it was without a good prior wetting. The edge of her garment crackled when he poked it and it was virtually cemented to the ground from the ice. He conjectures she fell and lay in the rain. Then the temperature dropped and the moisture frosted over."

"That makes it about seven hours, then," Graham calculated. "I'll have to find out if someone knows when the rain stopped. I don't think it lasted long, for all its punch."

"So even if she came out toward the end..."

"It fits with the lack of blanching, which normally occurs six to eight hours after death. But of course the full body rigidity that one would expect to find after twelve hours doesn't mean a thing. Don't look so astonished, Taylor. I've been to enough crime scenes and have been subjected to years of post mortem reports."

"You certainly know about the medical side of this, sir."

"Not all of it. What else?"

"Ramona's lips were white."

Graham frowned. "Did Ramona look like that yesterday?"

I shook my head. "The pathologist believes it's not from the cold, but more likely the result of something chemical. He said those are classic conditions of skin death."

"If it's chemical, would he find anything in her after all that time in the cold?"

"He believed so. He said cold wouldn't have affected it."

Graham nodded, frowning as if he were considering something.

I let half a minute elapse before I told him of

the rope strands under Ramona's body and the sample cut from one of the bundle of branches. "I thought it good to have something for comparison. I know Talbot supplied the rope for that bundle. I saw him make it."

"Excellent."

My blood tingled at the comment and I wanted to smile, but I didn't. I cleared my throat and said, "Isn't it rather odd, sir, that we have two cases involving rope?"

He blinked, as though snapping back to the present. "We don't know if this death *is* a case yet. 'Case' refers to something other than natural death, Taylor."

"But if it turns out to be—"

"Murder? Who'd want to kill a respected, well-liked woman like Ramona?"

"Who'd want to kill a respected, well-liked man like Steve Pedersen? You know as well as I do, sir, that motives run deep. Especially in villages."

"Well, I hope we can rule out Arthur. I don't think I can stand the thought of a besotted lover killing his intended."

"It's fortunate for us that Ramona fell where she did."

"Why?"

"If it is murder, and the rain obliterated any footprints or small clues outside, the body, by falling on the rope, protected it."

"That sounds planned. Look, Taylor, I'll go along with your murder suggestion. I hate rushing fences, but it looks suspicious with the whitened skin of her lips. The killer had to be a local. Would leave the house at night for anyone but a local, someone she knew?"

"Unless she was carried to the lawn after death." The words were out before I knew it. My throat threatened to close as near panic set it. I hadn't meant to contradict or best him. Merely to suggest another scenario. I glanced at him, barely daring to breathe. He rubbed his chin and nodded.

"How'd your questioning of Uncle Gilbert go?"

"Nothing to get me a promotion. Uncle Gilbert, as you won't be surprised to hear, both denies thought of borrowing rope or knowledge of loan of rope. He seems to have minded his own business for once. I hope you had better luck."

"I found Liam, yes, and broke the news to him. He'd spent the night at Arthur's, in one of the band member's rooms. All four of them had a long night of drinking at several pubs and ended up at Evan's establishment." He paused as I glanced around the room and murmured I should've asked Arthur about Liam when I was at the manor house. "You didn't know, Taylor. Anyway, Arthur vouched for their late arrival. They had to be let in. It seems no one had a key."

"Do you believe that?"

"Are you suggesting they needed Arthur to establish an alibi?" Graham leaned forward, his eyes dark and troubled. "Do you really think Liam killed his mother?"

"I don't want to think it, sir, but it strikes me odd that on the one night he doesn't sleep at home his mother is killed."

"What's the motive, if that's true? Did they have a history of fighting? Seems to me she was accommodating of him, getting him the gig at the bonfire, for starters."

"I don't know if they didn't get along." I was angry and sad and exhausted, and I didn't like the suggestion I'd made. "I'm just saying that it looks awfully strange that's he's not there the one night she needed him."

"That's as may be, Taylor, but he said he chose to stay at Arthur's because the lads got back late and he didn't want to wake her by getting home at that hour."

"Considerate."

"I'll have someone look into Liam's history with his mother. I don't believe he killed her, but I agree it is odd this happened at this time. You don't look any happier. What's troubling you?"

"If Liam didn't kill his mum, I wonder if the killer knew Liam wouldn't be home last night."

"You think it was one of the band members?"

I made a face, trying to think through the scenario. "They'd know Liam wasn't home, sir."

"I can have Salt or Byrd check at the pubs to see if they were all there. Liam gave me a list."

"Accommodating."

"If you want to go with that suggestion, Taylor, it wouldn't have to be a band member. Anyone in the village who saw Liam out with his mates would know he wasn't at home. It didn't take Einstein to figure out Ramona was alone."

I agreed that made sense, then asked if he'd been able to talk to Talbot.

"Yes. It was short and succinct." Graham shook his head, telling me that Talbot admitted tying up the bundles during the weekend, but that he ended the job Monday. "And you could have told me that much, Taylor, for all the help Talbot's narration provides. I believe anyone could have done it. Talbot's rope isn't uncommon, and it's lying about, most likely, contrary to his claim to have it under lock and key." He paused to let his meaning sink in, that Liam, a band member, or a village could have easily found a piece at the bonfire area or elsewhere.

"Not much help, sir. Although I was told again that Ramona had been married. And, no, I don't know her husband's name."

"Maybe Uncle Gilbert and Talbot are related. Do fraternal twins share similar cerebrations?"

"I don't know about that." I was momentarily thrown by Graham's word choice. "But Uncle Gilbert's not too strong on the headwork."

"The only interesting item I came upon was Tom in the middle of the road. He was taking photos of the pub and post office reflected in rain puddles."

"He's certainly creative. Is it instinctive or does he walk around his subject before he shoots?"

"I wonder how many memory cards he goes through on holiday," Graham said. "Well, he's bound to have an interesting album. I tire of snaps of Aunt Edith reduced to a dot in the middle of a Sahara-like stretch of beach."

"Or the wedding party and guests, none of whom I know but should find interesting because so-and-so's niece was a flower girl. Why is a photo of the bride and groom stuffing wedding cake into each other's mouths so fantastic? Icing all over her makeup, fingers sticky...I should think a bride would want to forget it."

I waited for a murmur of agreement, for a commiserating word. Instead, Graham sat mute, as though he had not heard me. Or as though he was thinking of a similar situation, for his eyes stared past me, focused on something beyond the window. I watched his face, trying to read his thoughts, wanting to understand the private world into which he slipped periodically. There was a slight lowering of his eyelids and a tightening of his jaw muscles, which I knew happened when he was angry or impatient. A phrase, hardly above a whisper, escaped his lips.

"Beg pardon, sir?"

He stirred, as if the sound of my voice broke his mood. Shifting his eyes to my face, he seemed startled to find himself in the incident room. "Pardon?"

"I didn't catch what you said. Sounded like 'till death do us part.' You want me to check up on Ramona's marriage?"

Graham rubbed his face and said no, that he had just been thinking of weddings. I wasn't so sure. I thought he had mentioned Ray. A brother or uncle? Perhaps a best friend. Someone who had bested Graham in love? I busied myself with the papers in front of me. As much as I longed to ask him about Ray, I refrained. Graham would tell me if he wanted to.

I had just suggested bringing in some lunch when the phone rang. Graham muttered that it was getting as bad as mealtime at home and picked up his mobile. After a few verbal pats on the back, he rang off. "Care to guess who that was? I won't even make you lay a wager."

"You better tell me. I don't feel very lucky today."

"On executing constabulary business, our constables found a turquoise thread."

"Turquoise," I muttered, recalling the puckered threads in Ramona's nightgown. "And where was this found?"

"On a bush outside the back door."

"Not meaning to play devil's advocate, sir, but couldn't the thread be old? Days, months ago?"

Graham conceded the possibility. "Unfortunately, Taylor, I've had many a case that hung by a thread."

21

We were nearly finished with our meal in the public bar—a break Graham and I admitted we needed—when Derek limped into the pub's large room. He nodded at us before joining a group at the bar. It was evidently one of their usual meeting places, the stretch of empty tables patiently waiting for tourists or villagers. Mark, I noted, stood in the center of the group and was buying one of the men a drink.

"Derek!" Evan threw his damp towel beneath the bar counter, drew a pint of bitters, and set it down in front of Derek. "We were just saying before you came in that we're starting up rehearsals. The walk-around's just five weeks away, right?" Evan turned to one of the older men leaning against the bar, who gave an affirming nod. "Right. Five weeks."

"Not much time."

"Not much time, you may well say. So, we've got to get at our carol rehearsals."

"Hope it's not as damned cold as it was last year." One of the men lowered his head, hardly lifting the glass from the counter top, and took a long drink. "Damned near froze to death before it was over. Bloody snow. Like as froze me feet trudgin' through that muck."

"Aye," another of the group agreed. "Never knew the wind so fierce as it was up at Leadlove's farm. God, it was like I had bloody well nothin' on. Cut right through to the bone, that cold did. Ain't much better tonight."

They paused, turning toward the front door, and listened. The wind moaned between the door and its frame, rattling the brass knocker. A tree branch bumped against a window, as though it wanted to come in from the cold. Returning to their drinks, the men seemed suddenly colder and talked quietly of a past snow storm. "Never found his body till next spring, it were," one man reminded the group. "Found him up around Fenig's Hill, near the pool. Frozen solid as a board and twice as stiff. 'Course, it's near always certain death up there that time of year, ain't it? Cold."

Silently, I agreed, knowing that patch of Thunor Moor. It was desolate, wild land, planed by fierce wintry winds that left nothing growing taller than grasses. Sheep refused to graze there, seeking instead the warmer, more sheltered dales. A pool of bracken-infested water along a walking track further chilled the wind as it swept across the pool's black surface. Frost and ice, always thicker and more abundant on the pool's eastern shore, seemed to linger into the summer, when it took refuge in the crevices of ruined stone walls. 'Cold' hardly described the moor.

"At least it's not snowin' tonight," someone said as the branch scratched again.

"Maybe not," Derek said, "but there's the smell of it in the air."

"I can feel it more than smell it. Gets into my bones. Missus says it's neuralgia, but I don't hold with that. Seeps into my body, cuts right through my flesh when it's gonna rain or snow, don't it?"

"Maybe we should bypass Leadlove's," Derek suggested. "I don't know as they would miss us all that much, anyhow."

"Not as though they was regular Churchgoers. Wouldn't think they'd miss the carols, them not attendin'."

"It will be our fortieth year of caroling," Evan said. "Can you believe it? Most of us started as youngsters and we're the same group. Regular as clockwork we showed up."

"I wouldn't have given us that hope when we started," one of the group confessed.

"No," admitted Byron, walking up to the bar. "We sounded awful."

"I wouldn't say awful," Evan returned. "No one ever sounds like Kings College Choir right off. It takes a bit of work."

"We've done all right," Derek said. "We improved each year."

"That's where the hard work comes in. Makes it enjoyable when folks appreciate us," Byron agreed.

Evan nodded, then snapped his fingers. "We ought to have a celebration after finishing at the last house. We did for our thirtieth year. After Leadlove's farm we'll stop here at the pub for a drink and a bite, and toast another ten years of the Upper Kingsleigh Carolers."

"Ought to print up another fancy paper with members' names listed. Maybe do some fancy graphics on the computer to make it look official."

"Forty years is purty near a milestone. Ought to have a plaque made," suggested another of the locals. "Hang it here on the wall, if you aren't of a mind to say no, Evan."

"I'd be honored. Maybe it'd get a few more to join, if they see how we've fared."

"We'll have all our names engraved," Derek said. "Show our spirit—"

"Speaking of spirit," Byron said. "If I may interrupt your meal, Mr. Graham..."

As though on cue, every head in the room turned to us. I felt their curiosity, their eyes darting between Graham and me.

"Are you any nearer to an arrest?"

A few throats cleared, a few feet shuffled as the interested waited for the news.

Graham eyed me as though we shared a secret, then turned to the men. "The Constabulary, although dealing with many dozen cases simultaneously, has utilized all its available resources for the swift and successful conclusion of this case. It has received the top priority of the Chief Constable, since murder receives priority status. The expeditious completion and apprehension of the miscreant, although an honorary pursuit, must also be tempered with lawful procedures, else we should be confronted with a vigilante episode. I have conferred both with the Assistant Commissioner and the Chief Constable, and we feel that an arrest, while being of major concern to the emotional and mental well-being of the citizenry—not to mention their physical survival—is imminently pending."

Did he take a course on officialeze—I wondered, sharing a wink with him—or had he a natural talent?

The men nodded, mumbled that they had thought so all along, and occupied themselves with their drinks.

Evan wished us Godspeed and Derek mumbled that this was one November they would not forget for many years, so it didn't make any difference to him what happened, other than the seeing of justice served.

"You don't mind that it's upset your wife, then?" asked one of the men.

"Of course I mind." Derek's voice sounded strained, his face flooding with color. "But what's done is done. When the calendar turns to Guy Fawkes night next year, Kris and I will be reminded of this mess, certainly. But other than the police finding the killer and someone being satisfied with the trial outcome, it doesn't make a difference in our lives, does it? Will it yours, George?" he said, confronting the man. "Or yours, Byron? Or Evan? I doubt it one bloody bit."

I felt like saying, "More tea, Vicar?" but after an awkward moment, Evan cleared his throat and asked the group if they could get back to another topic. "If we're going to do this plaque, we haven't much time. We must make our decisions. There's bound to be something we can order from Buxton or Chesterfield."

"Are you thinking of donating it?" Byron prompted, setting his empty beer glass on the bar top and turning toward Derek.

"You're not worried about the cost, are you?"

"Not more than the next. It's just that, with Christmas coming..."

Evan frowned. "I might've known you'd let a few quid come between you and our anniversary. I've never seen anyone so fretful over a penny."

"What were you thinking, then?" Byron leaned across the bar, nudging the glass out of his way and eyeing the man. "I can't see you parting with that kind of lolly. Must be talking of fifty quid or so, with the engraving, if we do it up right. Nothing cheap."

"If you're so money shy, what say we all contribute toward the cost?"

Murmurs bordering on consent greeted Evan's suggestion.

"You can always grab a spare job washing windows or making beds up at the Manor," someone joked from the back of the room. "Maybe earn a few pence washing Arthur's Jaguar. 'Course, you'd have to sign away the remainder of your salary in precaution of your scratching it."

"Better yet," Evan declared, grinning at Byron, "get your boss to donate the plaque. Save us poor working chaps doling out our own meager savings. Then we could have a proper party. You want the other half of that, Byron?"

The man looked up, seemingly startled. "No, no more. I've had my limit, thanks."

Talbot, the lone occupant at a table, coughed loudly, drawing the carolers' attention to him. He drew his handkerchief across his mouth. "You can have your party if you want. I'm not the man to stop any of you, but it's kind of silly, if you ask me."

"Well, nobody's asking you, then." Byron kicked a chair and sent it crashing into its neighbor.

Evan shook his head slightly at the man, as if silencing him, and asked Talbot what he meant.

Talbot stuffed the handkerchief into his pocket, picked up his glass and stared at it. "It may be forty years for you, Evan Greene, and most of your others, but Mr. Derek Halford, here, has only been out carolin' with the lot of you for thirty-nine years. He weren't here in '79, or don't any of you have the intelligence to remember that?" He finished with a sort of flurry, draining his glass.

"What the hell are you talking about?" demanded one of the men.

Evan's hand went out to the man's arm. "It's true. I'd forgotten. It's not the sort of thing you normally make it a point to recall each year, is it? Derek was back by the following spring, but anyway, it's the group that's been going for forty years, and that's what's being celebrated, not the individual members."

Talbot stood up, pushing back the chair with his leg. He remained at the table, staring at the men. "You can give out whatever the hell you like. Might as well do it. Next milestone's fifty years, and the way the world's goin', I doubt any of us'll be 'round then to enjoy it. Party while you can."

Ray of sunshine, I thought.

"Thanks for your permission, Talbot."

"Lot of nonsense, all this time spent on singin'. The telly's got whackin' good programs. So's the radio. I can hear better on recordings any day of the week than I can from you lot. Who needs you?" He grabbed his coat, struggling into it as he stomped out of the pub amidst an array of angry protests, the loudest being Byron's

Mark angled his back toward the man, set down his glass, coughed, and grabbed Byron's glass. He wandered outside, pretending to drink from it, took out his mobile, and walked to the pub door.

Evan ignored Mark's departure. It was common practice for people to take their drinks outside to stand around drinking and talking.

Graham murmured, "What an extraordinary exhibition. What's got into Talbot?"

I nodded and emptied my glass. "The lady doth protest too much, methinks."

"Truer words, Taylor. Come on." We followed Talbot at a more leisurely pace.

We were several yards behind him when the connecting door to the vestibule banged open, revealing Uncle Gilbert. Upon seeing Talbot, Gilbert grasped the handyman's arms in affection. "My boy!" gurgled Gilbert, all excitement. "I was going to drop by later this evening, but you've saved an old man a trip. How are—"

Talbot shrugged off the unwelcome hands and stepped backwards. "I'll save you a trip anytime, then, for I won't let you in. And I'm not your son. I wish to hell you'd stop natterin' on like that. I asked my dad once 'bout you and him. Know what he told me?" Talbot squinted through the smoke of his cigarette, studying the man before him. "He said he never knew you. You were in the same regiment, all right, that you and Kris's dad was mates, but that was it. So bugger off afore I get good an' mad." Talbot brushed past the man and slammed the outer pub door in his exit.

Embarrassed at being caught in a melodramatic pronouncement, Gilbert averted his eyes from us, mumbled something noncommittal, and slowly entered the public bar.

"Amazing," Graham said as we walked to the stairs leading to our bedrooms. "What's it mean?"

"What'll come of it is my question."

A chatter of raised voices inside the public bar turned our attention to the commotion. Peering through the door's glass panel, I could see Gilbert getting friendly with a group of women seated at a table.

"Amazing," Graham repeated. "Rebounds from rebuke by his pseudo son and transforms to amorous octopus in less than five minutes."

"The man's got stamina."

"Or hope. Ooh, that hurt!" Gilbert just received a slap from a middle-aged blonde. Although his back was towards us, the woman's face told us her attitude to the man's strategy and attack. Graham's jaw muscle tightened. "Serves him right, I don't doubt. They don't look very happy with his technique."

"As good as a Buster Keaton movie." I pressed my nose against the glass, trying to hear.

"Don't insult Keaton. He had class and dignity while being funny. Gilbert's just pathetically funny."

The man approached another member of the group, only to receive the same answer, though delivered differently. Gilbert finally seated himself at a lone table and occupied himself in studying the fire.

It was my turn. "Amazing."

"You can dream about the second reel. Good night, Taylor."

"'Night, sir."

I went to my room but stood behind the closed door, listening for Graham's door to close. When the latch clicked, I counted to five hundred, making certain he hadn't forgot something and would go downstairs. But when he remained in his room, I felt it safe to leave, so I returned to the public side of the pub.

Evan was laughing at something and wiping the bar top when I walked in. He looked up, seemed surprised to see me again, and asked if I needed something as he reached for a glass.

"I'm fine, thanks." I declined the offer of a nightcap. "I'd just like to ask you a question, if I may."

"Certainly, miss. Something not to your

liking with the room?" He seemed concerned, perhaps hoping he wouldn't have to tackle a plumbing problem at this hour.

"The room's fine. It's not that. I just would like to know if Liam and Ramona got along well."

A hint of confusion swept across his face before he recovered his composure. He might have thought it an odd question any other time, but a police investigation may have given it new meaning. He cleared his throat and leaned toward me, obviously wanting to keep the information between us.

"There was the odd teenaged rebellion, but it weren't serious. No episodes of running away or staying out with his mates to defy his curfew. So on the whole, I'd say him and Ramona got on fine. 'Course, he was at university in America for four years." He paused, as if I should infer the meaning. When I merely looked at him, Evan continued. "That's four years' squabbles that they didn't have. I think Liam grew up a lot in America. He came back more mature and considerate. Make sense?"

"How about the hols? When he came back home for Christmas and semester breaks did they get along?"

"He stayed there for Christmas." Evan said it as though it was the saddest thing he'd heard. "I suppose it were too much money to keep flying back and forth. But he came home each May, when the school year ended. He got himself a job here or in one of the neighboring villages. I gave him something to do. Not that I really needed Liam, but I wanted to help him."

"That was nice of you."

Evan shrugged. "But there you are. They never really quarreled over anything major, if that's what you're wanting to know. America did him good in more than his learning. He came back a real pleasant man. Wouldn't hurt a fly."

I sat on the bottom step of the stairs that went to the bedrooms, waiting for some of the older residents to leave the lounge area. As they entered the vestibule, I stood up and asked them the same question: if they knew of any personal problems between Ramona and Liam. Each person confirmed Evan's account; mother and son loved each other and got along well.

I trudged up the stairs to my room, thinking Ramona hadn't got along very well with someone.

22

I like to walk in the early morning, and while in Upper Kingsleigh I saw no reason to discontinue my habit. The walk not only focuses my mind on the day's activities but it also gives me a chance to bird watch.

I followed a much-used trail, entering the woods by Arthur's estate. The quiet, cool blend of sanctuary and November morning enveloped me. Old leaves and pine scented the air. I zipped up my jacket against the cold.

Several yards away a green woodpecker hopped among the branches of a dead tree. Despite the bird's large size, he had been difficult to see at first, for the sunlight had not penetrated this section of the woods. He was resplendent with red crown and nape that offset his practically all-green body. I watched him pursue his breakfast until a noise disturbed him. He rose in a flurry of flapping wings and loud laughing call, settling somewhere out of my sight. The tree seemed vacant without him.

Farther along the trail I came upon several nuthatches. A bit of fluff on the wind, this small bird was half the size of the woodpecker. But size didn't diminish its beauty: it was equally as striking with its subtle blue-gray back and orangish belly. Neither bird was on the endangered list, but I was thrilled to see them.

I crossed Rams Dyke Creek. In the village, the stream announced its presence by vociferously clambering over moss-slick rocks and gurgling around half-submerged logs. Here in the midst of the woods it slowed. Perhaps it had no reason to impress the villagers with its frantic pace. Perhaps the land lay flatter here. The channel widened and filled with leaves. The stream, it seemed, needed the earlier white water rush to clear itself of strangling vegetation. I stopped, dipping my hand into the water. Pure liquid ice. I wiped my hand on my slacks and crossed the stream. A growth of burdock, withered by frost, clung to the bank and brushed against me as I reclaimed the forest floor. Beneath my feet, fallen leaves and twigs crunched, scaring the birds into loftier branches.

As I came to the farther edge of the wood I saw the noose.

It hung from a tree limb, barely stirring in the slight breeze. I stopped abruptly. My heart beat racing, I glanced around the area, waiting for a cry of "Surprise!" or a laugh or a rush of kidnapping hands. When nothing happened, I finally approached it. There was nothing to indicate a connection with me or Steve's case. Yet, why was it here?

The rope was new, still smelling of hemp fiber. Was it another warning? Or some local kids playing at their own Guy Fawkes hoisting? Perhaps Mark was joking with me, having somehow learned of the other episodes in my room. Perhaps he had been the original instigator all along, and this was just Chapter 4 in his bag of pranks. I stared at it, wondering what he had waiting for me at the pub when I returned. Another dead bird? It would be like him to do this, I thought, grabbing the noose and savagely tugging it from the tree. Some strange trial to see if I was on a level with the boys. I peered at the rope's cut end. Of course without the lab's help I couldn't determine how long it had been weathering here. A call for their expertise would raise questions. And I was still determined to keep all such incidents quiet. So, I was stuck. Damn! as Graham often said.

I threw the rope to the ground and kicked it against a tree. The dull 'thud' did nothing to lessen my anger. I picked it up, hit it against the trunk, then flung it onto an open patch of ground where I stamped on it. After burying it beneath armfuls of leaves and rocks, I emerged from the woods near Talbot's cottage considerably happier.

The village was also in the midst of its early morning routine. The usual clank of bottles as Evan set out the empties for pick-up, and the roar of a car acceleration soared into the air. A voice called out a last-minute message to someone. A door slammed and two dogs barked. But, on the whole, it was quiet. Much quieter than the morning rush at Buxton.

Mason Conway and Talbot stood near the edge of the lane at Conway's Gift Shop. Mason leaned on his broom, evidently taking a break in his morning chore. Talbot turned as I approached and, for some reason known only to him and God, called out good morning and tipped his cap to me.

"If the murder hasn't scared them away, we'll have tourists." Mason's face was flushed. The first rays of morning sun fell upon his features, revealing his paper-white complexion.

"Christmas brings many folks out," Talbot said. "You'll see. They like a piece of the past to connect with ancestors, to see how our customs evolved. It's too soon to worry."

"Unless Arthur has Liam play for our pantomime. A bloody farce that will be, music during a pantomime."

"Arthur's given no indication he's thinkin' of doing that, has he?" Talbot sounded worried.

"How do I know what he's thinking? He made a farce of the bonfire by letting Liam and his group in, and if he wants a repeat performance for Christmas—" His neck muscles stood out in relief.

"I thought Liam was stayin' just the few days."

"So he is. But he's graduated now. He can return any time he's invited. And, he has to live somewhere." Mason bit off the last words. "Bloody musicians." He rubbed his nose so vigorously that I half expected to see blood when he stopped. I tried not to stare as I approached.

"I wouldn't worry about that yet. Anyway, it's early days yet, both for Liam bein' asked to return and to see how the murder will affect shop sales. Besides, maybe a bit of modern in with the old will be nice. We need to give it time, see what comes of it."

"Lot of folks do like the pageantry." Mason seemed to consider the other side of the argument. "Kind of puts a spark in their ordinary days, I agree. And most years we do all right. I get half my profit for the year around Christmas. But the point is—"

"The point is," Talbot said, his index finger poking Mason's chest, "we can build up the trade here, 'stead of seein' it die. With a little education from the right people, in the right spot, we'll be put on the map and have nothin' to fear, and it don't take no rock group to do it. We've got plenty enough talent in the village without outsiders comin' in."

"Liam is hardly an outsider, Talbot."

"If he don't live here no more, he's an outsider. We can increase trade without goin' to such extremes as Liam wants. We'll build up a group of traditional shops and events that will attract tourists lovin' the old ways. And they'll take us serious. You'll see."

"What are you talking about? Who's doing this education, as you put it, and where?"

"Never you mind that." Talbot took a cigarette from his jacket pocket and lit it. He was about to throw away the match when he held it toward Mason. "Like this match, now. Unlit it's no good. Just a bit of useless wood, for all its potential. But strike it at the right time and apply its flame to the right place—" He imitated an explosion. "Whoosh! You got somethin' movin' and dramatic, and all from a bit of education. Same thing here in the village. Trust us, lad."

I glanced at Mason as I passed. Evidently he was as nonplused as I. Mason opened his mouth but Talbot said, "You'll see. Once we get goin' you won't have to worry no more. About anything. Includin' modernization contaminatin' the customs."

Without appearing obvious, I couldn't slow my walk. I was out of listening range in seconds, wondering, along with Mason, what Talbot was planning. And with whom.

I had just entered the incident room when Byrd called me to the phone. "It's the Vicar, Brenna. He asked for you or Mr. Graham, and since Mr. Graham's not here..."

I nodded and took the receiver. Lyle's voice shot over the phone and bored into my ear. "I know it's dreadfully early. I hope they haven't pulled you out of bed." He paused, as if expecting me to reveal my schedule. I assured him I was fully dressed and had breakfasted. "Really? I suppose I could have waited, but I wanted to catch you up before you left for the day. I didn't now if you'd be about, if I'd see you—"

"Has something happened, sir?"

"What? Oh, no. At least, not to me. I suppose I'm an alarmist, but there was that poor American, you know. Well, there's always the doubt if one keeps quiet."

"It's always best to tell the police anything connected with a case, sir, no matter how trivial you may think it."

"Yes? Well, that's good to hear. Dear, this is such a struggle. Perhaps I shouldn't say anything, but in light of what happened with Ramona, and this *is* rather unusual..."

"What's unusual, sir?"

Lyle exhaled so loudly that I shook my head. "I found some money on top of the offertory box in the sanctuary."

"Nice for you."

"It is, but you don't understand, miss. Besides the fact that the donator could've dropped the money *into* the box, there was a scrap of paper with the money. I guess he wanted to be sure I found the note, otherwise—"

"Is it a lot of money?"

"More than we usually find in such anonymous offerings. £35."

"That *is* generous. Did the note explain the donation?"

"I'll read it to you, unless you wish me to

bring it to you."

"That won't be necessary, sir. You can read it."

Lyle cleared his throat, as though he wanted every word to be intelligible. 'For the poor man's funeral. Can't spare more. Sorry.' It was written out on white copy paper. The kind that computer printers use. I thought if you wanted to analyze the handwriting, I could come now."

I told him that wouldn't be necessary, but to keep it in case Mr. Graham wished to see it. "Thank you, sir. You've been quite helpful."

"Oh, I'm glad you think so, miss. I didn't know if should ring you up, but I thought perhaps this might tie in with your case. I don't know what clues you need."

I thanked him again and hung up assuring him that I didn't consider the call a waste of time.

"A witness to Steve Pedersen's murder?" Graham had strolled into the room midway through my indistinguishable grunts, and was now searching for his pen among the papers on the table.

"We should be so lucky." I told him of Lyle's discovery, and added, "At least it's not enough money to suggest the giver is the killer, and made the donation to clear his conscience. Though, I admit it would've helped if Lyle had CCTV cameras in the sanctuary."

"My fantasy," Graham said rather dreamily. "Just once. Just one time before I retire, I'd like a witness who was at the scene, who took a video, whose word won't be doubted, who—"

"I think you're wanting Moses again."

"And what's wrong with him?"

"Nothing. He's just a little hard to get a hold of right now, unless you're not telling me something."

"Taylor, I tell you absolutely everything. That's the only way a good police team can work."

I must have eyed him rather dubiously, but he plunged into our day. "In case you've forgotten, we were working on that wonderful year 1979. We have Byron stating that because he had that tragic car accident in December, he left the village. Talbot spouts off last night about Derek's absence from the village during the winter of 1979. Doesn't that do something to your curiosity, Taylor?"

I suppressed a yawn. "To tell the truth, sir, it didn't keep me up last night."

"You have something for us, Salt?"

Mark nodded, handing the page to Graham, and stood in his best at-ease stance.

Graham looked up from the paper. "Anything else, Salt?"

"I'm on my way to check out the pubs Liam VanDyke mentioned, sir. I doubt it'll take too long, since all but The Broken Loaf are in the next village."

"Thanks. I'll be anxious to hear what you learn."

Mark tossed out a dazzling smile before leaving to find Evan.

The vehicle accident records for the area around Upper Kingsleigh in 1979 showed a fatal accident in December, attributable to the extremely hazardous conditions of the roads. Two people were named as occupants of the car: the driver, Byron MacKinnon; and a passenger, George Alton. "Well, well," Graham said as he read the report. "Here's something unexpected. A Good Samaritan stopped by. Do you care to venture a guess?" He smiled at me from over the top of the printout.

"Derek Halford."

"First rate, Taylor." He tossed the paper onto the table. "How'd—"

"I didn't guess, if that's what you're accusing me of. Does he say what he was doing out in the wilds of Derbyshire? Do you suppose he was coming home from Christmas shopping?"

"More likely he blew his wad in a Buxton pub. He was a bright young bachelor in those days."

"I don't think he spent his annual dole on anything for his place, sir. It could do with a new coat of paint and a few slipcovers on the chairs. What's he been doing with the money all these years? Three hundred quid is a nice bit of change. Not only that, does his wife question what happens to the money?"

"Maybe she's the one who's been running footloose through his wallet. Equality in marriage sometimes means he earns it, and she spends it."

I ignored his jest. "How long have they been getting the benefits from that dole? His father dies in 1978, and Derek becomes heir. That's about forty years ago. Forty times £300." I stopped to calculate the total. "Twelve thousand pounds!"

Graham suggested that Derek might have used the money in a different way.

"Such as?"

"Such as a new car, telly or fridge, lessons at the Open University, bill at the dentist, spay the dog—"

"He doesn't have a dog."

"Maybe he did until recently, Taylor. Anyway, if Kris doesn't question the suspicious dwindling of their fortune, why should you? Evidently Derek is of a philanthropic bent."

"Charity starts at home."

"He can give some of it to charities and still

have some left over for his dog. What now?"

"Remember our first interview Sunday night? Arthur Catchpool, when he was telling us about how he had to turn part of his mansion into the B and B establishment? Well..." I hurried on after Graham nodded. "He mentioned in passing, though I've my idea he was rather proud in a one-upmanship sort of way, that he'd made Derek a loan. Remember? Arthur tossed it out when he told us Steve stayed Friday night at the house and left Saturday to stay with the Halfords."

"He didn't let drop the generous amount of his loan, did he? No, I don't recall it either. But I do recall Arthur mentioned the Halfords had enlarged their home. Something about it now being able to accommodate several guests. But if that's not it, I don't know what he's using his money for."

"I thought you liked his dentist. Or vet." picked up the phone, dialed the Constabulary, and asked the obliging listener at the other end to email us information on any planning applications made by Derek since 1979. When I'd hung up, I said, "She'll phone the planning board and let us know."

"Your idea being..."

"We'll at least know the extent of any alterations or whatever in his house, and make a fair deduction of the amount of the loan. If it's a whole extra room, it probably set Derek back a bit. I don't expect he makes all that much at his present position. And, inheritance aside, he can't have paid back the loan all that quickly if it was a nice, fat sum. At least it gives us something to go on."

"A simple coat of paint and those slip covers wouldn't have warranted Arthur's pocket-dipping."

"You don't suppose Derek used the loan money to help Kris with her dad's funeral. He didn't have all twelve thousand pounds then, and if she was financially strapped, it'd be one way to win a hesitant maiden's heart." The background noises of ringing phones, computer printings, and convivial conversations receded into a whisper as I waited for Graham's Judgment.

"But she was engaged at the beginning of November to Byron. Why wouldn't Byron do the funeral favors?"

"Couldn't afford it?"

"I wonder..." Graham gazed at the report. "Do you think it just a little too pat for Derek to be present at the car accident?"

"Unusual, perhaps, but it's a main thoroughfare. I'd think it more strange if they happened to meet in the middle of the A838 in Scotland."

"Damn it, Taylor, this thing just doesn't smell right. Kris' father dies, and Derek steps into Kris's life as her husband, supplanting Byron, who'd been engaged to her up to that point."

"Byron said he didn't feel he could marry her after the accident."

"That's it. *Byron said*. We have no witnesses. The obliging statement given to our man-in-blue at the time of the accident says that Derek was passing by and stopped to take up his Good Samaritan role. He was there before our boys were."

"You think it was planned, then?"

"I don't know if it was planned, but something's sticking in my throat. Steve, as former fiancée, turns up here in Upper Kingsleigh, and two days later he's dead."

"You think Kris is responsible for both deaths? But why should she want to kill her father or Steve?"

"I don't think it's Kris we have to focus on, Taylor. I think it's Derek."

"Derek? Why him?"

"Nothing concrete, I'm afraid. That's the problem with the entire supposition. But I was wondering if Derek could be unsure of his wife's love, maybe even jealous of Steve."

"I wonder what it feels like to know you're third best."

"Exactly. It can't do much for anyone's ego."

"So you think Derek eliminated his old rival?"

Graham rubbed his forehead, the strains of putting motive to action starting to tell. He eventually looked at me, his dark eyes serious as he explained. "Derek planned his conquest, if you want to call it that. First he eliminated Byron— probably slipped him a hefty check to get him out of the running. Then Derek gets rid of Steve by coaxing him into taking the effigy's place. Neat, succinct. He's taken care of both rivals, and feels relatively secure with his wife's affections."

"*Absit invidia.*"

"Let there be no envy, indeed." His mouth tightened.

"We can't prove it, though. You said it was your instinct, sir. I've worked with you on enough nebulous cases to trust you, but what set you off?"

Graham tapped the case notebook. "What your friend Talbot said last night at the pub."

"His ranting about the caroling? What's a bit of caroling got to do with this?"

"It's not the caroling per se. It's the expounding about the group's gala anniversary. Or, one of the group who isn't entitled to the loving cup."

"Derek? Evan said he'd only been with them for thirty-nine years."

"Derek was absent from Upper Kingsleigh from December '79 until the spring of '80. Three months. What did he do in that time? Where did he go? I need to find out. There's no such thing as coincidence in a murder investigation, Taylor."

"That soul of discretion should be able to tell you, sir."

Graham grabbed his mobile and punched in the vicarage number. Almost immediately he was speaking to Lyle. "My day will be much better, thank you, sir, if you can give me a bit of information. I know I've bothered you enough with this dreadful affair, but if you have a moment—"

As they talked, I had an image of the vicar sitting at his desk, his bald head warmed by and throwing back the yellowish light of his desk lamp, his round cheeks expanded like air-filled balloons as he held his breath in expectation.

Minutes later, Graham thanked the vicar and hung up.

"Did the vicar remember Derek's absence?"

"Derek left them rather abruptly. He just called up the vicar one day to tell him he'd be leaving."

"Where did he go?"

"Derek told the vicar he was going to do some hiking and skiing in Germany."

"Nothing so unusual in that," I said, feeling let down. "My cousin's wife has been to Germany."

"The point is, Taylor, when Derek returned, he brought Lyle a Bavarian stein."

"Was it the kind with the hinged lid?"

"There are other places than Germany in which to buy German gifts, Taylor. A stein doesn't prove he was there in '79."

"And your idea of his hideout is..."

"I'm going to find out. He had to have been somewhere for those three months."

"Just because a man lies about a trip, whether to impress his neighbors, or the girl he loves, doesn't mean he's guilty of murder. You can't take him in charge for Steve's murder on your suspicions of an unsubstantiated holiday."

"Of course not, but I can find out what our efficient government records show about his passport."

Inwardly I groaned. I knew Graham's bulldog tenacity, the way he set his jaw once his teeth were into a case, the way his back stiffened as though protecting his soft, vulnerable belly. He wouldn't release his bite or drop his shoulders until either he had his suspect in charge or had been declared dead by a qualified physician. And even then, I mused, listening to Graham's tackling of the poor official on the other end of the phone, I wouldn't put it past the man to haunt the guilty party into insanity or confession.

The minutes ticked away as Graham stayed on the phone, waiting for anything the computers could find.

"No Derek." Graham slammed down the receiver and glared at me. "So where the hell was he?"

23

"Why make such an obvious lie when it could be checked so easily? Why not just say he wintered at Brighton or someplace?"

Graham ran his hands through his dark hair and down the back of his neck. He kept them there, clasped, and leaned his elbows on the tabletop, speaking more to the pile of papers in front of him than to me. "1979 will take a bit of research, I agree. It's not like a crime committed last year, say, with the information easily accessed via computer."

"I doubt if the villagers really cared where he went. We'll have to employ an army to look through boxes of old files."

Graham tossed his pen at the stack of papers obscuring the edges of the table. Silence closed around us while we considered it.

"So where's the motive in all this for Steve or Ramona? In all these happy villagers and tourists, someone hated either him or Derek, if you want the mistaken identity theory. And enough to do something about it."

As though the Olympian gods were

directing the affairs of humans below, PC Byrd entered at that precise moment. There was something in his face, a glint of triumph in his eye that suggested this was not a normal report. He strode over to Graham, stood stiffly by the chair, and handed him a sealed plastic bag.

"I thought you'd like to see this, sir."

"Thank you. A postal card?"

"Yes, sir. During the examination of Ramona Van Dyke's front room, I found it. It was displayed rather prominently. I thought it a bit strange. It's from Newquay."

"Cornwall. A West Country town." I swallowed slowly, feeling my heart rate increase. "If it's a gilt card, I remember seeing it when I talked to her." Would Graham demote me for overlooking the clue? I felt my throat closing and wiped my palms against my slacks.

He didn't seem to consider the card rank-breaking. "Newquay's the boyhood home of Talbot Tanner, I believe. The place where his adoption proof resided."

"It's been printed, sir," Byrd said as though anticipating Graham's next question. "It may be useless after all these years, but..."

"No doubt we'll have your dabs on this, Taylor," Graham said.

I felt like throwing up.

Byrd frowned. "It was propped up on a small wooden plate rack. I almost tossed the thing aside, there was so much in that room."

Graham muttered that he had heard about it.

"Yes, sir. But if you'll look at the message--"

"Thank you, Byrd."

The man's shoulders inched backwards slightly as a blush of pride colored his cheeks. He answered Graham's remaining questions, then left.

"No expense spared on this." Graham angled the card so its band of gilt edging caught the light. This same brilliance had been applied to the group of sailing vessels. He turned it over to the message area. "Did you read Conan Doyle as a child, Taylor?" He leaned forward, positioning the card between us.

"I was reading them when most kids were reading Pooh Bear, sir."

"I bet you were." He read aloud, "'My month's nearly up. I'd like to stay longer, but I need to leg it at the end of the week. Been hunting in all the antique shops for that dry tie, but I can't find it. Beginning to think it's taken an ocean voyage. Could Cain have felt happier?'" Graham looked up, slightly amused by the apparent code.

"Who's Cain?" I said.

"Cain and Able, Taylor. Surely you know enough bible to know those two."

"What's he mean about Cain feeling happier?"

"The obvious thing that comes to mind is murder."

A silence settled over us as we studied the card's possible meaning. "Who sent it?" I angled the bag to eliminate the glare from the overhead light, scrutinizing the postmark. "March, 1980. That's a long time to keep a postcard. There's no signature. Was Ramona supposed to know who was in Newquay in March, 1980?"

"That's why I hoped you were up on your Conan Doyle."

"And this bit about a tie..."

"Not a silk one, if that's got you confused. My guess is a family one, that adoptive tie Derek's so hot over. Look, Taylor, it all fits. Antique shops are just Derek's clever way of telling Ramona he's been hunting for Talbot's adoption papers, the 'antique' part referring to old business or Talbot's age or something. I'm assuming for the moment it is Derek who sent the card. I don't know anyone else interested in disproving Talbot's adoption."

"How about Arthur? He provides the money."

"I can't see Arthur particularly interested. So what if Talbot proves he's the rightful heir? According to the will, Arthur still has to fork over the money. Either way, he's out his yearly £300. No, it's got to be Derek who sent this."

"But the reference to Cain, sir. Why talk about Cain if Derek hadn't committed murder? And he obviously didn't. 1979 was nearly forty years ago. Talbot's walking around, healthy as can be. Same with Derek and Arthur. Why Cain?"

"Perhaps," Graham said, slowly, "Derek meant it symbolically. Since he could find no trace of Talbot's adoption, Talbot has no legal or family ties to the money. He's dead. Gone. Buried. Derek had nothing to fear from Talbot."

"Good riddance to a potential brother."

"Like Abel. No more bothersome sibling. Or perhaps Esau and Jacob would have been a better comparison than Cain and Abel."

"Pardon?"

"The two sons of Isaac. Jacob stole his older brother's birthright. In the Old Testament."

"I never was too strong on the bible. Sir, if Jacob stole his older brother's birthright, do you think—"

"Talbot is older." He exhaled loudly and rubbed his forehead. "I don't know, Taylor. We're getting into more speculation than we should. It's so easy, so tempting to build a case this way."

"The Super will have your guts for garters if

you do, sir."

The expression was not lost on Graham. He sighed. "Unfortunately, he doesn't need much provocation."

"Getting back to something more solid…" I glanced at him to see if he was angry that I took the lead in the discussion. He looked slightly amused, but the serious spark in his eye told me we had best get on with our job. "So, if Derek was the real driver of Alton's car, with Byron actually the Good Samaritan, Derek no doubt got his game leg from the car crash, wouldn't you say?"

Graham nodded and patted my hand. It was in a careless manner, as though praising a dog for correctly executing a trick. I wish it had been more heart-felt. His voice heightened as he talked through the scenario. "If he got his limp from the accident, he couldn't let the villagers see it. If they knew he drove the car, sure, it would make sense, but it would take a bit of explaining how he ended up with the limp by playing the caring passer-by."

"So he ducks out of Upper Kingsleigh, holes up to heal, thinking Germany's as good an alibi as any. No one'd be looking for him on the continent. And the skiing accident would sound logical."

"But he goes to Newquay, the town that keeps popping up in Derek in and Talbot's pasts like a thorn in the foot."

"Lyle said that Derek returned in the spring." Like pigeons to roost. Or a sparrow to a waste bin, bedecked with homecoming flowers to mark the errant loved one's welcome, and to speed the dead to heaven. I looked out the window, at Evan waving to Mason, at Uncle Gilbert talking to the American tourists. How many final days did any of us have? The chirping of the sparrows on the windowsill broke my reverie. "Do you think Kris knows anything about all this?"

"About Derek's West Country holiday?" Graham shook his head and picked up the bag, staring again at the picture on the card. "All this was before he married her, Taylor. She was engaged to Byron before her dad died, remember? Derek became her husband only after Byron bowed out."

"But why does Derek write to *Ramona*? What's her interest in this? They weren't married."

My question remained unanswered, for Margo burst into the incident room at that moment. She hurried up to Graham and handed him an impressive assortment of official documents, each one consigned to constabulary paper.

"The lab report on the rope fiber found beneath Ramona VanDyke." Margo's voice was even and emotionless, as if she were choosing a piece of cod from the fishmonger's.

Graham looked up and accepted the papers.

"And the p.m. report, sir. The lads found something slightly unusual at the deceased's cottage. A small glass jar, like for marmalade or something similar. We don't know for certain because the label's gone."

"Why's that unusual, Lynch?"

"Well, sir, the jar was located outside, near the back door, under a bush."

"What is this jar holding, or have the contents washed away in the rain?"

"Not completely, no, sir. It's diluted somewhat, but the smell's still there, and we're about to take it to the lab. It smells like turpentine." Margo smiled when Graham praised their work. "And Brenna," Margo said, almost as an afterthought, "here's the information you asked for."

I thanked her and opened the envelope, not bothering Graham, who was occupied in his own pursuit of knowledge. It was a report of the Halfords' bank account. Even with the generous handout of the dole money, it was little better than mine. I scanned through the pages, back through a decade of deposits and withdrawals. It was all fairly steady. No drastic money juggling anywhere. I thanked her again and laid the paper on the table. She turned smartly and made for a paper-laden table, humming under her breath.

"Would you have expected turpentine, Taylor?" Graham read the reports as he talked to me, yet looked up when I replied it was common enough in most households. "She could have been cleaning something."

"Or Talbot may have done. He *is* the odd jobs man for the village."

"It may have been a very odd job," Graham grunted, handing me the reports. "What does one use turpentine for? Removing paint, cleaning off grease, asphyxiating Ramona."

"Damage to kidneys, intense congestion and swelling in the lungs and brain..." I turned briefly back to the report to make certain of the facts. "She died within minutes, from the pathologist's estimate. It's got to be murder, sir. No one, even the most determined suicide, would use turpentine. It'd be far too painful to swallow, and more than one sniff..."

"Aside from the fact that she was intensely happy with her forthcoming marriage, why commit suicide? It had to be murder. The killer no doubt doused a rag, and clamped it over her nose."

"That whitish skin around her nose was the area where he held the rag."

I envisioned the struggle. The man—it had to be a man. Who else would have the strength to hold a turpentine-soaked rag to a struggling woman for minutes while she inhaled lungful after lungful of this odor? Ramona, whether inside or outside her house, would have clawed at his hands trying to break his hold. He had worn gloves, for no one I had seen in the village had scratches on his hands. And he had been callous. A swift gunshot in a heated argument is one thing, but to deliberately hold a struggling woman for minutes... I shuddered.

Graham didn't notice. He was intent on the post mortem report. Facts were what solved murder cases. Not emotions. And I had started to get as emotional about Ramona as I had about my dead sparrow.

"No doubt, Taylor. The report also suggests the body was moved sometime prior to its discovery. The blood is stagnant in the upper body cavity, not along the back as we would expect since she was found lying on her back."

"The blood settled in her chest area." I stood up and read aloud over Graham's shoulder. "Fixed lividity generally occurs six to eight hours after death." I looked at him, a long, emotionless stare. He returned it, unblinking. "It fits our timetable, since we know she was lying there during the midnight storm and found at seven the next morning."

"So sometime during those seven hours her body was shifted. Why, Taylor?"

"To place her outside, or to extract something damning?" I tried to voice my nebulous thoughts. "Something incriminating that was torn off during the struggle, perhaps.

Something like a button or whatever that could point to the murderer."

"Do you think she was killed inside, and her body arranged in the back yard?"

"The report pushes me in that direction, yes. It'd be easier for him to lure her outside, to kill her there. Then he wouldn't have to carry her. Plus, her slippers were free of mud. Even if it rained like all hell it wouldn't have washed her slippers completely clean. Something would have clung, no matter how miniscule."

"And our lab boys would've found it." We were nearing the wrap-up of the case, and he was anxious to end it. Being close to naming the murderer propelled him ever faster in his work. I tried to understand him, tried to read the man within. His eyes gave me no information other than his solemnity. Yet, there was something else in their depths that I couldn't read. A second later, it had vanished and he sighed. "If not carried outside, Taylor, we at least know she was moved, though why..."

"Could it have to do with her hand positioned behind her back?"

"The rope fiber?"

I nodded while he assessed the possibility.

"We have no proof. And I hate coincidences."

"Perhaps we should go about this as to who could have killed her, which might lead us to the reason for the body shift."

"So whom do you favor as the murderer?" I asked.

The incident room was quiet. Most of the officers were either at the scene or on errands. In the silence, the sounds of the village sifted through the pub's walls: a dog barked, people talked, an occasional car horn honked. Common, everyday sounds, far removed from murder on a cool, tranquil evening.

"Well." I was eager to show Graham I could put two and two together as perfectly as he could. I stammered as Mark returned to the room and went over to Byrd. I tried to ignore him. "I, uh, we've focused on Derek due to the dole money, sir."

"You're suggesting we are off track, then." Graham's eyebrow was cocked slightly, his head tilted to one side as he studied my face.

"Yes, sir, I think we are. He loves his wife. Of course, no one can decipher the inner emotions of another." I averted my eyes from Graham, pretending to refer to the bank account statement. "I think we can take his love as real."

"Even with Steve, the ex-fiancé, showing up?"

"Kris made no move to go with him," I reminded Graham. "She could have said something to Derek, granted, but she didn't pack her luggage. And Derek is devoted to her. And if you're thinking that Derek paid off Byron annually with the dole money so he could slip the wedding ring on Kris's finger, that's another dead end." I handed him the bank statement and waited for him to read it. "The £300 is deposited in November or December for the past dozen or so years."

"So he wasn't keeping it out for Christmas gifts." Graham tossed the report onto the table.

"If Derek was paying for Kris, as I said, why would he suddenly quit? No. We have to focus on a different motive."

"Then, if you don't like the love rival elimination as motive—"

"There's money involved, yes, sir."

As though underscoring my statement, Byrd

took out his wallet to make change for Mark. His fingers closed over the coins and he patted Byrd's shoulder. They could've been playing the parts of the dole participants.

When I continued, my voice cracked. I coughed, covering my anger. "It's the money of tourism."

24

Mark chose that moment to come up to us. For once he was Professional Police Officer, ignoring me and concentrating on delivering his information to Graham.

"I checked the pubs Liam and his band frequented last night." Mark held his notebook open but evidently had no need to consult it, for his voice never faltered. "Evan said the lads closed up the place at one a.m. Of course, this was the last place they patronized. They started their pub crawl in Tideswell, hitting three establishments there, then returned here to finish up the night."

"What about the group members? Were all four of them present the entire time?"

"All present and accounted for, sir. The three pubs in Tideswell are spaced throughout the village, of course, but even so, there is no way someone could've left the group as they staggered to the next local, drive back here, kill Ramona, drive back to Tideswell, and catch up with the other three before they hit the next pub. It was a few minutes' walk between the three locals. And, even accounting for slow staggering or a stop to talk with someone on the street, it still would take less than ten minutes to get to the next pub."

Graham exhaled heavily. "I doubt if even Superman could've flown to Upper Kingsleigh, committed murder, and returned in ten minutes."

"No, sir. They all traveled in the one car. It's the same one they use all the time for local gigs. They've a designated driver. That's all the time, not just for nights when they drink."

"I suppose the driver's statement doesn't mean a thing, even if he swears everyone was in the car going back."

"Not unless we check the odometer for two round trips, no. Besides, we have no beginning mileage. But even more than that, it still goes back to the time element. There simply wasn't time to do all that even if they left someone behind at Tideswell. That's a twelve-mile trip on twisty two-lane roads, over hilly terrain and at night. I've driven it myself many times. You can't safely get above thirty or thirty-five miles per hour."

"It'd take them about a half hour to drive between Tideswell and Upper Kingsleigh," I said.

"Which'd make anyone's absence at least an hour and a half, counting committing the murder."

"Ninety minutes is more than enough time to be missed if the rest of the group wasn't in on the plan." Graham leaned back in his chair and stretched. "So it doesn't matter if the driver swears on a stack of bibles that they were together the whole time."

"Not really, sir."

Graham nodded, looking slightly defeated. "Well, it had to be checked. Thanks, Salt."

"I'm sorry it fizzled out, sir." Mark looked genuinely apologetic he hadn't been able to hand us a killer. He closed his notebook and wandered back to his computer, leaving me with the impression that he could be a decent guy when he wasn't trying to impress me.

"It seems like we're back to the motive I was considering a minute ago, sir, if you've time to hear it.

"Of course, Taylor." He settled back in his chair again. "You were talking about tourism. In my opinion, the foremost tourist enticer is Arthur. Are you saying he killed Steve?" A note of disbelief rose in his voice. "Motive, Taylor. Why? He didn't even know the man."

"Not Arthur, sir. He's involved in tourism, yes. So are Byron, Mason Conway, and Evan. They all have a lot to lose if tourists sidestep this village."

Mark, I noticed, took the change he got from Byrd and left the room. The door hadn't closed completely and his loud laugh echoed in the pub's entryway. He was busy flattering Paula, one of Evan's staff. Either he got a quick 'yes' or was just passing the time of day for once, for his voice faded as he left the building. I saw him pause just outside the front door and consult his watch. Calculating how much time he'd have to kill before his date, or seeing if he could rig up Surprise Number Five before I finished up with Graham? I grabbed the bank statement, crumbling it in my hand.

"And there are others," I said, "indirectly affected, whose livelihood would be threatened by the loss of tourists."

"Ramona, by marrying Arthur, would have had her fortune linked to his. And Uncle Gilbert, who clings to Arthur's wallet tighter than any barnacle ever did to a ship."

"Arthur admitted he needs the B and B

business to keep his head and hall above water. Byron also needs the B and B, for as Arthur's fortunes go, so do Byron's."

"Mason Conway has the gift shop, which depends completely on tourism."

"And Evan, though not totally dependent on the tourists, certainly gets a strong percent of his yearly income from them."

"Six people whose lives hang on the whims of tourists." Graham stared at the names he had scribbled down. "But why kill a tourist? We just agreed these six need tourists."

"They do. And Steve's murder is coincidentally connected to tourism."

"Guy Fawkes Day, yes, since he was dressed as the Guy. So who among this list committed the murder? And is it linked to Liam's unconventional entertainment that, unfortunately, has stirred up pros and cons about this very same tourism topic?" He asked it as one colleague to another. There was no mockery in his voice, as Mark would have done, taunting me to explain, to lay open my heart and then shred it with laughter and ridicule. Graham wanted to know my reasoning, to see if I had thought logically and applied the clues and facts of the case to my choice. He was writing something opposite one name on the list. Probably writing down his own deduction, I thought, for he finally raised his head and looked at me, ready for me to continue, as student looking at teacher.

"As much as the rock group has stirred up controversy, I don't believe it has a thing to do with the murder."

"Go on."

"It's Byron." I had said it louder and more forcefully than I intended. There had been no derisive laugh, no mocking rhyme.

Graham angled his head, looking interested in my logic, and waited patiently for more, knowing I would explain.

"Yes, sir. Arthur told us during our first interview Sunday evening that Byron had been near to bankruptcy years ago."

"His business had failed," Graham recalled. "And Arthur was extolling Byron's virtue in repaying his friends who had loaned him the business money."

I nodded and smoothed out the wrinkled bank statement. "This confirms it. Derek was probably paying Byron the dole money for those fifteen years, since there's no sign of it in the bank account. But after that, the Halfords suddenly become richer by £300 each year."

"Byron had repaid everyone and, being the virtuous fellow Arthur insists he is, refused anymore of Derek's dole money. It fits." He chewed on a pencil, waiting to see if I had pieced together the rest of the scenario.

"So, if Byron's need for money is legitimate and verifiable, which it is, we turn to a different angle. If Steve wasn't killed for *himself*—"

"We'd be daft to say he was. No one except the Halfords and the American knew him. And we've eliminated them."

"Then perhaps he was killed, not so much as a symbol proper, but as *result* of a symbol. As a result of loving that symbol and depending on it to bring guests to Arthur's B and B so he could be assured of employment."

Graham was drawing the effigy along a margin of the notebook page, rendering a remarkably lifelike face. He decorated Steve's shirt in the stripes of the Union Jack flag. "This whole weekend was peppered in symbolism, Taylor. The Guy itself, Derek with the symbolic crutches at the dole—" He threw down his pencil. "So what's the motive, if you're going along with this reasoning?"

"I was on bonfire duty Sunday," I reminded him. "Early afternoon Byron, with considerable pride, was explaining the history of Guy Fawkes to the Americans, who, I'm sad to say, didn't quite take it seriously. Steve was the worst of the lot. Byron sounded offended. He might've fought with him later that day. As we worked out earlier, sir, the bruising on the jaw indicates Byron probably KO'd Steve with his fist. Once on the ground, he kicked him. He doesn't know his strength, if you remember him kicking the chair in the pub. Anyway, if Steve had merely stumbled, there would be more general bruising, as on hip, knee, and palm. All places where he'd break his fall. But the concentrated area of bruises, plus the cracked ribs, led me to conclude he was assaulted as he lay on the ground. Byron probably then hit him with a stone or log. There were a lot of nice-sized pieces of wood about. One correctly-placed hit..." I shut my eyes, sickened by the image of Byron, overcome with anger, striking out in a moment of patriotism, pushing Steve, perhaps a little too hard, picking up a stone, not meaning to kill...

Graham was staring at me when I opened my eyes. His voice was soft, as though not wanting to frighten me. "Some people have more homeland love than others, I agree."

"There's also one other bit of evidence, sir. The hoisting itself. Normally Ramona raises the effigy, but her son hanged it early so they could use it in their act."

Graham nodded. "Byron lucked out. If it'd been the usual hoisting, Ramona would've discovered immediately the difference in weight between a straw effigy and a man."

"But he had an ace up his sleeve. The last time I spoke with Ramona she told me she wasn't convinced she should've asked Arthur if Liam's group could perform. She had second thoughts about disrupting the tradition. But Byron sided with her and talked Arthur into it, stating it might be a good thing for tourism. When Arthur consented, Byron knew no one would raise the dummy and discover the weight discrepancy. He was safe."

"So even if the effigy switch was discovered early, Byron could claim innocence. Who, me? Liam and Josh were last seen hanging the Guy... What a nasty piece of work Byron is, trying to entrap two innocent lads." He gazed out the window, in the direction of the fire circle. "Do you have any ideas why he dressed Steve as the Guy instead of leaving him in his own clothes?"

I nodded, proud he wanted me to think it through. "That threw me for quite a while. Byron probably viewed Steve as a sort of defiler, an uncouth, ignorant bloke who didn't even try to see another point of view, who ridiculed the other fellow's beliefs. For someone like Byron, who loved the village and was struggling out of debt, the Guy was the perfect symbol of a traitor, a fitting shroud for such a despoiler."

Graham sat, studying my face. There was no hint of mirth or ridicule or puzzlement in his eyes. I wondered what he was thinking, what he might say. We had no proof of Byron's part in this, other than the conflicting weight of effigy and corpse. But it was common sense to anyone's logic. And it certainly made sense to clothe the object of Byron's anger in that handy shroud. Graham finally leaned forward, put his hand on mine, and squeezed it. He spoke in an even, warm voice. "Well, Taylor, it all fits, the motive and opportunity. Byron knew everyone's time table and jobs. And he would lose just as much as Arthur would if the B and B guests stop coming."

"I don't think he thought of that at the time. I think it was a crime of passion originally. He just struck out at Steve in anger for ridiculing the ceremony."

"Remember, remember..." Graham began, then let his voice die away as though he was remembering something dim and past and painful. "You've done a first-class job with Steve, Taylor. What are your views on Ramona?"

I dismissed the possibility of an amorous Gilbert. Even if he had come for a fling and been thwarted, he wouldn't have come prepared for murder. Arthur didn't make sense, for he was engaged to her. And a 'Sorry, old girl' would be a more sensible way to break the engagement, if he had wished it, than murder. And Talbot, though the rope fiber and ropes tying the twig bundles in her yard were the same, anyone could have cut a piece from the rope. I bent my head, massaging the back of my neck. I was tired of thinking about the two murders and about my own dilemma. I wanted a good night's sleep and a holiday in Jamaica. "I really haven't thought that far, sir."

"Yes, you have, Taylor. You're just not using your head. Mind if I give you a hint? The body wasn't as we're used to seeing it." He folded his arms, leaned against the back of his chair, and waited for me to continue the reasoning.

I could imagine the scenario at Ramona's. A dark night that kept folks inside. The man with the limp body in his arms placing it on the ground, then coming back much later to shift it, placing something beneath it. My voice was barely audible as I said, "Ramona's sprained wrist. She wore no sling. She had been ready for bed."

"Which suggests…what?"

"If she was dressed for bed, or even *in* bed, she wouldn't open the door to a stranger. It had to be someone she's comfortable with."

"And?"

"And we know that she was pretty helpless, that Arthur or Byron brought her meals, and looked in on her."

"Bingo! We have our player and a logical house access."

"Good so far?"

"First rate, Taylor. What else?"

"As Arthur's secretary, Byron knew days earlier that Liam and his group would have the Guy up before Bonfire Night. He could switch Steve's body for the effigy, and then hoist it up again just like it was never altered. He was safe, innocent. After all, Liam and his group were the logical suspects because they had raised the dummy. They admitted it and everyone knew it. Ramona's faint and subsequent wrist injury were just coincidental." I took a breath, waiting for Graham's verdict on my reasoning.

"But if it makes no difference when the effigy is hoisted, why does Byron have to kill Ramona?"

"Ramona must have known about the '79 accident. Of course she did! In the pub, when she and Byron were talking. We didn't catch much, but she said at the end something about 'your secrets' being safe. It could be singular 'your,' but I don't think so. Not when, in the same breath, she wished him and Derek—"

"—a good evening," Graham finished, his voice taking on a hard edge. "She knew about their role reversals from the car accident. It's the only reason that makes sense. But Byron, like most amateur killers, got scared."

"He probably thought he couldn't trust her in light of Steve's murder investigation and all the questioning, though I agree that if she hadn't said anything in all this time she was probably good to retain her silence. Still, murderers get scared."

Graham added a crutch to his effigy sketch. "It's easy to let loose a bit of information you intend to keep secret, especially if you're nervous. If Byron was afraid she'd say something, he very easily would've killed her."

"He has his own quarters at Arthur's. He could slip out with no difficulty. He'd stick to the edge of the woods. It's unlikely anyone would see him at midnight, especially in the storm. Arthur, the only one to ask embarrassing questions, had just returned from dinner and was bunked down for the rest of the night."

"All the little birds to their nests." Graham had wandered to the window during my speech. We had been asking questions and dealing with possible motives and suspects for hours, unaware that morning had slipped into afternoon, impervious to the waning of precious autumnal daylight.

Graham stood looking out the eastern window, staring at the saffron-tinted light of late afternoon, stretching his chair-weary muscles. I bet he could sit by the hour and watch the changing light. He loved the late afternoon, the early evening when the growing darkness creeps into sunlight-splashed regions. At the light-flecked fringes of the fire area, giant, bare arms of the oak stretched out, canopying the burnt wood beneath it, scratching at the lilac-hued clouds above. Graham's voice came slowly, as though drugged from sleep. "Ever notice how dark it is in these villages with no street lights, Taylor? Dark as the grave." He turned from the window—reluctantly, I thought—and looked straight through me. His eyes were vacant, as if he saw something other than the pub room.

He'd rather be out there, I mused, wondering what captured his attention, what private world held him. Was it his broken engagement, some ministerial tie or past trouble, boyhood memory? I wished he would tell me, include me in his world, let me hold him. He seemed so alone, so vulnerable, so melancholy. Twilight does something to him, pulls at his soul or memory. Perhaps it's the link with something ancestral to all of us, of Homo sapiens huddled protectively around the midnight fire. Or something whispering to him of holy things.

I focused on his face, and tried like so many other times, to envision Graham in clerical garb. I was never happy with the image. Not that he wouldn't have lent a sympathetic ear, but there had to have been more restraints in the church—even if it had been the more radical Methodist religion—than he'd been subjected to with the Force. And for the impatient, incautious Graham, the dogma and rules of religion must have been frustrating.

"Byron knew she was taking Mogadon." I was talking again to Graham's back. He didn't turn around but I continued. "She might've been groggy enough not to put up much resistance."

I closed my eyes. Sunday evening's scene burst into my mind. I was back at the village green. Evening spread across the sky. A cloud momentarily masked the moon. From somewhere in the darkness, a match scraped against something rough. The smell of sulfur filtered downwind, and a small blue and ochre flame flared in the blackness. A stronger scent of kerosene as the batting ignited, and the vicar's face leapt out of the dark, bathed in crimson, gold and yellow. He lit the torch and handed it to Byron, who smiled at Ramona and handed her the torch when she was at eye level with Steve. I shuddered, opening my eyes to find Graham gazing at me, back to being all cop and concerned that something was wrong with someone else. I smiled weakly.

"Byron and the effigy. It was so easy. The woods were close by. He could drag Steve out of sight, redress him there, then easily pull him out when no one was looking."

Graham gave me a final appraising look. "If anyone happened to see him, he could say he came upon Steve and had stopped to render help. It wouldn't matter if Steve were dressed, half-dressed, or nude. It's his word against anyone else's."

"It was dark, probably near teatime." I trembled, imagining the clothing switch that had happened a hundred yards in front of me that late afternoon. Like a damned, incompetent first-day constable on the job, I had let him get away with staging the murder.

"Anger is a strong force in murder, Taylor. Nearly as powerful and prevalent as love and lust."

I was afraid to respond, afraid my voice might betray my burgeoning feelings. Instead, I asked about the knife.

"Byron, you don't need reminding, is virtuous. On the way from delivering meals to Ramona, he stopped in to console Kris. And while he was fixing her a cup of tea perhaps, he got the idea and the implement. The box of goodies Steve brought with him from Kris's mother was sitting out."

"The opal ring and her dad's scout knife. It looks about that vintage."

The telephone rang as Graham uttered a complimentary remark about my reasoning. I let it pass, assuming I would soon hear an uncomplimentary remark about letting Byron redress Steve.

Graham picked up his mobile, listened for a minute or so, made vague, responsive sounds, then said, "Meet us there, will you? I'll phone you," and rang off. As he punched in the number, he said, "That was Tom Oldendorf. He said— Oh, Vicar." During Lyle's response, Graham mouthed 'I'll tell you in a minute' to me, then spoke a few sparse sentences to the vicar before ending the conversation. He angled his body so he could look around the room. Byrd was still there, lingering over a report. "Byrd, do you have a minute?"

"Yes, sir." He stood up.

Graham consulted his watch. "Byrd, I hate to ask, but would you mind running back to Buxton for a search warrant?" He jotted down the particulars, handed the note to the constable, then looked up as Mark entered the room. He held out a sheet of paper as he came over.

"Sir, the report's in from the DNA test that you rushed through."

I frowned, and Graham explained that he'd requested an overnight analysis of Byron's saliva on the beer mug Mark had purloined the previous evening.

"Here it is." On handing Graham the report, he said, "It's a match to the red hair on the shirt Steve was wearing, the Guy clothing, I mean."

"And he wore a jacket that was buttoned up," Graham reiterated.

"Yes, sir, so it couldn't have blown onto him outside. It'd have to come from the owner of the shirt or from close contact with someone."

"Bingo!"

25

Hours later, our prime suspect looked vaguely uneasy and surprised at seeing us at his door, but he welcomed us inside. A batch of posters, freshly printed in vibrant graphics, leaned against a wall opposite the doorway. A mockup of a brochure, along with architectural sketches for display cases and room arrangements lay scattered across his desk. Paints, brushes and mat board leaned against a battered easel.

An electric teakettle whistled madly on the counter, and Byron asked if we would like something. "I was just going to have a cuppa." He poured the water into the teapot. "Sure I can't get you anything? Beer?"

Graham's sigh was just discernable above Byron's chatter. His jaw muscle tensed, for the scar shone prominently against his skin. He wants to get on with the arrest, not play at Suzy Homemaker.

As though sensing Graham's impatience, Byron said, his voice faltering slightly, "I guess that's the wrong thing to suggest. This has to be an official visit. Forgive the mess." He blushed, obviously embarrassed by the paper and books stacked around the room. "You caught me behind my chores. I've got a little project on. We want to develop a visitor's center." He saw me staring at an unwashed mug, the interior of which was ringed with tealeaves, a section of the exterior rim stained by a lipstick mark. Gesturing toward the table, he asked if we'd like to have a seat.

Graham shook his head, saying we'd only be a minute or so. He let Byron finish his tea making, then asked where he had been Tuesday night.

The spoon rattled suddenly against the sides of the cup. He gently removed it, set it on the countertop, took a sip of too-hot tea, and tried to smile. It was forced, the kind that is used in awkward situations and accompanied by a quick change in subject. This time Byron could not change the subject. He coughed. "Tuesday night? Why, either here or in the office. I'd been to Ramona's to deliver lunch, and Arthur went down for dinner. Even if she could fair for herself, what with Steve's—" He flinched at the subject and stared at his cup. "I just sat around, read and listened to music. Why? Something to do with Ramona?" Graham nodded and Byron gushed on. "Well, you would ask, wouldn't you, seeing as how it was probably someone in the village. I suppose you want to know if I saw anything. I can't say I did. The Manor's too far away to see anything there. I'm sorry I can't help." He waited, probably hoping we'd gathered what we wanted and would leave.

We didn't. Instead, Graham delivered the murder theory. The hot tea splashed onto the tabletop as Byron jerked sideways. He stood open-mouthed, his eyes bulging, his cheeks flooding with color. "You can't mean it!"

Graham issued the usual warning. "You do not have to say anything—"

"Nice to know the individual has some rights left to him in this country."

"You do not have to say anything." Graham repeated it, as though forcing Byron to listen.

Byron's eyes fixed on Graham's face, his fingertips attempting to dig into the cup. "You're damned right I don't. And if you think I'm going to say anything without my solicitor—"

"—but it may harm your defense," Graham continued, rolling over Byron's bluster, "if you do not mention now something which you later rely on in court."

"Not bloody likely to, am I?" Byron's anger was stronger than his discretion. "You've got it all thought out—the howdunit, the wheredunit, the whendunit. It's obvious, you two are so adept at this fictionalization of my completely innocent actions. You should've spent your time watching 'Police Action Live' to see how reputable, responsible coppers work, instead of slandering us innocent chaps."

"Anything you do say," Graham went on, "may be given in evidence."

"Are you two wired, then?" Byron gestured with his free hand toward Graham's jacket. "Your cronies back at the station, or perhaps parked outside the gate, listening to all this over a mic, jotting it all down? Is that how you use my words in evidence against me? Hold on!" He snapped his fingers as though the truth exploded before his eyes. "You have a tape recorder in your pocket or secreted inside your pen, or fashioned to look like a warrant card. Your lab boys are so ingenious these days. Bloody marvelous!" He laughed, his voice full of irony and resignation at his situation.

"You have a right to legal advice, should you choose," Graham added, although it was unnecessary. "I suggest you send for him, Mr. MacKinnon. Your situation is very grave. This really is not a laughing matter. I'm confident we have a water-tight case against you."

The laughter died abruptly. His eyes widened. "Well, you would say that. It's all part of the plan to scare me into confessing and make me think things will go easier if I own up. It just won't go, lads. So, unless the heavy gang is lingering about and ready to beat a confession out of me, I'll take my chances with the judge. Unless you've already got to him and bribed—"

"You're probably safe with a trial, Mr. MacKinnon." Graham's words rose sharp in his anger. "Though I can't guarantee it. I couldn't afford much of a bribe. Just the minimum acceptable."

Byron's gaze shifted between Graham and me, as though judging which of us would be the more sympathetic. He focused on me. "You can't really think I killed that American and Ramona."

"I'm sorry," I replied, "but we do."

"We don't rank this as fun and games." Graham's voice filled with the hardness that claimed him when about to make an arrest.

Byron fumbled for the back of a chair. A laugh, tinted with the rudiments of hysteria, burst from his throat.

I handed him the cup of tea. "Perhaps you'd feel better, sir, if you had a sip of this. Do you need to sit down?" I pulled out the chair nearest to him, offering him the physical support and emotional breath-catching he needed.

Murmuring something that might have been 'no,' Byron ignored both offers. He turned his gaze from my outstretched hand to Graham's eyes. The hardness that lay in his voice also lay behind his unwavering look. Byron swept a shaky hand across his lips, letting his teeth nibble slowly at his knuckles before responding. "You haven't any proof. You can't have."

"Why can't we?" My lower, quieter voice contrasted greatly with Byron's rising pitch. I turned to Graham. "Do you know of any reason why we can't have any proof, sir?"

"I can't come up with any, no."

Having recovered from his shock, he delivered his first defense. "What's my motive for these murders?" Byron said. "Isn't that a usual consideration? My motive is damned thin if not nonexistent. The man was a stranger. I didn't even know he would be here. He arrived with Tom Oldendorf. They booked two separate rooms. And you're insisting I planned this whole thing and killed him? This is a bit thick, Graham. You're clutching at straws."

"Strange you should mention straw." Graham pulled the plastic-bagged scout knife from his pocket and held it in front of Byron. "This whole case wallows in straw, you might say. Have you seen this before?"

Byron barely glanced at the knife before replying smugly, "Yes. In the corpse."

Carefully laying the knife on the table, Graham asked if Byron was certain he hadn't seen it elsewhere, prior to the murder, and urged him to look at it again. The rivets, dotting the wooden handle like eyes in a potato, stared at him. Blood had dried to a brownish smear and imprinted the brass section separating the blade proper from the handle. The corroded release mechanism faced Byron as though silently urging him to close the blade and obliterate the revolting spectacle.

Shaking his head, Byron denied he'd seen it

in any other setting. Once he glanced at it, however, it mysteriously held his gaze.

"Murder motives take many forms, Mr. MacKinnon. It can be triggered by many things, too. In your instance," Graham said, "the rock music performance threatened to ridicule the tradition that you loved, for one thing. Add to that Steve's rude scoffing about the Guy. Perhaps that was the last straw in a stressful week. National pride can be a powerful motivation, especially when foreigners do the ridiculing." He paused, studying Byron's face, the hand still crammed into his pocket.

Byron lifted his head and returned Graham's gaze. The initial fright was gone; his voice was steady when he spoke. "I don't know what you're talking about."

Graham reached for the folded piece of paper. He held it out to Byron. "This is a search warrant, Mr. MacKinnon. If you read it, you will see it gives me full authority to search your rooms and remove just this sort of thing." He gestured toward the can of turpentine sitting on the floor beneath the easel. He tapped lightly on the warrant. "Do you want to change your story about Tuesday night?"

Though visibly shaken, Byron managed to keep his voice calm. He sniffed, drawing in his upper lip as though he were smelling something rotten. "You're arresting me because I've got turpentine? I bet most houses in Upper Kingsleigh have it. I use it to clean my paintbrushes, or haven't you noticed? I'm in the middle of a project. And anyway, I was home, like I said. All night. You think I'd go out in that hell of a storm?"

I excused myself and exited the office area by the front door. A few moments later, I reentered. Byron's fingers gripped the edge of the countertop when Tom Oldendorf came into the room.

Tom glanced at Byron, then took a deep breath as Graham asked him to relay what he had seen Tuesday around midnight.

Tom began haltingly but gathered confidence the more he went on. "I saw a man at Ramona's house a little after eleven-thirty."

He took another breath, as though to finish in a rush of facts, when Byron's tirade stopped him, "You saw a man at Ramona's. Big bloody deal. I suppose I'm that man. That's why you're here, right? How could you see any man, how could you identify me as this man if it was as late as you say? Ramona doesn't have a driveway lamp. How you going to beat that, Inspector?" Byron turned to Graham, his eyes enlarged by his anger.

Graham quickly asked Tom to continue. "I was standing on the main road. It was just after eleven. I had a flashlight with me, but I'd turned it off because I wanted absolute darkness for my photos. I do nature photography," he explained to Byron. "That's why I chose that spot. I'd driven down, parked in the pub's lot, then walked about the village for a bit, glancing at the sky, noting where the lightning flashes were. I liked the looks of the road Ramona lives on. It's quite dark, since it has no streetlights or driveway lights. I walked down the lane, then stopped opposite her driveway. That's next to the Halfords'." He glanced at me. "They have that old tree in their front yard. I thought it'd make a great photo if I could get the bare branches of the tree with the lightning flash behind it.

"So I waited there in the dark, my camera set up on the tripod. I'm a very patient man." He grinned slightly, glancing apologetically at Graham, who remained straight-faced. "You have to be patient if you do nature photography. Anyway, I saw the lights go on and off twice in Ramona's house. Ordinarily I wouldn't think a thing of a light going on or off, but twice in rapid succession? That sort of drew my attention. I looked to see what was going on. I thought maybe something had happened and someone was signaling. When the lights went out for the last time I saw a man slip out of the front door and practically run up the road."

"And if I'm that man," Byron said, "how come I didn't see you?"

"I was farther down the road, angled toward the tree but past her front door."

Byron grumbled something about this sounding rehearsed and everyone but he having a ready-made answer.

Graham nodded for Tom to continue. "Well, I got my lightning flash photo. Two of them, in fact. By that time, it was just beginning to rain, so I scrambled back to my car. I came back to my room around midnight." He waited, watching Graham, who still remained rooted near the table.

Byron broke the silence, his voice high and his words rapid. "You saw someone slip out of Ramona's house. That doesn't prove it was me. It could have been Liam. He's staying with her." He fumbled for another defense. "It doesn't mean a thing. Dark shapes. Jesus Christ! You've all met to concoct this, because you can't think of anyone else to pin it on. If I'd suspected what was going on, I'd have invented some ironclad alibi. Else why am I the only one—"

This time my movement to the door and signal to someone outside stopped him. The door swung open and Lyle walked in.

26

Lyle began in his usual haphazard way, saying he hoped he wasn't inconveniencing anyone and apologizing for his duty as he phrased it, but eventually told of his errand of mercy Tuesday evening. "Arthur rang me up close to eleven-thirty. He was worried about Gilbert. The man had been drinking all day, evidently, and was now hallucinating. You know how he gets."

I mumbled that I did indeed, even after so short an acquaintance with the man.

Lyle grimaced, as though reliving the scene. "He was screaming that he saw the devil and was scared to death of going to hell. He kept calling for a vicar to save him. So Arthur phoned me up. It was the only way to calm the dear man." Lyle's fingers stroked the edge of his jacket as he paused in thought. "I went, had a talk with Gilbert to make him understand God's love and that he should forsake his drinking. I finally got him calmed down a few minutes before midnight. As I was leaving the manor, I saw Byron."

"How'd you see me?" Byron cocked his head forward as if to catch every word.

"By the light from the front door," Lyle said. "When I opened it, the light fell across the yard. I saw you just entering the door to your suite here."

"So." Byron's eyes darted from Lyle, who was looking very uncomfortable, to Graham, who was looking quite comfortable. He nearly bit off his words in his anger. "This is as inane as the first piece of fiction! So you saw me enter the Manor. That doesn't prove a thing. I enter it each day. Most people do enter their homes. That doesn't make me a killer."

"No, it doesn't," Graham said, slowly. "However..." He waited for what seemed minutes. In the quiet I could hear Byron's labored breathing, the call of a cat outside and the tap of Graham's fingers on the tabletop. I knew it was a waiting game to test Byron's nerves, but it was tensing my already-taut emotions. As I was about to motion to Graham he said, "By your own admission, Mr. MacKinnon, you have stated before Sergeant Taylor and me that you were home all night. We have this witness, however, who will place you at the crime scene at the exact time. We have another witness who saw you arrive home. And before you can flip us off, we also have something else that will prove definitely that you murdered Steve Pedersen."

He stepped back slightly, as though giving me the floor. He walked over to the clothes dryer. Folding his arms, he leaned against it. When I cleared my throat, Byron jerked his head back to me. His eyes were wide and wild looking, like a trapped rabbit.

"This year," I said, "Liam came along and wanted his group to play for Bonfire Night. You persuaded Ramona to talk to Arthur, who gave his consent. You learned that the Guy would be hanging for the ceremony, that there was no need for anyone to raise it. You couldn't let the opportunity slip by. It was the perfect alibi, you felt. You killed Steve Pedersen and dressed him as the effigy and then hoisted him up again."

The room turned deathly quiet. The teakettle, shiny and squatting on the counter, had hushed. On the desk, the electric clock whirred noisily in preparation for the hour, then sank back into anonymity. Outside, the tomcat had relinquished his serenade, seeking more fruitful pastures elsewhere. The wind, underscoring Byron's anger only minutes before, now merely sighed, as if exhausted or surrendering to the futility of denial.

Byron opened his mouth but I continued with our reasoning. "The shirt, jacket and trousers belonged to Arthur. Why are we so fixated on the clothes? A red hair on the shirt puzzled us, for Steve Pedersen didn't have red hair. Neither do most of the villagers, except Liam VanDyke and you." I paused, letting the significance of the hair declare itself. "The hair DNA matches your DNA."

He found his voice then, squawking that he never gave a sample.

"But you discarded it last night in the pub."

"In the pub…"

"On your beer glass. You shoved it aside, and told Evan you were finished with it. The lab extracted your DNA from the mouth of the glass and, as I said, it matches your hair. How did your hair get on the shirt Steve wore? No, it couldn't have blown onto him. It was lodged *underneath* the jacket. It came from you when you dressed his body."

I looked at the group. Lyle was fidgeting with his collar, running a finger along the inside of the fabric, as though the subject was too vivid or recent for his comfort. Tom eyed the posters, his artistic eye perhaps evaluating the placement of graphics and text. Byron sponged his forehead with his hand, then blotted it on his jeans. Graham, I was amused to see, leaned against the clothes dryer. His long legs were crossed at the ankles, his arms folded across his chest, as though he had all the time in the world. He looked at Byron, urging him to speak.

"I didn't mean to kill him." Byron spoke with sudden resignation, his eyes on me. He sighed, knowing his own cleverness had trapped him. When he spoke again, it was nearly *sotto voce* and with a gentleness in contrast to his earlier violent outbursts. "It was an accident. I was damned angry with him, I admit. Mocking our national symbol and our history. But I only meant to push him. I swear that's all! He came back later to check the lanterns and torch for firecrackers."

"That must've been when I was walking around and was stopped by that French couple to answer questions," I muttered, my stomach tightening. If I had returned minutes earlier, perhaps... But Graham, I saw, was not reproachful when he glanced at me. What had he said earlier, about understanding that I had had to walk about? He did not hold me responsible, even now as Byron was relating the fight timetable.

"He got into it with me then, and I was angry. I pushed him. He pushed back, then he threw a punch. Something snapped in both of us. He started swinging his fists like all hell had broken loose. I couldn't shake him and so I pushed him again, but he came back at me like he was tormented. I picked up a large, heavy limb." He lowered his head, wiping his eyes. "I ought to have left him there. I know that now. I'd walked away after the fight but I kept thinking of him, so I went back a bit later. No one had found him. He was still sprawled on the ground, his arms and legs all at different angles. I dragged him into the woods and clothed him as the Guy, using its clothes. I guess that's when my hair got on him. I didn't notice. Anyway, I heard a couple of kids run around the fire circle so I squatted in the woods till they'd gone, then dragged him out and strung him up. No one'd seen me. I was mad as hell at the time, but now..." He looked at me, pleading with his eyes for my understanding.

I shook my head very slowly, envisioning the scene. Steve must have had a war flashback, if he fought Byron so savagely. As if realizing I wanted proof, Byron rolled up his sleeve and showed me the bruises. Not that it proved the American had done it, but I believed him.

"I killed Ramona, too. That was planned. I admit that. I'm sorry, especially for Liam. But I had to. You see, I was afraid she'd tell about the car accident, about how I took money from Derek to pay off my earlier business debt. I owed them and didn't want to see them suffer bankruptcy due to my own failure. I loved Kris. but I had to give her up. What is two people's happiness when compared to all my friends' financial futures?"

"And after you paid back your friends," I said, "you let Derek keep his dole money."

Byron lowered his head. A great shudder claimed his body and he grabbed Lyle's hand as though any contact with God would steady him. "I don't say it was a gallant gesture in taking the dole money and abandoning Kris, but I had to choose between that and my friends. Derek's turned out to be the best friend I ever had."

"But why kill Ramona? Even if you were

nervous, as you say, it has been years since this all happened. Why would you fear she'd talk now?"

"She told her husband and Mum years ago. The mother lives in Glasgow now, but when someone's that talkative, and there are police about asking questions... Well, I couldn't take the chance, could I? I couldn't risk it. I was scared you'd interview the mother, and she might remember it and talk. Hell, Ramona might talk if she got scared. Her tongue was such an undisciplined thing."

I understood his anger and fear. There's a desperation that claims those who kill, an imagination that hears footsteps and gossip. The surest way to silence both is to eliminate the sources. I heard Byron's voice and wondered what I had missed.

"I hadn't planned to kill Ramona until Tuesday evening. I couldn't chance she'd say something about the accident in 1979. She'd been blackmailing me before this...oh, nothing huge. Like £25 or £50 a week. Whatever amount she seemed to need or want that day. It'd never bothered me much. Well, yes, it bothered me, but I thought it small enough to pay her and count myself lucky." He took a breath, as if reliving his emotions. "But in the summer she increased the amount. I hadn't the money for that kind of payment, at least not if she kept up her demands, which I assumed she would. I was angry at first, figuring I'd more than compensated for the incident. But then I got bloody well mad. What right had she to keep bleeding me like this? Especially with her upcoming marriage? I'd not hurt her. She wasn't even involved in the car crash." His gaze met mine, and his eyes seemed to be begging me to understand. He looked away, and lowered his head slightly. "I know Arthur's not filthy rich, but he's better off than I am. And Ramona wouldn't have had to worry about money. The quid she was getting from me would seem like pocket change in comparison to what she'd get her hands on through Arthur. I couldn't go on paying her. She'd kept quiet about the accident for this long, but with her increased demands and her taunting... And then she began insinuating that she'd been quiet long enough, that her conscience was bothering her, that it wasn't right that I shouldn't pay for what I'd done." His mouth twitched, as though the next words were difficult to say. "I was frightened she'd talk. She said she would if I was late with my payments. I...I couldn't endure it anymore."

I was tempted to say that I understood, but I didn't interrupt his explanation. Byron cleared his throat, as though steadying himself for an interrogation, and continued.

"I'd stood outside her place for a long time. Nearly an hour and a half. Arthur had been there for dinner, and he didn't leave until eleven. I waited for a few minutes, making certain he wouldn't return to reclaim some forgotten item, and wondering if Liam would return. When he didn't, I figured he was out with his mates for the evening, so I banged on her door. I had the turpentine all ready for her, you see. Poured a bit onto a cloth when I saw the light go on. She was surprised to see me. I grabbed her arm, pulled her outside, and—

"I carried her to the middle of the garden. I turned off the light when I went inside her house. I was afraid someone would see me. Then I had an idea about making it look like burglary, so I turned on the lights again. But when I realized the police always see through that, I changed my mind and turned them off." He glanced at

Graham, silently acknowledging the Force's talent. "I came back later. Not for the turpentine jar, because I figured it was safe there. I'd worn gloves, so there were no fingerprints to connect me with it. It would look like she could've dropped it there, for all anyone would know. But I did come back much later. When I first returned here, after killing her, it was raining."

"That was when Lyle saw you," Graham said.

Byron nodded. "I didn't know anyone was out. It was then that I got the idea of implicating Talbot with a fragment of rope. Everyone knew he'd done that job of work for Ramona. He made no secret that he always had rope. I thought it rather a brilliant idea. But I waited for an hour or so before returning to her place. It took a lot longer than I thought, setting up that fiber bit. Several times while I was sawing away at that damned rope I'd hear a dog bark or a noise in the woods. I kept glancing back at her, half expecting her to get up. I thought I'd never get out of there. Did you ever trying cutting a thick rope with a dull knife blade in the dark?"

"You got the knife from the Halfords, hoping to implicate them?" I asked.

"Yes, from Kris and Derek, but I didn't think they'd be suspects. The knife was awfully old."

"And awfully common," Graham said.

I envisioned the strange scene—a corpse lying on the cold ground, a stormy sky with occasional bursts of ominous thunder and lightning, a desperate man cutting a rope in near pitch blackness, his hands encased in clumsy gloves, looking over his shoulder, perhaps, for the damning witness. And all the time that damning witness was out there in the dark, waiting to catch a flash of lightning, never realizing he was going to help catch a murderer.

"I knew you'd find the rope," Byron went on, automatically, hurriedly, as though he was afraid of running out of time. "I didn't realize you could tell she'd been moved, though. That was a mistake. I see that now. But I had to kill her." His voice slipped into a sort of whine, pleading for empathy. "She was like that, you know. She always has been. Teasing, so you don't really trust her or believe her. She said she wouldn't tell, but you know how things get out."

I nodded, my eyes fixed—as if by hypnosis—on Byron. I remembered Ramona's laugh at the pub, the way she teased Derek.

"I understand your action." Graham's voice was low and strained. "Even if I don't condone it, I understand. Now, Mr. MacKinnon..." Slowly, almost as though he was offended by everything that had been revealed, Graham laid his hand on Byron's shoulder.

Before Graham could take him outside, I said, "It was you, Mr. MacKinnon, who rigged those atrocities in my room, wasn't it?"

Graham looked at me in surprise.

"You wanted to frighten me into leaving the case because I had heard the episode with the two Americans Sunday at the bonfire. You were afraid I would remember your anger and deduce you killed Steve."

Byron nodded, turning toward me.

"Lyle mentioned that you take group photos of the guests here." I nodded toward the camera on the counter next to the sketches. "I also saw it when Mr. Graham and I questioned you the day you were talking to Talbot. It's an expensive model. You go in for all the gadgets, including telephoto lens."

"I was afraid to get too close to you, afraid it

would give me away if you saw me take your photo."

"Actually, sir, your career gave you away."

"Being secretary to Arthur?"

"No. Bookkeeper. You also keep Evan's books. You work in his office. Mr. Graham mentioned it Wednesday morning."

Graham was about to say something but I cut him off, not wanting his praise in public. I wanted to finish with Byron. "You have access in that office to all the pub's keys, Mr. MacKinnon. They're probably conveniently labeled and hanging on hooks. That's how you left the photos and the...other things in my room." My excitement ebbed somewhat and I needed to take a breath. "I admit I originally thought of two other people as possible perpetrators, but they really couldn't have been. I'm glad I didn't accuse either of them." I mentally made a note to be nice to Mark, now that I had cleared him of my suspicions. And Talbot, running a close second, had no room keys. When emptying waste bins in the pub, he had to knock on people's doors.

I got to put my mental note into practice that evening when we were packing up our equipment. Mark was unplugging his laptop but looked up as I approached. He eyed me with a hint of curiosity, but the smart aleck attitude was absent, even from his speech.

When I complimented him on nabbing Byron's glass in the pub, he thanked me and said there was nothing wrong with my detective skills. "I heard from Margo how you discovered who played those pranks on you. That was a grand job, just brilliant."

I smiled, muttering my thanks.

"If something like that ever happens

again—and I pray it doesn't—don't hesitate to ask for help, Brenna. That could've had a very different outcome."

"I don't think I really was in danger, Mark. It just unnerved me at the time."

He stared at me, suddenly very serious, and it was evident that he realized I hadn't wanted to ask for help, hadn't wanted to appear the scared, incompetent female among the lads.

He cleared his throat. "Well, you never know about people like that, Brenna." He held my gaze, but allowed the hint of a smile at the corners of his lips. Holding out his hand, he said, "Truce?"

"Truce." I grabbed his hand. His grip was warm and firm. He held my fingers for longer than I thought necessary but there was no mocking tone in his voice when he said I was a real asset to the team.

He resumed packing up and I wandered outside. The moon hovered on the eastern horizon and the air was chilly, but I still felt the warmth of Mark's handshake. I'd survived my trial. Maybe he wasn't a berk after all. At that moment he seemed like a potential friend, just an ordinary guy.

Jo A. Hiestand Books

Mysteries steeped in tea and tartan!

Available through Amazon.com,
barnesandnoble.com, Kobo, iBooks, overdrive,
and the author's website

A Staged Murder
Shrouded in Holly
Cold Revenge
Last Seen
Shadow in the Smoke
Brushed With Injustice
An Unfolding Trap
No Known Address
An Unwilling Suspect
Arrested Flight
Cider, Swords & Straw: Celebrating British
Customs

A sneak peak at the next Peak District mystery

Shrouded in Holly

I

I had never believed in ghosts. They seemed more the stuff of fiction and ancient castles than of churches. But as the massive door closed behind me with all the heaviness of a coffin lid settling into place, I considered there might be some basis for the stories after all.

It was the hinges that first startled me—great, metal things groaning into the stillness like an atmospheric prerequisite of a gothic novel. The disturbance echoed against cold stone and hard wood; it multiplied into a dozen voices that tumbled down the aisles or rolled up the tower steps, dying as they nudged a bell into song. A deep tone, soft as an angel's voice, sighed from the tower and cajoled sympathetic ripples from neighboring bells. In the ringing chamber below, their ropes swayed as if pulled by invisible hands, the sallies dancing ghost-like in the dark.

I could relegate these phantoms to their nether lands by flipping on the lights. But I wanted to experience it as it probably had happened. So I sank against the wooden slab, letting my eyes adjust to the gloom, letting my mind reason through my sensations.

Scents of pine, hot candle wax and wood polish floated over to me, and I breathed deeply of the fragrances that stirred a thousand Christmas memories—the pine tree decorated with gingerbread men and orange pomanders, the bayberry candles gleaming against frosted window panes, the tins of homemade chocolates and spiced tea, Uncle Ernie's after shave lotion that clung to me after his bear-hug greeting. Yet, just as quickly as the images rose before me, they dissolved. A window rattled and the candle flames cringed. An organ pipe droned with no mortal hand upon the keys. And a whisper—as though from a great distance—moaned somewhere beyond the pinprick of light. A sighing of wintry wind buffeting the windows, or a lamenting banshee?

I had no real desire to find out, to leave the relative security of the door, however cold it was, and cross the vast expanse of darkened floor. But a path of water droplets taunted me, cajoling me to follow them into the darkness. Remnants of an innocent visitor, or the reason I was there? I tapped the snow from my boots, and pulled on my paper shoe covers and latex gloves. Flicking on my torch, I stretched out my arm and felt my way forward as though blind or sleepwalking.

Even through my half-frozen boots I could feel the texture of the flagstone floor, the rough and smooth stones, the grade of the rocky slabs that had tilted during the centuries, asserting their individuality among a sea of apparent flatness. Patches of near-black near the nave altar spoke of centuries of worshiper's feet trafficking the area. Lighter stones shone dove-gray in the dimness, chiseled with ancient names and dates to commemorate or remember.

A rectangle of brass gleamed among the sober tones, repelling the surrounding stone, sanctifying this body-sized space. I detoured from my path and shone the light on it. The monumental brass depicted an armored knight. The wording, as were parts of the tablet's edging, showed slight wear from the thousands of feet that had walked across it. The knight, however, still stared distinct and unmarked into the future. Between the raised lettering above his head small drops of water had accumulated. I bent down to sniff them but could detect nothing odd. Snow from a recent visitor? If so, how fast had it melted in the mid-50 degree temperature of the chancel?

Clumps of melting snow lead me past great, white bulks of carved chests, gargoyles and alabaster statues that jumped out of the shadows. A sliver of gold flashed out as the torch discovered two gold candlesticks, then left them as I threaded my way between the low houselling benches and the white nave altar cloth, floating phantom-like in the gloom, the silvers, peacock and cornflower blues, reds and golds of the needlework mesmerizing. Wondering what it would look like at evensong, I snapped off the torch. The satin cloth shimmered like moonlit white sands; glass beads and gold sequins sparkled as if on fire. Its beauty was almost enough to lure me back to a church service.

But I wasn't there to worship. Shifting shadows thrown by the candlelight gestured toward the murkiest part of the church. On the far side of the wooden pulpit, a black bulk in the gloomy reaches of the chantry screen called to me. Snapping on the torch again, I walked over to the shape.

It revealed itself slowly, bits at a time, as though being pulled from the night—first the good, sturdy boots, then the black slacks still damp from snow, the dark jacket and finally a ghost-white hand. All part of the inert body lying facedown on the floor. All expected but the scattering of holly, a sprig of pine, and the glint of metal above its back. The knife seemed jammed into the flesh, for the victim's jacket nearly swallowed the knife blade. Yet, I kneeled beside it, reached for the left hand and felt for a pulse. There was nothing I could do. Had he, before joining his ancestors, been my whispering phantom, urging me to capture his killer? I gazed again at the knife blade, and waited in dead silence for Graham's arrival.

2

'Flashy' was not a word to describe Olive Lindbergh. She was younger than I had thought, on learning she was the wife of the vicar. Possibly in her early twenties, she was teenager slim with a baby-smooth complexion and short-cropped blonde hair nearly as light as the snow. Add to that teenager clothes: tight jeans, a baggy yellow sweatshirt with 'Yellow Submarine' stamped across the front, and gold ear cuffs. It all conveyed action and energy. But she seemed drained of both, now, for she trembled and looked as though she wished she were anywhere but here as she related her discovery of the corpse.

"I'd just finished with the holly, miss," Mrs. Lindbergh said, not knowing whether to look at me or her handiwork. Her voice quivered and her gaze shifted to the church door.

I, too, glanced at it, but I wanted Graham and the police team to pour through it, unlike Olive, who probably wished for escape. I, Detective-Sergeant Brenna Taylor, been first police officer on the scene, called from my warm office in Buxton for preliminary investigation in this snow-wrapped village in England's upland Derbyshire. Olive had been calm enough when I had met her half an hour ago. But now that the investigation appeared Official, complete with written statements, she was seized with nerves. I let her take a deep breath and smiled encouragingly.

"I like holly on the altar on St. Nicholas Day. Though there are some in this village that call it heathen to put Druid greenery there, so close to God. But Trueman explains that we've come to embrace other heathen symbols, and I don't see the church any worse off for the sprigs of holly, do you?"

We were inside St. Nicholas Church, a limestone edifice warding off sin and evil with all its stalwart enthusiasm of medieval gargoyles, buttresses and towers. In the half-darkness at the foot of the nave altar, the corpse remained mute, staring with sightless eyes at the ancient gold rood as though seeking divine explanation. Or help. The rood was flanked by two statues that gazed at the crucified Christ. We waited, busy with our thoughts, a tree branch scraping against a window uncommonly loud.

Silently, I agreed with her assessment. Besides, holly seemed made for Christmas—red berries and green foliage.

Perhaps needing to break the quiet. Olive added, "I brought it from home. I do it every year. I'm in charge of the hanging of the greens. Which sounds important, but only one other villager helps me."

"Committees of two usually accomplish more than larger groups." I smiled and glanced at the door again.

"We've a sexton, who sees to the main manual labor, but it's just us two for the other things, like changing altar cloths."

I nodded, recalling the church as I had seen it on my arrival.

A path had been shoveled from the lych gate to the church porch, yet even now nature was reclaiming this land, for snow continued to settle into the faint depressions scattered along the walkway. A red bow, starched from icy wind, stood crisply on the south door. A sprig of holly, already defeated by Nature's blast, sagged in the bow's knot. Below it, as though shaken by the force of the door's closing, several berries dotted the snow, blood-red drops on white.

"Anyway," Olive said, tugging her well-worn cardigan over her hips, "I got a good armful, then took up the basket with the boughs of yew, pine and boxwood, and came over to the church."

"You must've brought quite a lot."

She frowned and opened her mouth, but I added, "There's quite a lot of holly strewn over the victim's back. I just wondered how much you carried over, if there's any missing from another area of the church, for example."

She glanced around the sanctuary as though comparing what she saw with how she'd left it decorated. "Only the basket by the altar, miss. I'd filled that on my arrival, then got some more cuttings from home."

The basket held several berries and a broken leaf. "What's the meaning of the…holly and pine on the body? Has it something to do with St. Nicholas?"

"I don't think so." She looked like she wanted to say it was in the realms of police investigation, but instead said, "I was tying up the greenery on the chantry screen. That's when I noticed the basket empty and the holly on the...the body." Her bravado wavered under the retelling of the event. She grabbed the hand of the man standing behind her, pulling him to her side, and lowered her head.

"A terrible shock," I said, eyeing the man now that the light better illuminated him. "It's a good thing you were nearby, sir."

The vicar, a mid-30s pillar of strength with a take-charge voice, must have thought I needed more elucidation, for he said, "I had just finished with the last of the St. Nicolas gifts when I heard my wife's scream. At first I couldn't tell where it was coming from. It echoes rather badly in these all-stone edifices, the hard walls, lofty ceilings."

I nodded, thinking it a blessing and a curse. One solo voice echoing in a cappella song sounded as near to angelic music as I could imagine, but sermonic speech was rather difficult to understand at times. Taking my nod as a sign of understanding, he said, "I entered the sanctuary and I found Olive by the nave altar. That's here, just behind us."

We turned as if one body, I imagining the shaken woman over the body, Olive reiterating her scare, and the vicar acting as guide as he pointed to the spot. I asked, "Was the body there? Is that why you crouched there, Mrs. Lindbergh, trying to comfort the dying man, perhaps?"

"I touched him once, miss, on his neck artery, to see if he was breathing. I couldn't detect a pulse. I think I stood up and screamed then."

The man's arm encircled her shoulders and he kissed the top of her head.

"Such a stupid thing to do, but I've never encountered a dead person like that. I thought maybe he'd had an accident or illness and had fallen from that, but then I saw the blood..." She squeezed her husband's hand and she murmured she wished she'd found him earlier. "I started to call for Trueman, but my throat had tightened. I could hardly move or think. I kept staring at the body, wondering how it'd happened, trying to think if I'd heard him fall. I wish I had. I might've been able to help him. He had that great wound and knife in his back—" She clamped her hand over her mouth, as though speaking the word would inflict more painful memories.

A shake of her head induced me to ask, "Did either of you move the body to the screen, then?"

The vicar blanched at my question, uttering an emphatic assertion that the body was exactly where and how they had seen it. I tended to agree, for there was no accusing trail of blood that suggested the attack had been other than the place of his death. And the vicar wouldn't lie, for he was a man of God. But he was also a man of the world, so he had pulled his frightened wife from the altar, given her a cup of tea, locked the south door, and phoned the police. Nothing, he swore, had been touched. Not the melting snow on the floor, the knife in the victim's back, or the burlap bag that enveloped his head and shoulders.

"Murder, isn't it?" Olive said, finally breaking the silence.

"What makes you say that, Mrs. Lindbergh?"

"The gash on his head and the pool of blood. There's nothing he could've hit that would cause that wound. Someone assaulted him."

I replied that the Home Office pathologist would determine everything, but right now the Murder Team from Buxton would do the preliminary investigation.

"I doubt there was much of a struggle, or Trueman or I would've heard it. Things would've been disturbed. Though I didn't hear the killer enter or leave…"

We turned quickly as a window rattled under a buffeting of wind.

Trueman spoke over the clatter. "I only hope your lot aren't having too much of a struggle getting here, miss." His eyes shifted from me to the south door, as though he expected the whole of the Derbyshire Constabulary B Division to suddenly appear. "I wouldn't fancy the drive from Buxton myself, not through these twisty roads. It's blowing up a storm worse than any I can recollect."

December was blowing into the village of Bramwell in a swirl of snow and wind laced with North Sea coldness as sharp as village gossip. Snow shrouded rooftop, car top and treetop. It christened the pub sign, a wind-driven splatter flocking the already white swan and masking the pallid letters that read "The Snowy Cygnet." Snow lay like a vast winding sheet over the churchyard, camouflaged tombstones, nestled against the building.

The church itself, an expansive pile of medieval architecture with Victorian 'improvements', stood dark against this snowy whiteness. Doors and bell louvers closed as much against the elements as against burglary, and the building seemed a carcass silhouetted on the bleak hill. Yet, a glimpse of life called the traveler from the storm, the believer to the play. A whisper slipped from the tower shutters, the faint voice of a bell singing to Aeolus. A lancet window glowed with welcoming candlelight. Like a cat's eye in the darkness. Watching your journey across the frozen ground, assuring you of a sanctuary. The window danced within the solid black shape. Yellow, purple, blue and red diamonds spilled onto the snow, their jeweled shapes stretching and convulsing as the candlelight behind the windows flickered.

Within the church walls, pine roping looped across choir stall and pews, scenting the cold air with hints of the season. Garlands of tiny silver bells twined amongst the greenery while, hanging from the wooden rafters and suspended from the railing of the west gallery, groups of three golden balls threw back the candlelight. The church's acknowledgement to its namesake, St. Nicholas.

"And you're decorating already for Christmas?" I asked, trying to keep the astonishment from my voice. "Isn't 6 December a bit early?"

"It's St. Nicholas Day," Trueman explained. He appeared to be all biceps and chest, able to hold his own in a physical combat. And that same strength emerged in a voice that would probably take no nonsense from anyone. "It's for tonight's St. Nicholas festivity. Or, rather, it was. I suppose now, with the inquiry into the death, it's canceled."

"St. Nicholas festivity?" I asked, looking up from my notebook.

"A bit of a mix, actually." He crossed his arms over his chest, and his muscles pressed against his shirtsleeves. "We do a bit of reverse role-playing with the stockings. You know, instead of hanging up your stocking with the list of what you want for Christmas, we give out St. Nicholas gifts."

I replied that the people of Bramwell were starting their Christmas season in the right spirit.

"We try to, Sergeant. Or should I say Miss Taylor?"

I smiled, saying either was fine, and he went on.

"They're nothing extravagant. The church ledger bleeds every time I open it. So we limit the gifts to just a few trinkets for the children. We have a lot of help with the buying and the wrapping. Most of the boxes are rather plain, just red and green paper and a ribbon run around the box. But those silver-paper ones with the wired bows are done up by Joel Twiss, a parishioner who excels at anything creative. Pity I'm not like that, but God gave us different talents, didn't He? My wife, besides owning the bookshop, is good with the holly and carnations. And we've a villager who likes to help with the cloth banners and penning a brass fanfare or two."

I said that it was fortunate he had so many talented helpers.

"But the gifts and decorations are only part of it, of course. We see to it that our needy parishioners have a bit of bread."

It was certainly more than a bit. I gazed at the foot of the altar where the baskets of freshly baked bread rose mountain-high, and tried not to focus on the aroma.

"St. Nicholas was real, certainly. More than our cartoon Santa Claus. Martyred in 305 A.D., we believe. He aided the poor, giving money and bread. We, bearing his name, do the same. Little things in their way, but it means so much to those on the receiving end. Especially during the Christmas season, when the rest of the world seems to be wallowing in excess. But, then, that's what the church is really for, relieving suffering and trying to overcome the blatant commercialism of late."

"As long as the jobs are decent and law abiding," his wife said, "you shouldn't judge how others make their bread, dear. People have got to live. Many could say the same of me and my bookshop. You make a decent wage, so why do I have an outside job?"

"I'm not saying no one can live," he began. Then, as though realizing his statement, he looked in the direction of the victim, and coughed.

I followed his gaze, straining my eyes against the dimness beyond the altar and tubs of wrapped packages. The corpse was no gift from Santa Claus, as most of us call the saint. It had been difficult to see at first, dressed in dark colored clothes and slumped in a shadowy section of the church. The vicar had offered to turn on the overhead lights. But I had restrained him, thinking it better to see the scene as it may have been originally. It was dark, nearly pitch black, by the chantry chapel screen, the rectangular, wooden enclosure that sits in the north aisle. A splendid spot to delay the discovery of a body if one needed time to escape the scene. Or establish an alibi.

Scattered pinpricks of candlelight stood out like spotlights in the gloom. Like the pockets of warmth issuing from the space heaters that slowly chased away the chill. They had been turned on, I had been informed, that lunchtime, so the church would be comfortable for the evening's St. Nicholas celebration. But for all of the vicar's foresight, the murder team would still have a cold job processing the scene.

I had taken a step toward the corpse but stopped just outside the shadowy region of the chantry. The vicar stood several yards behind me, his voice low yet echoing in the stillness of the vast interior, hesitant at first to speak, as though unsure if I should be disturbed. When I turned and looked interested, he continued.

"It's not our bread knife, Miss Taylor."   I must have looked bewildered that he had read my thoughts, for he added, "We don't keep one on the altar for the St. Nicholas bread.   The killer must have brought his own."

Reviews for Jo A. Hiestand Books

A STAGED MURDER:
"A good and original story with good dialogue."
- Anne Perry, author of the Pitt and Monk series

"Ngaio Marsh's Roderick Alleyn is back to work and has changed his name to Geoffrey Graham. If you like Marsh, you'll like Hiestand." - John Dacres-Mannings, cousin of Golden Age mystery novelist Ngaio Marsh

"It looks like I'll have to watch my back now that Jo Hiestand has moved into the Peak District!" - Stephen Booth, author of *Black Dog* and *Dancing With the Virgins*

"Set in a small English village, Jo A. Hiestand's *A Staged Murder* has all the smarts and intrigue you'd expect from a good mystery. And something more: an authentic sense of wit and a wonderful, moody feel for the English countryside." - John Dalton, author of *Heaven Lake*

SHROUDED IN HOLLY:
"I don't usually read mysteries, but this woman's descriptive writing was so beautiful I just had to … Intriguing characters … clues that will keep you guessing wrong. What more can you ask?" - Connie Anderson, *Armchair Interviews*

"Atmospheric, intriguing and compelling. I wanted to savor every well-written passage, while racing toward the conclusion. A gem of a story." - Karen Cahill, R.J. Julia Booksellers

Forthcoming Books:
"Immaculate research, attention to detail and an elegant style are the hallmarks of Jo Hiestand's writing." - Peter Lovesey, author of the Sergeant Cribb and Peter Diamond mystery series

"Jo Hiestand has made the Derbyshire Constabulary her own!" - Charles Todd, author of the Inspector Ian Rutledge mysteries

THE McLAREN MYSTERY SERIES:
"The setting [of COLD REVENGE] is vividly described, the characters are well crafted and full of human qualities, both good and bad, and atmosphere is both comfortable and believable." - Mary Fairchild, *Mystery Lover's Corner*

"*LAST SEEN* is a mystery to sink your teeth into. Not only was the murder investigation top notch but also the peek into the life of the investigator added another layer to the mystery. A mystery worthy of sinking your teeth into; *LAST SEEN* is a keeper." – *Coffee Time Romance & More* Review, 4-stars

"*SHADOW IN THE SMOKE* presents a truly original investigative main character, a wonderful study of human emotion and motivation, and a perfectly satisfying mystery. This reader is excited to find a wonderful addition to the classic British mystery! Five stars and an absolute must read for fans of Agatha Christie, Ngaio Marsh and the like." -- 5-star review, *Long and Short Reviews*

"If this is your first Hiestand novel [AN UNFOLDING TRAP], go for more! If you're a long-time fan, this one will not disappoint. She delivers an intriguing, action-filled story that lures you in like the shifting darkness of Scotland's deep, unfathomable waters." - Reviewed by Drake Morgan for *Suspense Magazine*

"I enjoyed the mystery, the suspense, and the drama [of NO KNOWN ADDRESS]. Jo Hiestand has a nice writing voice that was easy to read. This is the sixth book in the McLaren Mystery series but it stood alone just fine...I have to say the ending was completely unexpected. I did not see that coming at all...I will say there are going to be times you might need to reach for your [tissue] box." -- *Reviews by Crystal*, Crystal's Review: 4 out of 5 Stars

Jo A. Hiestand

Jo A. Hiestand is the author of two Derbyshire-based mystery series. The Taylor & Graham series uses British customs as the backbone of each book's plot. The McLaren Case Mysteries feature ex-police detective Michael McLaren, who investigates cold cases on his own. Her cookbook, Cider, Swords and Straw, is a companion piece to the Taylor & Graham novels and features over three hundred recipes based on the customs highlighted in the plots.

Jo's insistence for accuracy—from police methods and location layout to the general "feel" of the area—has driven her innumerable times to Derbyshire, England, the setting for her books. These explorations and conferences with police friends provide the detail used for McLaren's cases.

She has combined her love of writing, board games and music by co-inventing P.I.R.A.T.E.S., the mystery-solving game that uses maps, graphics, song lyrics, and other clues to lead the players to the lost treasure.

In 2001 Jo graduated from Webster University with a BA degree in English and departmental honors.

Jo founded the Greater St. Louis Chapter of Sisters in Crime, serving as its first president. She is also a member of Mystery Writers of America.

Her two cats, Chaucer and Tennyson, share her St. Louis home.

Peter Lovesey, author of the Sergeant Cribb and Peter Diamond series, praises Jo's writing: "Immaculate research, attention to detail and an elegant style are the hallmarks of Jo Hiestand's writing. An atmospheric novel."

For more information about Jo, or to keep up to date with new book information, scheduled talks and signings, visit her on the web at www.johiestand.com

Printed in Great Britain
by Amazon

64410951R00190